Perfect...

Eve Hightower

Crimson Folio
publishing

Edited by Kathy Bradshaw
Designed by Alexandra N. Segal
Printed in the United States of America
Published by Crimson Folio Publishing, Springboro, Ohio
ISBN: 978-1-958919-00-2
Library of Congress Control Number: pending
Ordering information: Special discounts are available on quantity purchases by bookstores, corporations, associations, and others.
For details, contact the publisher at:

sales@crimsonfolio.com

For questions or comments about this book, please write to:

info@crimsonfolio.com

Crimson Folio
publishing

Prologue

THE DAY BELLE ERICKSON'S LIFE FELL APART started rather mundanely. The sky was a bright blue with puffy clouds as she drove her son, Oliver, to school. He sat in the back seat, singing to the tune of a children's song as she hummed along with him. Should she have seen it coming? Looking back, she couldn't help but think 'yes' despite the fact there was no omen to betray the coming doom of her perfectly crafted life.

So, Belle and Oliver sang as they drove down a two-lane road with hedges on either side. Not ten minutes later, the SUV came to a stop in front of a private elementary school. Belle got out of the car and unbuckled her son from his booster seat.

"Have a great day, sweetheart!" She gave him a tight squeeze, taking in a whiff of his sunshine, baby powder, and crisp green apple scent before waving him off.

His little legs carried him over to Ms. McGrady, his kindergarten teacher, around whom the other students gathered, but Belle didn't linger. She didn't want to be roped into volunteering for yet another school bake sale; she was already running herself ragged fixing a costume for Halloween.

Belle dallied a couple more seconds after getting in her car, watching the infamous Tommy Jenkins sneak up behind her son, who jumped up in fright before dissolving into giggles. She chuckled as she turned to put on her seatbelt. A hard knock on the window startled her, causing her to jump.

She looked up with an apologetic smile, thinking it was a traffic monitor telling her to move along. An apology was on the tip of her tongue as she automatically pressed the button to crack the window, but the words died with her smile as nausea overtook her. She clutched the steering wheel.

The man knocked again, but this time Belle shook her head.

"I'm perfectly fine with causing a scene," his voice announced through the small crack of the lowered window. His voice was an octave louder than necessary for good measure.

Belle blanched, quickly opening the window the rest of the way.

"Glad you remember me," he said, his voice softer.

She couldn't breathe as she stared into the golden-brown eyes of a man that she hadn't seen in five years. The stink of cigarette smoke flooded the car, drowning out all the other comforting scents. Bile crept up her throat as his thin lips curled in that lecherous smile, bringing back memories that she had fought so hard to bury in the deepest recesses of her mind. He looked older and a bit more haggard—but, unfortunately, still as handsome as the last day Belle had seen him. If evil wore an ugly face, people would know whom to stay as far away from. He had long, dirty-blonde hair and boy-band good looks; Danton Stanley knew how to draw women to him like honey enticed flies.

"Danton." Her voice was barely audible, even to her, but his smile widened when she uttered his name. Supporting himself with one arm over the roof of her car, he shook a cigarette free from the breast pocket of a suit jacket that looked like it had seen better days. Belle wanted to ask how he'd tracked her to her son's school—knowing Danton as she did, their run-in was no coincidence. While her throat worked to spit out words—any words—Danton lit his cigarette, took a huge puff, and blew out the smoke into her car.

Belle's face contorted in disgust as she fanned the smoke away.

"Ya know, I couldn't believe my eyes when I saw you here a few days ago. Cute kid you got there." His baleful gaze drifted to Oliver and his friends. Belle cursed to herself when she spotted her son and three teachers looking over at her car with curiosity.

"What are you doing here, Danton? What do you want?" Belle hissed.

"Heard you got yourself hitched to Maxwell Erickson. Moved on up in the world, haven't ya? You're a millionaire's wife now." He chuckled derisively as his eyes roamed over the visible parts of her body, lingering on her breasts. Belle's stomach twisted in knots. She needed to leave before Danton exposed her in front of Oliver's teachers and friends, not to mention the other parents.

"I have no idea what you're talking about. Now, if you'll excuse me—" she said through gritted teeth, turning the key in the ignition. Danton reached into his pocket, took out a piece of paper, and threw it at her. As it fell in her lap, Belle flinched like it would grow fangs and bite her.

"My room number at the Oasis Motel," he explained. "I'll meet you there at noon tomorrow. Don't be late." His eyes shone with amusement but also something darker—more feral—at her obvious discomfort.

"I don't do that anymore!" Her voice was quiet but severe. She unconsciously twisted her engagement ring and wedding band. "Go find your fun somewhere else and leave me alone!"

"But darling, no one does it like you." He feigned a wounded look, clutching at his chest dramatically. He dropped the act, his brow smoothing out as he leveled a hardened glare at her. "You'll be there, dear, sweet Belle, or your husband will receive some interesting photos in the mail. Does he know how flexible you are? I'd be happy to give him some pointers, though ol' Maxwell seems like the conservative sort."

"P... pictures?" The blood drained from Belle's extremities as she put two and two together. "You're bluffing!"

"I assure you I'm not. Now, 'less you want your husband and the damn PTA to know who you were before this soccer mom schtick, you'll be there tomorrow. Noon, and don't be a minute late." He looked down at her with his usual smarmy, self-satisfied smirk and added, "Don't forget to wear that cute little number you used to."

"Jokes on you, I burned that garbage long ago," she growled.

"Pity," he claimed with a chuckle. Looking her up and down, he winked, tapped her chin playfully, and said, "Later, sweet cheeks." He knocked twice on the roof of her car and left. She watched him saunter away without a care in the world, whistling an unrecognizable tune.

Belle sat frozen in her car, clenching the piece of paper in her hands as everything around her faded into the background.

She considered the possibility that this was just a ruse. That it was a ploy to blackmail her, but she knew he was *exactly* the sort of man who would film her without her consent or knowledge. If she'd eaten breakfast that morning, she would have vomited all over the newly upholstered seats.

How did this happen?

CHAPTER 1

Six years Prior...

BELLE CLOSED HER EYES, letting out a loud groan that sounded more like a pig than a woman. Her fingers dug into the sheets, holding tightly for leverage as he continued pounding into her from behind. Her knees ached from the rough treatment, but that was nothing compared to the fire in her arms as she held herself up. His thrusts became more erratic and desperate. It was a feeling she didn't share. She tried not to cringe when she felt his seed fill the condom inside her.

Her eyes snapped open, looking up at the faded puke green wallpaper. Finally, he finished. She shuffled forward, his now flaccid member slipping from inside her. He fell onto her back with an exaggerated huff, sweaty and smelling of rotten seaweed. Her gaze focused on the ornate ceiling fan that sluggishly spun above them, causing her to wonder if one had ever fallen on a person? Well, death by decapitation didn't sound bad to her anymore, she reasoned. If she were dead, she would be saved from having strange men shove themselves inside her chaotically, uncaring for her pleasure, or whether they caused her pain from their rough treatment. Some of the men might have known what they were doing, occasionally having the ability to squeeze an orgasm or two from her stubborn pussy. With Danton, it always felt like he'd just discovered his cock for the first time. He seemed to have no clue what he was doing when he blindly stabbed it inside her.

If this hadn't been the umpteenth time he called upon her, Belle would've assumed he was a virgin. He had absolutely no imagination in the bedroom. He lacked everything a man of his age should have known, especially originality and rhythm. Without fail, he always missed that one spot inside her that was forever neglected. He often talked of the numerous porn videos he watched, yet he failed miserably when it came to understanding that women didn't get off on penetration alone.

Realizing that Belle's response wasn't as enthusiastic as normal, which was a telling sign she wasn't even close to coming, Danton crawled down onto his belly and began slobbering at her pussy. He was like a dog slobbering over a bone. She idly wondered why he even bothered trying to make her come; they were doing this for *his* pleasure, not hers, after all.

Time for the real acting to begin....

"Fucking cum for me, sweet cheeks," he growled, stabbing

three fingers into her without warning. It was only through practice that she managed to hide her wince of pain and flash of irritation behind a flirty smile. She'd been doing this for almost two years by now, and with so much practice, she was learning how to control her outward show of emotions.

"I'm so close!" She moaned, loud enough that if the room next door had occupants, they would've heard her.

Danton was the sort of customer that appreciated a show, so she always moaned extra loud for him. For him, he enjoyed a sort of exaggerated whining noise that echoed off the walls. Whenever she whined, it would help him come faster, and the event would be over sooner.

Belle cried out, hoping he wouldn't pick up on the fact she was faking it. One last yelp, and she fell limp on the bed. She cringed inwardly at how pathetic she sounded but silently applauded herself when he seemed to buy it, yet again. Danton wasn't the type to linger, and for that, she was grateful. She sighed in relief when he kept to his usual routine of dressing as soon as they were finished. Without so much as a *wham-bam-thank-you-ma'am*, he left, shutting the door behind him with a gentle click.

Belle laid motionless on the bed for several minutes, her fake flirty expression melting from her face like butter on a summer day. Yes, two years of practice helped her adjust to the raw feeling between her thighs, but not to keep the raw feeling in her chest from squeezing her heart.

She slowly slipped from the bed when she was sure he wasn't going to return. He didn't make a habit of returning often, but she liked to be cautious. On the ground, by the bedside, sat the used condom, stretched out and oozing with his vile cum. The sight nearly caused her to vomit. Her shame wouldn't allow her to leave it for housekeeping to find. She had more class than that, which wasn't saying much for him. Carefully, she wrapped the condom in toilet paper and disposed of it in the bathroom trash bin. After, she rushed into the shower to rinse off Danton's scent of cologne, cigarettes, and sex, a combination that caused her stomach to churn as much as the sight of the condom. Besides, she needed to get ready for her nightly gig as a data clerk for Titan Telecom, a startup that was rapidly expanding into foreign markets.

"Funny how a mundane 9 to 5 job makes me more excited than a night of rough sex," she whispered, chuckling to herself.

As she exited the shower, her phone rang. She wrapped a towel around herself and rushed to find her phone. She found her phone in her jacket pocket, hanging from the back of the desk chair. Her heart raced into her throat as she grabbed her phone. A deep sigh of relief deflated her tight chest when she saw that it wasn't her mother or the hospital calling. That feeling was quickly squashed when she realized that Romero's name was flashing on the screen.

"Hey, Romero," she answered dryly. She could only guess the reason why he was calling. "Just finished with Danton. He paid upfront, and I'm in the process of wiring you your cut."

Belle was an escort, not a prostitute, even though her actions looked contrary. Typically, she would accompany men to events or office parties, those sorts of things. However, on occasion, if the money was right, she considered going further... especially if it meant earning some much-needed extra cash.

Which meant it came with shame.

Shame... shame was her constant companion. Shame pressed upon her soul every moment of every day. She wore her shame like a coat crafted from a thousand daggers, jabbing into her mercilessly, yet not allowing one drop of crimson blood to spill. There was little she could do at this point. She liked her entry-level position at Titan, but that was the problem—it was entry-level. Which meant it came with an entry-level paycheck, which was hardly enough to cover the medical bills stacking up haphazardly on her bedroom nightstand. Bills that the insurance failed to cover.

"You don't sound like you enjoyed it much, kitten," Romero replied in a lazy drawl.

Belle shrugged before remembering that Romero couldn't see her. She put the phone on loudspeaker as she grabbed her clothes off the floor. The white motel towel fell onto the floor in a moist heap, allowing her to redress.

She grabbed the phone again, placing it to her ear. "Did you need something? I have to get to work."

She returned to the restroom to comb out her hair so she could braid it.

"Ah, damn! I was hoping you'd have the night off.

Got a big spender that's requesting my best girl for a golden experience."

That was Romero's code for a client who wanted a happy ending at the end of the night. In other words, a girl to fuck.

"You have more than one of us, Romero. I'm sure another girl would appreciate the money. I need my job at Titan as much as this one," she replied, not about to give in to his flattery. Even if she didn't need to work that night, she would have made an excuse. Belle had one rule: never sleep with more than one client per night.

Keeping her one rule was the only way to make her feel human and not some horrible creature that men only used and tossed aside.

"I know, I know," Romero said in a soothing, *'I'm here for you, babe'* kind of voice. She could hear laughter and soft music coming from his end and reasoned that he was at the lounge—the front for his escort business. "I know that your mom's health is declining and thought you might need some extra dough."

Son of a bitch, she thought with a growl.

Belle picked up the phone, turning out of the speakerphone. Her fingers wrapped so tightly around the phone that her knuckles were turning white. She knew why he brought up the medical bills. He liked to use them as leverage, and they were fast becoming his favorite weapon against her. It was yet another bid to force her to work for him 24/7. Unfortunately for him, Belle simply wouldn't be bullied. She knew if she immersed herself too deeply into this life that she would never be able to escape, and Romero was causing that to happen!

Normality was why she loved her job at Titan. If only for a few hours a day, she could feel like a regular twenty-three-year-old with a plain, boring job.

"Well, I guess you thought wrong," she replied tersely. "Ask someone else. I'm busy." She hung up without giving him a chance to reply.

"Hold the elevator, please!" Belle called out, running across the white marble floors of the foyer. The office building she worked at stood twenty floors tall, and it typically took either of the two elevators forever to reach the lobby. If she didn't arrive on the fifth floor in the next five minutes, she'd be late, and the bald pervert who supervised her would threaten to dock her pay.

She nearly stumbled running to the closing elevator doors, cursing the fact she didn't wear flats.

A large hand slipped between the sliver of space of the elevator doors right as they were about to shut. "Thank y—" The words shriveled on her tongue when she saw who the only other occupant was. She hesitated, wanting to offer him to go ahead and that she would just catch the next one, but she was already skating on thin ice at work, and he'd already opened the door.

"Good evening, sir," Belle greeted quietly, gripping onto the yellowed straps of her faux leather handbag.

Belle felt like she had entered a lion's den. She stood uncomfortably against the wall on the other side of the elevator, unsure of what to say. Beside her stood Maxwell Erickson, the CEO of Titan Telecom. He gave her a brusque nod, then continued to text a message on his phone. The ride to the fifth floor took only a few seconds, but to Belle, it felt like hours. He was engrossed on his phone the entire way up; it allowed Belle a moment to look him over.

At 5'7", Belle stood taller than most women. Maxwell Erickson stood a good head taller than her. In his presence, she couldn't help but feel tiny and insignificant. Everything about the man screamed intimidation from his cold, almost emotionless blue eyes to his lean but still muscular body. He had a talent for cutting people down with only a few words. Belle recalled seeing him reduce one of the software engineers to tears with only one well-timed remark two days prior. His callous and detached demeanor had earned him the epithet 'Iceman' from his employees... and it was well deserving.

Being the low man on the totem pole, Belle rarely interacted with him. Yet, she couldn't help but feel the *Iceman* was off. She felt like she was standing next to a livewire. He crackled with so much energy that she could feel the hair on her neck rise. She held her breath, hoping none of his past negative energy would be unleashed at her.

The elevator glided to a stop. He waited for her to disembark before following. Belle briefly wondered why he was heading to Human Resources. His office was located on the research and development floor seven stories higher.

"Have a good night, Ms. Aston," Maxwell told her. He didn't raise his voice, but it still carried over the open-plan office space. A few colleagues looked in her direction out of curiosity. When they noticed the boss, though, they quickly returned to their work.

Belle remained where she stood in stunned silence as she watched Maxwell. Her jaw dropped as he walked away in the opposite direction. His back was turned to her, so he didn't see her disbelieving expression. Her chest felt warm and tingly in a way, much like how she felt as a child on Christmas morning. She didn't understand why it made her happy, but it did. The smile on her face didn't wane even as she dove into the countless mind-numbing reports set aside for her that night.

Maxwell Erickson knew my name!

"You need to stop fussing so much," Annaliese Aston wheezed as she watched her daughter flutter around the room like a restless butterfly. Her breath rattled in her chest like a handful of bolts in a tin bucket. Each time she blinked, she struggled to stay awake. She could feel the medication's grip on her eyes, forcing her closer to slumber. It felt like all she did was sleep, but she fought away the need so she could spend this brief moment with her daughter before Belle left for work.

"I need to make sure you're warm and have all the medication near you...." Belle trailed off in a moment of indecision before adding, "Maybe I should take the night off. You don't look like you're doing too well today." She bit her bottom lip as she placed a humidifier on one of the bedside tables.

She was extra agitated because the home nurse wasn't able to come today... or even tomorrow. Her mother was hardly in a position to take care of herself.

"Nonsense," Annaliese replied weakly, playfully smacking the back of her daughter's hand as Belle attempted to tuck the duvet tighter around her body. All day she had been complaining that she was dizzy, probably from her lack of oxygen. Even the four blankets piled on top of her weren't helping to keep her freezing body warm, though, she'd never reveal this to Belle. She knew it would only make her worry more. Besides, there was nothing Belle could do. God, she hated her damned disease for stealing the light from her daughter's beautiful eyes.

Annaliese struggled to remember the last time she saw a genuine smile on Belle's lips. A really happy, wide smile that would cause a dimple on her left cheek to appear. Even though Belle hid her dimple under layers of makeup, Annaliese knew that dark circles haunted the skin under her eyes. She knew it was from working late nights at Titan. When she finally did come home, she spent less time sleeping and more time anxiously hovering over her mother's deathbed. She knew Belle hated it when she called it that. She was dying.

Her sweet little girl simply refused to accept the situation for what it really was.

Annaliese reached out her frail hand for Belle to take. She smiled as Belle knelt next to her, allowing her to cradle her cheek with a palm. Belle frowned, but she said nothing. Fear lived in those hazel eyes. Belle's irises had a starburst pattern of golden-brown around her pupils that gradually bled into a moss green, surrounded by a ring of darker green. Her eyes once were full of life, with vibrant beauty, but they now only carried hopelessness, exhaustion, and fear. They might have been a looking glass mirroring Annaliese's own heart.

They were the only two left of their family. When she died, she feared that Belle would have no one to take care of her. Would there be no one to pull Belle from the dark chasm of despair she would surely descend to?

Now wasn't the time to worry about that....

"You've been stuck indoors with me all day, sweetheart. You need to step away from this stench of sickness for a while, even if it's just for work. You deserve a life outside of caring for your dying mother. No one will begrudge you for having fun." Annaliese's words were beginning to slur, and she could feel her eyes drooping. "Besides, I'll be asleep for... most of the night. You should go. Don't you worry about me."

"That's like asking the sky not to be blue," Belle responded softly. "I'll always worry."

"I know, darling. Still," she patted her daughters' hand once more, "do me this one favor and... have a night for yourself. You've already made me feel better spending some… quality time… with you."

"Alright, if you're sure. Goodnight, Mom," Belle whispered, kissing her mother softly on the forehead. As she pulled away, a stray tear slipped down her cheek. The tear landed on Annaliese's brow. Belle continued to watch her pale mother slip into unconsciousness, "I'll stop by in the morning," she said, though she needn't.

CHAPTER 2

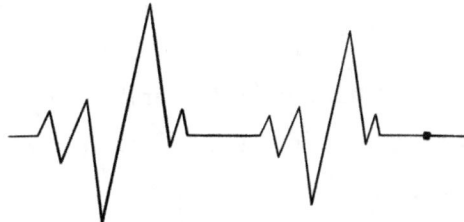

WEEKS TRUDGED ON as summer melted into autumn. To Belle, it appeared that her mother's time was running out. She spent her twenty-third birthday in the hospital looking after Annaliese. Her mother had come down with a severe case of pneumonia. Instead of birthday cake and wine, they had dry bran muffins and apple juice so clear it looked like water, purchased from the hospital cafeteria.

The hospital was fast becoming her home away from home. Belle only left her mother's side when she had a shift at Titan or Romero had a client lined up for her.

Dr. Fields, her mother's doctor, informed her that she wouldn't be discharged for a while. Then he broached the idea of an experimental treatment. He warned her not to get her hopes up. When she heard there was hope, she started sleeping with more clients. It was an act of desperation, in a way. If the experimental treatment were a viable option, she'd have to pay out of her own pocket. If somehow the treatment could cure her mother, then the few hours wasted as some strange man's fuck-toy would provide her with the funds she needed... and some much-needed numbness.

The waiting list was miles long and she had no special connections. Belle refused to give up hope. Her only reprieve from this existence of anxiety, fear, and emotional anguish was going to work every night at Titan. She had no idea why, but the eight hours she spent at night updating databases were helping her preserve her sanity. She'd come to look forward to the numbers she'd square away in a spreadsheet.

It was only when she was clicking away at her computer that she could disconnect from her real life. She relished being a part of something big, no matter how small that part was. There were also brief moments she'd catch a glimpse of Maxwell, usually from afar. He hadn't said another word to her since the night in the elevator, but she always got a quiet thrill from observing him... from the safety of her cubicle.

She wondered how he would react if she ever told him that she pictured his face when she was fucking a client, that it was *his* face she came to, *his* name she screamed in her mind the few times she'd climax. Belle laughed mirthlessly. Who was she kidding? He would fire her on the spot if he found out she was moonlighting as an escort.

"What's so funny, kitten?" Romero asked lazily. He lay in bed, propped up against the headboard amongst rumpled sheets. In the fingers of his jeweled left hand, he held a burning blunt. His caramel blond hair was in disarray, and his tribal chest tattoo was slick with sweat from their recent activities.

Belle couldn't believe how far she had fallen. She was now sleeping with her pimp for an extra buck so she could keep up with her bills.

She became the breadwinner when her mother was forced to quit her receptionist job. Not that Belle minded. It was her turn to take care of Annaliese. Her mother had single-handedly raised her, playing the role of both father and mother. All the while, she struggled to work, all the while battling cystic fibrosis, just to make sure Belle could have a decent childhood. Her mother's sacrifice was often her driving point to leave the lifestyle and earn a living doing honest work, but it was her fear that led her right back to Romero.

Until she could earn more money, Belle knew she was stuck. And she hated Romero for using it against her.

"Nothing," she told him, unable to meet his gaze, "I just remembered something funny." She put the hairbrush down on Romero's vanity, pulling her dark chocolate-brown hair into a tight ponytail at the crown of her head.

"Feel free to share," he probed. He just wouldn't quit. Belle chose to ignore him.

She examined her appearance in the full-length mirror on the back of the bedroom door instead. The dark circles under her eyes were, as usual, hidden beneath a concealer that complimented her olive skin. She was dressed in a sleeveless white maxi dress that made her look more like a middle school teacher than an escort. The way she looked in her dress, no one could have suspected she led a double-life. For that, she was thankful. Though, she was becoming tired of constantly hiding the truth... especially from her mother. She knew, if her mother ever did know the truth, it would kill her far faster than cystic fibrosis.

She checked the time on her phone. It was six in the evening. She was due for her shift at Titan at eight. She didn't bother to say goodbye to Romero. Her mind focused on where to grab dinner. Her stomach was grumbling, and although she wasn't exactly hungry, she did need to eat once in a while.

Two steps outside of the apartment building, her phone rang. People on the sidewalk gave her strange looks when they heard the *Jaws* theme and a toy poodle yipping as her ringtone. The song ended as the dog's yips quieted.

Belle originally bought the ringtone because it made her laugh. Since then, she had assigned the ringtone to a special person: her mother's doctor.

"Ms. Aston?" asked a youthful female voice. It was a voice that certainly didn't belong to Dr. Fields. The caller didn't wait before plowing on, "It's Abigail Stone from Trinity Medical. Dr. Fields asked me to call you." There was a loaded pause before the nurse continued. On a subconscious level, Belle knew what was coming. Her heart tightened in her chest, making it difficult to breathe. "Your mother's condition is deteriorating. We believe it's best if you come here immediately—"

"I'll be there in a few minutes." Belle cut her off. She searched the busy streets, looking for the quickest way to get there. On the corner, across four lanes of busy traffic, she spotted a cab. She waved her arms in the air, attempting to gain the cab driver's attention, but it was of no use. She ran across the street, dodging oncoming traffic just as a couple were about to get in. She pushed them aside, apologizing profusely. Their protests and insults landed on deaf ears.

In breathless words, she gasped, "Trinity Medical! Step on it, please! It's an emergency!" She held her hand to her fast-beating heart, then motioned for the driver to drive. "Now!" she screamed, fist thumping against the back of the driver's seat when he just stared at her like she was an alien.

"Alright, sheesh!" The man grumbled under his breath as he merged into rush hour traffic. Every few seconds, he kept throwing Belle glances via the rearview mirror, which she studiously ignored. Her leg wouldn't stop bouncing against the sticky floorboard. The ride seemed to last for an eternity. Belle's growing fear was nearly swallowing her, that her mother was going to die surrounded by strangers. The mere thought brought tears to her eyes.

The cab drove to the front of the hospital, stopping at the curb.

"That will be—"

"Keep the change," she offered, practically throwing her cab fare at the driver. She left the door wide open as she ran into the hospital. She flew through the lobby and to the bank of elevators. There, she repeatedly pressed the elevator call button before throwing her hands up in the air in frustration at its slow arrival.

"Why the hell was everything moving at a snail's pace today of all days?" she grumbled. "COME ON!" she growled.

Once inside the elevator, Belle scowled at each floor and every person who had the audacity to interrupt her ascent. Couldn't they see she was in a hurry? Couldn't they understand that something more important was happening than their silly need for a goddamn elevator ride?

She caught a glimpse of her reflection on the metal doors. She didn't bother to grimace. Her hair had fallen from her bun, and her eye makeup was wild and smeared down her cheeks from her tears. When she finally arrived at her mother's floor, she pushed past the objecting passengers and sprinted down the hall, ignoring the calls telling her not to run.

"Mommy?" her voice cracked the moment she stepped into the room.

Dr. Fields and his female nurse turned to her. They were all crowded around Annaliese's bed. Belle's eyes were drawn to the figure that lay still and silent. Her mother was attached to a ventilator, her body thinner and frailer than Belle remembered. She looked like a skeleton, her pale skin washed out by the harsh fluorescent lighting.

"She slipped into a coma about a half-hour ago," Dr. Fields began gravely, his gray eyes filled with sympathy, sympathy that brought Belle absolutely no comfort. "At the rate she's deteriorating, you should think about making preparations."

"I'm supposed to stand by and watch her die?!" Belle yelled, her anger overwhelming her sorrow as tears streamed down her cheeks. "You are doctors, dammit. Do something!"

"Ms. Aston," the other doctor began in a dispassionate tone, "Unfortunately, the ventilator is all that is keeping your mother alive for now."

"She signed a do not resuscitate order," Dr. Fields explained, rubbing his eyes in an uncharacteristic sign of agitation.

"What?!" Belle croaked, turning to her unconscious mother. Betrayal was written all over her face. "Why would she do that? Why would she not tell me?" She collapsed into the folding chair beside the bed and buried her face in her hands. Was her mother that determined to abandon her?

A warm hand squeezed her shoulder, and Dr. Field's floral scent wafted toward Belle from behind.

"She's been doing a good job hiding it, but your mother has been in excruciating pain for a while now, Ms. Aston." The unknown doctor said in the same detached tone as before. She wished he'd just swallow his tongue and stop talking. "Patients in these circumstances often choose not to prolong their suffering."

Belle wanted to yell at him for being so cold, for treating her mother's death like nothing but another day at the office. Then again, she supposed that's exactly what it was for him.

For Belle, however, her entire world was falling apart.

"We'll give you some time to say your goodbyes, Belle. When you're ready, have Nurse Stone call me, and we'll switch off the ventilator together."

"No!" Belle cleared her clogged throat and blinked back tears. "Let's... let's just do it now. I don't want her to suffer anymore." If what the doctor had said about her mother's constant pain had been true, then she didn't want to drag this out.

In what seemed like a numbing trance, Belle watched as the oxygen tubes were removed one by one from her mother's throat. With a few presses to buttons, the ventilator made its last descent. The heart monitor continued to beat at a slow, rhythmic pace. She clung to each beat as the next one followed longer and longer. The idea that she would hear her mother's heart beat its last, was like a knife stabbing into her chest, the blade heated and serrated as it cut into her.

She listened as her mother took labored breaths, and for one final moment, Belle wished she'd open her eyes, look at her, and smile that reassuring smile of hers that always told her things would be alright. Belle bit down on her chapped lips, tasting blood on her tongue as silent tears ran down her face.

The situation continued for ten agonizing minutes. The piercing sound of Annaliese's flat-lining heart machine was so incredibly sharp; more blood flowed into Belle's mouth as her teeth buried in her bottom lip. She hugged herself in a white-knuckled grip as she rocked back and forth in distress.

"Time of death, 19:15."

Dr. Fields continued to speak, but Belle could only focus on the lifeless body lying on the hospital bed. She stroked her mother's brittle, dark brown hair. Softly, she caressed her face, ending with a gentle kiss on her forehead.

"—ton? Ms. Aston? Is there someone I can call for you?" The nurse called out to her, speaking for the first time. Concern or pity, she didn't know which, maybe both, glistened in her eyes.

"I... need to go to work," Belle responded in a monotone voice. Immediately after, her tears dried, and her mind grew numb. Then there was the smell that she focused on. The stench of disinfectant and antibiotics were annoying her sense of smell. Her stomach tensed, sending bile into her throat. She needed to leave, to be somewhere other than being surrounded by doctors. "I'll contact you once the funeral arrangements are made."

Belle didn't know how she arrived at work, but she knew that her co-workers could sense something was amiss. Even her fussy supervisor didn't say a word about her arriving twenty minutes late. The thought of returning to an empty and cold house—one where her mother would never return to—made her physically ill. Instead, she chose to focus on work and her wonderful numbers.

She had never been as productive as she was that night. She didn't bother to stop and take any breaks except to grab a black coffee from the vending machine. When the stack of documents had been exhausted, she finally raised her head to see that nearly all of her co-workers had left for the day.

All the cubicles were empty, and only a couple of the private offices had lights on.

Dread filled her chest, forcing her to remain seated at her desk. There was no way she wanted to return home, let alone make funeral arrangements. Instead, she decided to force her way through the next week's tasks. As her hand reached for the paper beside her that explained her next assignment, a drop of clear liquid fell on her keyboard.

"What the fuck?" She whispered.

The drop was followed by another and then another. Where was the water coming from? Then she realized the liquid was her own tears. No matter how much she attempted to hold in her emotions, she knew that they would eventually gain the better of her.

Soon a choking sob broke the silence. She could deny her emotions no longer. Belle jumped up from her chair and rushed into the hallway. The ladies' room was too far, and she knew she'd fall apart before she reached the doors. Instead, she ran toward an abandoned corridor near the marketing department. They left early most days, so there should be no one to bother her.

She hid in a small space between a vending machine and potted fern, her body shaking uncontrollably. At first, she tried stifling the sound of her sobs with her hands, and when that didn't work, she attempted to hold her breath. Then when she remembered that everyone had left, she stopped holding back.

Her relief was short-lived. In the distance, she could hear footsteps muffled by carpeting, heading closer and closer. Before she could think or move, she felt someone stopping in front of her. She inhaled, smelling the clean scent of cypress and cedarwood. She gulped back her sobs, turning to see a figure crouching in front of her. Belle found herself drowning in eyes of cornflower blue.

"Are you alright?" Maxwell Erickson's deep voice reverberated through her bones as he held out a monogrammed handkerchief.

CHAPTER 3

BEAUTIFUL. That was the first thought that crossed Maxwell's mind when Belle's hazel eyes locked with his own. He didn't think someone could look so beautiful even while crying their heart out. There she was, cheeks the shade of pale rose, a reddened nose, and unnaturally bright eyes that held profound sadness. He found himself transfixed as he continued to hold out his handkerchief.

Max was on his way home after a tedious call with the director of a Tokyo-based smartphone maker when he realized he'd forgotten to ask his assistant to drop off some documents at Human Resources. *It can wait until tomorrow,* he'd initially thought. Then he picked up the folder and brought it to the fifth floor. Human Resources was on his way, and it's not like anyone was waiting for him at home.

The head of HR had already gone home but fortunately left her room unlocked, so he dropped off the files and headed back toward the elevator. As he waited for the elevator to arrive on his floor, he heard a woman crying. He wanted to ignore it, but his damn conscience gained the better of him.

What if she were hurt or in need of medical assistance? he thought.

That's why he was now standing beside Belle as her heart-shaped lips trembled before breaking into another bout of absolutely heart-wrenching cries. She dug her fingers into her scalp, making Max worry she'd rip out her chocolate locks by the roots. Panic stretched its wings as the normally aloof clerk descended deeper into distress.

He didn't have a lot of experience with crying women. As a general rule, he went out of his way to avoid an emotionally distraught person if he could. He hated feeling helpless, so he pulled his employee into a platonic embrace, patting her back in an awkward attempt at comfort. "There, there. You'll make yourself sick if you continue crying this hard, Ms. Aston. I'm sure whatever is bothering you will be better after a night's rest."

He cringed at his own words. They hadn't sounded the least bit sympathetic, which was apparent by Belle's worsening cries. His shirt was drenched, and her nails painfully dug into his chest. What was wrong? Was she sick? In pain? He didn't see any outward injuries, but that didn't mean much. Perhaps she was having a panic attack?

"Are you feeling unwell, Ms. Aston? Should I call for an ambulance?" He asked softly, and Belle finally looked up at him, agitation shining clear through the tears.

"No! No more hospitals, please! No more doctors! Anything but that. I'm fine. I promise you I am fine!" Her body tensed in his arms before she pulled away from his embrace. Her face was ash white as she wiped away her tears with the back of her hand. It did nothing to stop her tears from overflowing, however. "I'm really fine, Mr. Erickson. I'll stop crying, just..." She let out a shaky breath, her long lashes fluttering furiously as she attempted to keep the tears at bay.

"No more hospitals," she finished in a broken whisper.

Max frowned in confusion, unsure of the next step. He offered her his handkerchief again, and this time she took it with trembling hands.

"Forgive me for being direct, but you're clearly far from fine." His voice was firm as he watched her gingerly dab at her eyes and nose. "If you don't want to go to the hospital, then why not tell me what's wrong? I might be of some help." He surprised both of them with that.

Belle's lips parted for a few seconds before she found her words. "Why would you help me?" She asked suspiciously. "You don't even know me."

Max's knees were beginning to protest from kneeling. Pins and needles started shooting from his toes to calves. He moved to stand before holding his hand out for Belle. "While most of the terrible stories you've undoubtedly heard about me are true, Ms. Aston, I'm not *so* callous as to turn my back on someone in need of help." He didn't let go of her hand. Instead, he led her to the kitchenette nearby.

Belle mindlessly followed beside him. She flinched when he switched on the lights. The room was bathed in a cool white ambiance that was far too bright for this late hour. It didn't help that everything in the room was also white, which helped to accentuate the harsh glow.

"Have a seat." He gestured to a chair in the corner of the room. He cleared his throat uneasily when he realized how demanding he sounded.

Belle stiffly walked to a small, round table at the center of the room. She watched him switch on the electric kettle. Afterward, he searched the cabinets for mugs. This wasn't his floor, and he probably wasn't accustomed to making his own beverages, Belle mused—so it took him a few tries. She quietly started the breathing exercises she'd learned in a recent *YouTube* yoga video, hoping it would calm her nerves. The breathing exercises worked well, at least for a few seconds, until her mind replayed the scene where she freaked out on her boss after he suggested medical attention.

The next few seconds sent her into a downward spiral. All of a sudden, all she could see were images of her beloved mother—who hated dark, enclosed spaces—being buried six feet in the ground. She thought she heard someone call her name but was too distracted. All she could focus on was the nasty monster called *Grief* clawing at her chest and stealing her breath away. She felt a pair of hands on her shoulders, shaking her.

"Breathe, Ms. Aston, breathe!" Maxwell's harsh voice startled her out of her trance. "Come on, Belle, breathe with me. In through your nose and out through your mouth. That's a girl," He patiently instructed as he held her to his chest, allowing his breaths to guide hers.

She was riveted by the seemingly endless blue of his eyes. Their faces were so close she couldn't help but notice the violet-blue flecks around his pupils. She saw reflection within and focused on her image, willing herself to breathe in and out as her heart rate slowed to normal.

Maxwell's voice lulled her racing mind, "Good girl. Now drink this." He passed her a warm mug. It wasn't until the heat spread through her fingertips had Belle realized her hands were freezing. She took a tentative sip, blinking slowly in surprise. She wasn't expecting to taste sweetness rather than the bitter coffee flavor she expected.

"Hot chocolate..." She murmured, her lips curving into a shy smile. She inhaled the comforting scent of the beverage.

"I've read that chocolate is a good treatment for shock." Maxwell's smile was as shy as hers. She took a bigger sip, wincing as she scalded her tongue.

He pulled out the chair next to her and sat down close enough that their knees were touching. He looked like he didn't quite know what to do. However, he was the type who looked a person right in the eye in general conversation, which made Belle incredibly uncomfortable.

"Won't you tell me what's upset you, Ms. Aston?" He cracked a half-smile, loosening his navy tie as he added: "If some jerk out there needs their butt kicked, I'm your man. I have a black belt in taekwondo."

Belle let out a dry chuckle, "If only it were that easy, Mr. Erickson."

"Please, call me Max. Mr. Erickson was my father, and you're only a few years younger than me?" The last part sounded like a question. Belle nodded, a gesture *Max* returned satisfied. "But only after hours. I wouldn't want the whole office getting the wrong idea. Your name is Belle, correct? Short for..." He trailed off, waiting for her to finish his statement.

Belle remained suspicious, unused to him acting friendly toward anyone, let alone her. In her experience, men were only friendly when they wanted something—usually sex. Some didn't even bother wasting time on kindness, choosing to treat her like nothing but an inanimate object. They didn't care about her as a person—that much was obvious—and they certainly wouldn't have taken time out of their schedules just because she was crying.

There had to be more to his kindness than what she was seeing. She couldn't help but wonder what Maxwell Erickson's angle was?

She couldn't help fret over his motives, jumping to conclusions and fearing he was the same as her clients. She was a pretty face with long legs, a slim waist, and round, perky breasts. What if that was all he saw? What if he turned out to be like the rest of the men in her life, shallow, selfish, and self-serving? She wasn't sure if she could handle that. She loved working at Titan; what would she do if that were the case?

It was too much on her already overloaded brain, and she could feel the waterworks nearly well over again.

He smiled, and it completely transformed his face from harsh lines to a softer and more youthful expression. The wrinkles between his brows smoothed, as did the lines around his thin lips. Even the way he carried himself changed; he slouched in his chair and didn't look like he was carrying the weight of the world on his shoulders. Even his honey-brown hair, which was typically slicked back, was tousled at the top. In this slightly disheveled state, he looked like an ordinary twenty-something and not an up-and-comer who routinely made his employees cry or tear out their hair.

Belle was awestruck by this transformation. Max was a tall guy, standing proud at over six feet. With his broad shoulders and long legs, she briefly wondered if he played sports in university. He had a strong jawline and elegant features that complemented every part of him. Despite his reputation, countless women in the office were attracted to him.

She was one of them, but unlike some who were bold enough to try to approach him, Belle was satisfied with admiring from afar.

"...Isobel. It's Isobel," Belle replied at last, realizing she had been staring without giving an answer. She spelled out her name before draining the rest of the drink. She set the mug on the table and cleared her throat. "No offense, but I doubt that you can help me, sir. I mean, Max." She closed her eyes and pinched the bridge of her nose, feeling the sting of tears again. "Unless you know someone who can bring back the dead." Her last words were barely audible, her breath shaky and a lump of emotion in her throat, but Max heard.

They sat in silence for a moment before Belle removed her hand from her face and placed them on her lap, staring down at them and picking at the already chipping white nail polish.

When Max's larger hand covered hers compassionately, Belle instinctively gasped, taking a moment to marvel at the warmth, before looking up at his sympathetic gaze.

Belle hated that look. She'd had enough of that same sympathetic gaze from the doctors and hospital staff, and from her mother's friends that gradually stopped visiting as her mother's time was nearing its end. Seeing that same sympathetic gaze on him made her want to lash out uncontrollably.

"You've lost someone," he stated matter-of-factly. She didn't bother with a response, choosing to look away. "My condolences, Belle. I recently lost someone close as well. Losing someone who you love is incredibly painful. I know it must hurt more than you thought possible, and I'm sure you can't see the light at the end of the tunnel right now, but you will get through this dark time. I'm not promising the hurt and grief will ever stop. It'll always be at the back of your mind, and there will be days when the sadness and anger might overwhelm you, but it does get better with time. You'll learn to live with it. I know it's cliché to say this, but the dead are never really gone so long as memories of them live on." His eyes shone with sincerity, and Belle hadn't expected to be on the receiving end of that.

"You... you lost someone recently?" she gulped hard.

He nodded, his eyes growing misty as well. "My friend who was like my brother. He died in a car accident three weeks ago." He held out his hand to her. She accepted his gesture. "Who did you lose?"

"My..." she gulped hard, trying to dislodge her emotions from her throat, "my mother."

"I'm sorry for your loss," he returned sincerely.

Absent-mindedly, her fingers laced with his, and she found herself spilling her guts to him.

Her voice cracked as she spoke of her dear mother and their last moments together, of her struggles with cystic fibrosis and her life in the hospital. Belle expressed her lonely childhood as a single child raised by an equally single mother who sacrificed everything to provide for her. The reverence in her voice was hard to ignore despite the broken interruptions when tears decided to appear.

Max sat silently listening as Belle spoke of the financial hardships she had to endure to provide for her ailing mother and how much she sacrificed in order to ensure the woman who raised her would receive the best medical care possible.

Anger tainted her words as she spoke about the doctors and how her mother wouldn't make it on the waiting list for the experimental treatments.

Belle's eyes were wild now as she paced across the break room. "They hit me with the 'there's nothing more we can do' bullshit. And I just…" She stopped pacing, stopped speaking for a moment before whispering the last part, "…It was my fault. Mom should have lived much longer than she did. She would have been able to manage this illness if she hadn't had me."

"That's not true, Belle," Max finally spoke up. He stood and walked over to her. He took her shoulders in hand and forced her to look at him. "I'm no expert, but I know that those with cystic fibrosis aren't long for this world."

"But her health wouldn't have deteriorated so quickly if it weren't for the difficult pregnancy! On top of that, she was a single mother with no family to help raise an energetic brat like me. Mom worked so hard to give me everything! She put her own needs, her own wants, and her own health on the back burner until it was too late. She couldn't catch a single damn break until the end!" Belle raged, hazel eyes burning in fury at the world. She shrunk into herself, sniffing, "It's just not fair!"

"Life often isn't fair," Max replied somberly. "Sometimes good people suffer loss after loss, while bad people prosper. That's just the way it is."

"After all she went through, I wanted her to be happy," she sobbed.

If there was one thing Max was good at, it was listening. He learned that her mother was orphaned at an early age and was bounced around in the system because no one wanted a sickly child. The woman worked multiple jobs to afford college, and when her medical bills piled up, she took out loans and dealt with collection agencies on a frequent basis. Despite all her trials, she found love with a police detective and happiness when she discovered she was pregnant. Tragedy struck again when her husband passed away mere days before the birth of their child; all this after struggling to conceive for years.

"You make it sound like your mother was unhappy," Max pointed out. With the use of his finger, he lifted Belle's chin, so their eyes locked. "All I'm hearing is that your mother was a wonderful woman who loved her daughter beyond reason, who worked tirelessly to give her the life she didn't have. Instead of being angry about the sacrifices, celebrate them. Be thankful for the mother who cared for you so much. Not everyone is as lucky." There was a bitter edge near the end that made Belle curious, but she didn't have the courage to ask.

His words rang true, didn't they? How many times had her mother told her not to dwell on her death? How many times had she made Belle promise to unapologetically live the way she wanted to?

Unfortunately, this filled her up with a new sense of emptiness. What were her dreams? She didn't know. For the longest time, her life had been taking care of her mother.

That had been her sole purpose, and now it was gone. She felt like an unanchored boat floating aimlessly in a dark, endless ocean.

Maxwell seemed to notice this change. "Why don't I take you home?"

He took the hand from her chin, checking his Rolex. Belle gulped, seeing hints of the veins that likely ran up the length of his forearm and a sprinkling of hair around the metal strap of his watch. She finally realized how close they were. If she took one more step, then they'd be toe-to-toe, and if she took a deep breath, her breasts would brush against his chest.

If I rose on my tiptoes and he lowered his head just a bit, came a daring voice in her mind, *then I could kiss him.*

Her eyes fell to his lips. She could feel the desire to kiss them. Instead, she shook her head and backed away, trying to put some distance between them. Her butt met the countertop, and the back of her blouse received a wet surprise from a watery spill near the sink. She silently cursed.

"That's okay, Mr. Erickson—I mean, sir—I mean Max! Max. I can call an Uber. You don't need to go out of your way like that," she spluttered awkwardly. The thought of spending twenty minutes in an enclosed space with this man—with his scent, his warmth—sounded torturous.

Max smirked at her, eyes flickering in amusement for the first time that night. "You don't even know where I live, so how can you be sure if I'd be going out of my way?" Then his tone took a more serious turn, "And it would give me peace of mind if I saw to it that you got home. Go, grab your things, Isobel. I'll meet you by the elevator." All traces of laughter had disappeared from his expression, and it didn't look like he'd be accepting 'no' for an answer.

She sighed. Butterflies fluttered in her stomach at the way he said her name—the way the syllables rolled off his tongue—and she wanted to hear it a dozen more times. In this haze, she could only nod and obey his stern request.

CHAPTER 4

MAX HAD THE PERSONALITY of a man who would own a Tesla, Belle surmised. And so he did. His car smelled like leather, woody cologne, coffee, topped with a faint hint of tobacco.

"You smoke?" Belle asked without thinking. He didn't seem like the type to smoke cigarettes, maybe a cigar or a pipe, but not cigarettes.

"Occasionally," Max admitted, a touch sheepish. "Only when I'm feeling stressed, which... is every day lately." He watched her from the corner of his eye as his car drove out of the garage and onto the empty street. "Where do you live?"

Belle rattled off her address, then stifled a yawn. The crying had zapped her of what little energy she had left. She'd finished her shift on pure adrenaline and was surprised she hadn't crashed yet. The clock on Max's dashboard read 2:05 AM and Belle knew from the office rumor mill that Max would be back in the office in a few short hours. Sometimes the employees wondered if he slept at all, though she supposed she wasn't one to talk.

She shifted a couple of times in her seat before nodding off as the car began cruising down the highway. The soft, relaxing sound of jazz from the radio was her last memory before Max's voice—loud in the dead of night—awoke her. He opened the passenger side door, standing backlit by the neighbor's porch lights. It was difficult to make out his expression, but the light gave his light brown hair a golden halo.

"What?" Belle murmured. Her eyes were still heavy from the short nap. It took her a moment to gather her bearings.

Only as she spotted the hibiscus her mother had planted in front of the house did she realize she was home. The house was drowning in darkness. The porch lights had been malfunctioning for days now, but Belle hadn't had the time nor energy to fix them. Once upon a time, her home was inviting and warm; it now looked cold and foreboding as if it was warning her away. The house was a harsh reminder of what had changed and how her life would never be the same.

She closed her eyes and took a deep breath to center herself before stepping out of the car. She grabbed her handbag, clutching it to her chest like some kind of magic shield. Max stepped aside from the passenger door, giving her some space.

"Thank you for the ride," Belle said with a small smile, "and for letting me ruin your shirt with my makeup. I'll return your handkerchief after I wash it."

"No need. You can keep it or throw it away. Whatever you want." Max gave her a one-shouldered shrug, "I've got others at home."

"Okay," Belle dragged out the 'o' and laughed. She didn't know any other men who'd brag about their handkerchief collection in this day and age. "I guess..." she paused, once again close enough to be swept away in a sea of cornflower blue. "This is goodnight, or good morning, rather."

Max nodded, but neither moved.

Belle's gaze turned to the house that no longer felt like home. Her mother would never be there again. Memories, both good and bad, flashed through her mind, from echoes of childish laughter to epic fights between mother and teenage daughter to endless coughing fits that kept both of them awake. If she remained outside, maybe she could pretend her mother was quietly sleeping in the room next to hers. She could pretend today never happened, that her mother would be accepted into a promising experimental trial, and they would have a few more years together.

Loneliness emanated from the house in waves, dragging her deeper into her grief.

"Belle?"

Her sudden spiral into the abyss of dismay was cut through like a knife by the sound of his voice, so filled with concern as she stood there in a trance. She blinked and glanced at him pleadingly.

"I can't go in there, Max." Her voice was barely above a whisper as she admitted, "I can't be in there alone... I'll go crazy." She pushed into his personal space, looking up at him with her big hazel eyes. Hesitating for a second, she bit her lip and voiced her wish no matter how ridiculous it seemed to her, "Please stay with me tonight."

Max's tongue jabbed at his inner cheek, the imprint visible against his shadowed features. He looked at her contemplatively beneath his lashes. A powerful current zapped between them. It buzzed underneath Belle's skin and stole all rational thoughts. Perhaps it was the loneliness and sorrow that drove her following action, or maybe it was pure lust and attraction paired with a desperate craving for human contact. She dropped her bag onto the paved driveway and stood on her tiptoes. Her hands clutched into his shirt and tie, but his mouth remained out of reach. She looked up at him with acute longing, rolling her hips against his. She let out a quiet whimper when she felt his cock twitch against her abdomen.

"Kiss me. Please. I want you to hold me, just for the night. It doesn't have to mean anything.... I," Belle paused, staring into Max's eyes through the darkness. "I don't want to be alone tonight." She sounded needy and shamelessly wanton; a fire was spreading throughout her body, and her core felt slick with the first signs of arousal. Somewhere in the back of her mind, she was appalled by her behavior. It hadn't even been twelve hours since her mother's passing, and she was already throwing herself into the nearest available arms.

"You're vulnerable right now, Belle. You're not in the mindset to make such a decision, and I don't want to take advantage of you." Maxwell replied, pressing his forehead against hers. His large, warm hands cradled her face, and Belle closed her eyes, loving how the pads of his thumbs felt against her cheekbones as they languidly rubbed.

"If anyone is taking advantage, it's me. I want you, Max. I want you right now, at this very moment. More than anything. Yes, it might be the grief speaking, but that doesn't make it any less true. It's giving me an excuse to say something I would never have been brave enough to say otherwise."

The words barely escaped her lips when Max's teeth scraped against her lower lip, tugging at it and prodding against the shallow cut she'd made from biting down. There was a hint of iron, but no blood, as his tongue licked against the seam of her lips before he kissed her in earnest. She made a gasp of pleasure, giving him the chance to sneak his tongue into her mouth. Max kissed her with single-minded focus. He kissed her like he wanted to drink in her very essence, every last drop of her soul until he owned every single inch of her body. Belle melted into his arms as he used one hand to tilt her head for a deeper angle that had them both moaning. The other snaked around her waist, pressing her closer against him so that their rapid heartbeats hammered against each other. Belle had no other choice but to hold onto him as he plundered and ravished her mouth until her lips were bruised and swollen, and they had to stop for some air.

"I'll stay the night," he told her, his voice husky as they both gasped for breath.

He was making a huge mistake, but Max couldn't bring himself to care that he was breaking one of his personal rules at the moment. All the blood had drained from his brain and went south, and he was drunk off of one kiss with Belle Aston.

The quiet snick of the lock as Belle locked up the front door mocked him as if it were telling him that it was too late to change his mind now. Belle didn't bother turning on the light as she led him down a hallway of the single-story house, taking him past the living room with the kitchen located to its left. They passed by a half-open door that led to a bathroom to the left and another closed door opposite it which he assumed was the master bedroom.

Belle's room was next to the master bedroom. She swung the door open, taking Max by surprise when she switched on the lights. He remained rooted in the hallway as his eyes adjusted to the sudden change as Belle walked inside.

The decals on her periwinkle-painted door caught his attention. At the very top of the door was a silhouette decal of the pied piper playing on his flute and children following him. On the bottom corners were two fairies seated on mushrooms, legs crossed and facing each other as if they were having a conversation. At the center of a door were two Tinkerbelle silhouette decals sprinkling rainbow-colored pixie dust on a bunch of stickers spelling the name 'Belle' in gold cursive writing. Underneath the name was another silhouette decal of Peter Pan and the Lost Boys flying off into the distance.

His lip curled into a crooked smile at the small insight into Belle's surprisingly innocent and naive personality.

"I was obsessed with fairy tales as a kid. I especially loved the character Tinkerbell since we shared the same nickname." Belle's voice came from somewhere behind the bedroom door.

"I was fond of superheroes and Japanese anime characters," he said in reply as he entered, taking in the bedroom that was a bit more mature than the door—except for the golden Tinkerbell decal above her bed with a quote that read, "*All you need is faith, trust, and pixie dust*" against the purple painted wall that was darker than her door. The entire color scheme of her bedroom revolved around the two colors.

"I guess it's safe to assume purple and gold are your favorites—" the words died on the tip of his tongue as he swallowed down saliva in an attempt to wet his dry throat. He'd turned to face Belle only to find her dress and underwear in a heap at her feet. The mirror behind her gave him a good view of her round and very biteable ass. He breathed in deep through his nose, fists clenched by his sides to stop from mauling her like an uncivilized beast.

A girl like Belle, a sweet little flower, like her, not yet fully bloomed, deserved to be handled with care lest he unwittingly bruise her with his rougher appetites. His dick was weeping in his pants. There was probably a wet spot on his briefs since he'd been painfully hard from the moment he pulled Belle to comfort her back at the office and got a whiff of her citrusy shampoo and her sweet perfume.

"Well?" she arched a slender brow at him. Her shoulders were tense and her body rigid despite the confident demeanor she was trying to give off by cocking her hip and pushing out her chest. Belle was well endowed and would overflow in his hands; she had the kind of breasts that were made to be titty-fucked. Her nipples stood to attention, the points pebbled and swollen.

"C'mere," he managed to speak past the grip of lust that held him in a chokehold.

A flush of pink spread across her cheeks, her eyes flaring at the command, but she obeyed.

Max pulled the tails of his shirt from his pants and unbuttoned it, carelessly throwing it to the floor once he'd shirked it off, as well as the undershirt he wore. "Up," he commanded as he wrapped his arms underneath Belle's smooth thighs. It seemed brusque commands were all he was capable of at the moment, and she didn't seem to mind as she hoisted herself up, arms wrapping around his neck and legs around his waist.

He let out a pained groan when he felt her wet heat press against his lower abdomen, causing his dick to twitch in anticipation. Her eyes dilated in arousal, the hues of her green irises nearly nonexistent.

"Kiss me," she commanded before nipping at his ear.

Max hissed, fingers digging into her soft flesh as she licked at the same spot with little flicks of her tongue. She ground her center against his stomach, uncaring of how wet and desperate it seemed. She needed the friction, and this was moving too slow for her.

Growling, Max gripped her hips to stop her movements, smirking as she mewled in protest.

"More," she begged.

He was going to spill in his pants at this rate. "Patience," he told her. He needed to take the edge off first, and since she was already dripping down her thighs, she didn't need any preparation. The foreplay would have to come after.

"Don't want to wait," Belle panted as she tightened her hold to continue her gyration.

Groaning, Max had to admit his patience was running thin, and they had barely started. He wanted to press her against the wall and shove himself inside without any further consideration, but she deserved more than that. He just wasn't sure if he would last.

He lowered her body a bit, so her center brushed against the tent that had formed, and he pressed himself against her with a clear indication. The zipper and layers of clothing between them were infuriating.

"You okay with this?" he asked Belle with his face buried in her chest.

Her reply was more of an exhaled gasp as he sucked one nipple into his mouth, causing another rush of wetness to coat her soft folds.

Max laid her down on the bed and quickly divested himself of his shoes, socks, pants, and underwear. His cock sprang up like a jack-in-the-box toy, curving upward with need.

Belle glanced at his piece out of habit. It was something she did, sizing up her clients to judge how long of a bath she would need, but this time she did a double-take. To say she had seen all kinds of dicks was an understatement, but Max rated near the top in girth.

"Shit," she muttered. "Is that a penis or a weapon?"

Max paused before laughing. "Problem?"

Belle smirked sheepishly, "No, just... intimidating, I guess. You're definitely on the larger side than I'm used to."

"You've seen a lot of cocks, have you?" he asked arrogantly, injecting a teasing tone into his voice so that Belle didn't pick up on the gnawing and irrational jealousy that made him want to hunt down every man who'd ever been with her.

She didn't need to pretend to blush and act like a coy maiden, as usual. Instead, the color bleached from her face, and a sick expression came over her.

Max's heart dropped to his knees, and he cursed himself for his insensitivity. So what if she had lovers before him? He wasn't a celibate monk either.

Climbing onto the bed, he picked her up so that she was straddling him, his cock nestled between them securely.

"Fuck, that was a dumb thing to say." When she wouldn't meet his eyes, he said, "Hey, don't feel ashamed. I didn't mean to come off as slut-shaming you or anything. Obviously, I know you've been with other people, but then again, so have

I. I'm sorry, Belle. I didn't mean anything by it, okay?" he asked, brushing her hair away from her face.

It took her a second to swallow that gut-wrenching feeling of shame. Not that she wasn't used to hearing awful things considering the path she took, but hearing Max make an off-handed comment, no matter what harm he didn't mean, was brutal. Still, the look on his face was so sincere that she felt those old feelings melt away.

"Okay," she nodded, smiling shyly, her gaze darting between his lips and eyes.

"Okay," he grinned. Max leaned up to kiss her again and flipped them back over so that Belle was beneath him. She squealed, but his tongue muffled the sound.

"You got any condoms, babe?" he asked, kissing his way down her neck and onto her chest while one hand palmed her right breast.

"T-top drawer on your left," Belle gasped out, her fingers digging and kneading at his shoulders. He stopped in his ministrations and opened the drawer by her bedside, pausing when he saw how many condoms she had in all kinds of sizes.

He blinked. Maybe he'd underestimated Belle's naiveté, but that was a mystery for another day. He picked out a condom in his size and quickly sheathed himself.

"You ready?" he asked as he ran his hard length up and down her wet folds. He dipped his cock in a few inches, jaws clenched painfully when he felt how tight she was.

He heard her whisper a response and nodded sharply. His jaw clenched tight as he took his time entering. A slow and agonizing tease as the head of his cock slowly rubbed along her walls. He moved his hips closer to hers, his cock about halfway through when Belle's breath hitched sharply. Her nails dug into his shoulders.

He stopped, looking up at her in concern. The last thing he wanted to do in such a delicate moment was to make her feel uncomfortable.

His left hand clutched the top of the headboard, and his right arm gently hugged around her waist. "You... you okay? Did I hurt you?" His eyes were searching hers for any sign of displeasure.

To his surprise, Belle's hand gently cupped his cheek. Her legs were loosely wrapped around his waist as she wiggled her hips.

"Mmm... no, I need a minute to get used to it, that's all. Please, don't stop."

There was a mix of emotions that ran through Belle, sorrow being one of them. Out of all her emotions, sorrow was the last one she wanted to feel, and he made her forget everything. She felt like she was floating on a cloud drifting in peace. His rough hands gently pulled her closer. His smell was comforting and embraced her. The husky tone in his voice as he tried to steady himself grounded her. Every movement he made easily took her sorrows away and left her breathless.

When Max heard her request, he swallowed hard. *Fuck*, he thought to himself. She was slick with her tongue, and her body adjusted to him like a fitted, warm glove. The last time he worked this hard not to cum was when he lost his virginity.

If he wasn't careful, there'd be a repeat of that night, and he didn't want to embarrass himself.

Eventually, staying stationary grew to be too much, and despite her plea, Max held still for a bit longer to make sure she was truly okay. He began rotating his hips slowly in a circular motion, adjusting to the sensation that was her core wrapped so deliciously around his length. His thrusts were measured, and each time he slid back in, her walls would open up for him another inch until she had accepted his size in full.

The feeling felt so good it made him lean down to her. He clutched Belle as hard as possible, pulling her closer until there wasn't a single bit of space between their bodies. He wrapped all her hair in his left hand, yanking her head firmly to the side and revealing her neck to his teeth. His cock slid further inside while he nipped up the column of her neck to behind her ear. He was about to ravish in her taste, his eyes wild and his thrusts bordering on frantic. He leaned to her collarbone, lavishing it with attention. His entire being overwhelmed by the sensation of being inside her until...

He stopped.

Gently, he told himself.

Max's thumbs ran along both sides of her thighs roughly. His fingertips followed in what was like a sensual massage. He guided her leg higher. The palm of his hand cupped the under part of her knee. Her left leg, still wrapped around his waist. His hips moved rhythmically, building to a crescendo of euphoria. It was like a dance, as though he had music playing that his body responded to. Although there was no music, it was just the two of them both under a spell.

He felt her slick heat spasm and her soft breath hitch into a moan. "Hold me, Max," he heard Belle mutter softly. "Mmmpf..."

A heavy grunt escaped his throat, lustful in anticipation for what was to come. He adjusted her legs, wrapping them around his mid-back. His hips angled just right, causing her back to arch into him. His arms wrapped around her so that he cupped the upper part of her back.

The bed beneath them rocked precariously with each movement, and his forearm pressed against the mattress as he tried to leverage himself for faster strokes. Her arms circled his neck, fingers buried in his hair and nails scraping his scalp. Her breath panted into his ear, her lips ghosting the shell and sending shivers straight to his core.

He looked down at her, capturing her beauty at the moment before gently placing his lips over hers. It was a slow, tender kiss made up of small pecks that turned into long tongue-swirling kisses that left them gasping for breath. As the kiss deepened, so did his movements. Faster and faster until the headboard began to bang against the wall. Sweat trickled down their skin, causing friction as he stroked in and out of her over and over. They moved together so easily. It was as though they had become one.

His tongue followed the pulsing vein in her neck, tasting salt as he suckled a trail down to her breast. He could hear her pleas growing in intensity and her legs hugging his body to her.

"Ma... Max, please, don't stop!"

He grunted as he pulled himself up by his hands to rock harder. Belle pulled on his hair and brought his head back down to her chest demandingly. He chuckled breathlessly before complying and taking her left breast into his mouth while his hand tweaked her right. Her moans filled the room, her back arching.

"I won't stop," escaped Max's mouth as he continued to plummet her pussy. The bed gave an ominous creak, threatening to buckle from the force of their lovemaking. He wrapped both his arms around her back, pulling her into a seated position.

The adjustment was surprising, but Belle followed his lead. The air hit his back, and he hissed a bit at the burn where her nails broke the first layer of skin. He didn't mind, though. It wasn't painful to him at all, just a deeper sexual sensation. It was a sign that he was doing everything right.

Or maybe a punishment for the sweet, sweet crime of taking her body at a time like this. Yet, she had asked. It was the only thing she wanted from Max, and he had been craving to show her this side of him since he first saw her. He could still recall what she wore that day he noticed her in the office. She wore a cute and very tight little sapphire skirt suit with matching heels. The suit she wore wasn't entirely appropriate, yet he didn't mind.

He did what any man would do and answered her wish. He longed for this moment, dreaming that one day he would be in this exact place with her. There was nothing he wouldn't do for her.

His brain shorted out for a moment as Belle twisted her hips in the perfect angle. It took everything in Max not to blow his load right then. She continued to grind against his cock, her body falling and rising, and her eyes closing as a shockwave spread through her. Both her hands grabbed the bed behind her for support, her head tilting backward as she began to cry out loudly.

Max's grunts mixed in with her gasps, his grip lowering when she changed her position. She began to bounce on top of him frantically.

"Fuck me, Belle! Shit, that feels so... Mphf." His words wouldn't come. His words were a jumbled mess of inaudible sounds. He was about to climax, and there was no more holding it back. He yanked her back toward him, spinning her around and laying her on her back.

He rested on his knees, holding her legs up straight with both hands around her ankles. He watched as her voluptuous breasts bounced up and down. His movements became almost sloppy as his climax drew near.

Belle's eyebrows drew together with her determination. "Aaagh! Max, yes!"

Max could feel her walls tighten around him. She cried out in release. He stuttered, thrusting once, twice, and one final time, shooting his load into her sweet heat, filling the condom with his seed instead of her womb. Lowering her legs gently, he fell onto his hands above her and gave one more slow push, an automatic response during orgasm, before slowly withdrawing from her. He sat back on his knees, out of breath, his eyes glued to the beauty that lay exhausted beneath him. While her eyes were closed, Max took the opportunity to escape to the bathroom, pulling the condom off and tossing it in the waste bin.

When he returned, Belle's eyes had opened and were gazing distantly at him. She looked wrecked yet relaxed and at peace. He climbed back into bed, pulling her to him. She nuzzled under his arm, tenderly kissing his chest. Her fingernails ran along his abdomen, and his fingertips traced her spine until he drifted to sleep.

Belle brushed Max's hair from his forehead, watching him sleep and listening to his soft snores. He'd passed out almost immediately after they made love, mumbling apologies and saying he'd make it up to her after he rested his eyes.

She smiled, amused at how adorable he was acting while trying to fight back his sleepiness. He was obviously exhausted from the long hours he put in at Titan. He was a hardworking man, perhaps the hardest working of them all, and Belle was astounded he still took time out of his busy schedule to comfort her, even if their evening took a turn toward the unexpected.

She traced her finger up the prominent bridge of his nose, following the slight curve of his brow, before tracing his lips. He looked so relaxed and content. Asleep, he didn't look domineering or ill-tempered at all. The stress and wrinkles melted away from his face, giving him a youthful appearance. Belle released a dejected sigh. What was she doing sharing a bed with a man like Max? He was clearly going places, places that she could never dream of going. It was obvious to her that he had a very affluent upbringing. It was only a matter of time before some perfect heiress would snatch him up. Their night together was just a meaningless fuck; he was blowing off steam, and she needed something to take her mind off her tragic loss. They were using one another only, so she had no business admiring his good looks or his prowess in bed.

She knew full well that he'd never want her once he knew who she was and how dirty her life had become. But it was strange. Belle felt at peace sleeping next to Max, a feeling she'd only experienced with her mother, and yet, she also felt great unease about sleeping next to a man whose kindness she didn't deserve. A brief moment of doubt slipped into her mind as she contemplated his attempts to pity her with a good hard fucking, but Maxwell wasn't the type of man to do something he didn't want to. Rarely had she seen him take pity on clients or employees. She suddenly felt ashamed for allowing this line of thought to tarnish their night together, no matter how short it would be.

She fell asleep with those thoughts circling around in her brain. That night, nightmares of her dead mother disowning her from beyond the grave haunted her. She dreamt of Maxwell marrying a slender Barbie look-a-like. Some of her clients even made guest appearances in her nightmares, hammering in the fact that she was damaged goods, a cunt for hire, and many more derogatory slurs.

She dreamt that all these people, her mother and Max included, dragged her to an unmarked grave, stripped her naked, and dumped her in like trash. Her pleas fell on deaf ears as they buried her alive beneath the damp soil, dirt falling into her mouth and ears, silencing her pleas for help.

"No, please!" She was soaked in sweat when she sat up in bed, spitting out nonexistent soil from her mouth. Her blinds were drawn, but sunlight still peeked through the string holes. She clutched her sheets to her chest and looked to the empty side of her bed. Disappointment panged through her; Max had already left.

"It was all just a dream," she said to herself, pushing down the sheets to make sure there were no traces of dirt in her bed. She held her palm over her racing heart in an effort to calm herself. When she felt like she could finally stand, she grabbed her robe, sitting on the chair beside her, and stood.

What she needed was a hot shower to wake her brain up along with a strong cup of coffee, and then she'd be ready for day one without her mother.

The sound of someone moving about and whistling in the kitchen, and the smell of flapjacks, bacon, and coffee, caused her to pause in the narrow hallway. *It really was a dream,* the childlike voice in her head screamed. It was all just a dream. Her mother was alive and fine. She was making her favorite breakfast in the kitchen while whistling like she usually did when she was cooking. Her mommy was fine, and Belle still had her family.

Hope stretched like wings across her chest as her heart expanded with joy. Her feet carried her toward the kitchen at a breakneck speed. She bumped her toes and then her shin into a tall curio cabinet along the way but didn't feel any pain. Skidding to a halt in the doorway of the tiny kitchen, her smile melted from her face when she realized it was Max who was flipping pancakes over the electric stove instead of the willowy figure of her mother.

The crushing weight of reality slammed into her. All the strength left her, leaving her legs weak and unable to hold her weight. Max looked up when he heard her drop to the floor, his jovial whistling abruptly dying off. He made sure to turn off the stove—even though the pancakes weren't done yet—before rushing to Belle's side.

"Belle, what's wrong? Are you not feeling well?" He sounded alarmed as he searched for any signs of injury on her crumpled form. He almost asked her if she needed to see a doctor when he remembered her drastic reaction to the mention of doctors and hospitals last night.

An all-consuming sadness enveloped her when she looked up at him. It was as if Max had never seen someone look so defeated before, but he seemed to understand the weight of grief and all the other accompanying feelings of loss she was feeling.

"I thought you—she used to make me pancakes and bacon on weekends. When I smelled the food... I forgot for a moment. I forgot that she's gone, and I'm alone now." Her voice was muffled by the hand that she held in front of her mouth. She still looked as pale as she had been at the office last night. If he hadn't woken up and saw that she was sleeping like a rock this morning, he would have assumed that she hadn't slept at all from the sunken look of her eyes. But he supposed that just because she managed to fall asleep, it didn't mean that it was restful.

"You'll have moments like that often. Sometimes you'll see something that you know your mother would have loved or hear a joke she would have found funny, and you'll turn to see her reaction, only to find that she's not there anymore. It will feel like a hard slap in the face, a reminder that she's gone and you're still here, going on and living your life. But you have no other choice but to move on; the living should never envy the dead. It's disrespectful to both them and you, who still have the gift of life."

"Wow," Belle said in awe. "That was actually really profound. I didn't think you were that philosophical or in tune with people's feelings. No offense, boss, but I always assumed you have the emotional intelligence of a robot." She gave him a teasing smile that didn't match up with the look in her eyes.

"You know what they say about assuming, but if you tell anyone in the office that I actually have feelings, I'm demoting you to the mailroom," Max replied, flicking her nose, which crinkled adorably. He even managed to get a quiet chuckle out of her!

He led her to the dining table in the kitchen then returned to finish cooking the pancakes. Belle had to admit it: he certainly had a talent for drawing a smile out of her.

When he offered to help with funeral arrangements, she politely but firmly declined, saying she wanted to organize everything on her own.

Neither of them brought up what happened the previous night. There was an unspoken agreement between them that it was a one-time occurrence. He left her house around seven-thirty so he could change and ready himself for another day at the office, only after insisting that Belle take at least a week off as her bereavement leave.

CHAPTER 5

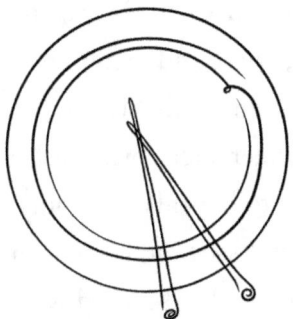

HIS RESOLVE TO FORGET everything that happened between him and Belle lasted four full days after their encounter. On the fourth day, he found himself in the HR files, searching for contact information. Once he had her phone number in his hand, he took a seat at one of the empty desks and stared at the slip of paper he wrote it on. Should he call her? Was calling her worth the risk? And what exactly was he risking? He closed his eyes, recalling their night together. Yes, it was worth everything, if only he could see her again.

Calling her may have been an abuse of his powers, but he told himself it was out of concern for her well-being and that, as a good boss, he should check in on her.

Max initially felt nervous about calling her out of the blue, but when she talked to him on the phone, she seemed happy to hear from him. Belle told him that she decided to cremate her mother's body instead of a traditional burial.

He regaled her with reassurance that her mother probably wanted it that way.

They chatted for over thirty minutes. During their conversation, Belle told him about how she planned to apply for a loan that would cover the remaining medical expenses and use the rest to pay her school tuition since she planned on going back to college. He loved hearing the sound of her voice on the phone. If he didn't have a meeting with his lawyer, Max would have kept her on the line longer. Her voice was so soothing and melodious; he could listen to her talk for hours.

After hanging up, he requested his assistant to send a bouquet of flowers to her house. He also added a card with the same message as the quote above her bed.

Later that day, while he was in a different meeting with the marketing department, he received a message from her. As soon as he realized the message was from her, a broad smile stretched across his lips. It was a picture of the bouquet. The flowers were of different hues of purple petals. The flowers sat in a vase by her beside table. Beneath the picture was a text. *Thank you - Belle*

He caught his employees eyeing him as if he'd grown a second head. He quickly switched the phone off, his mask firmly back in place. Now was not the time for him to act like a lovesick teenager. As matter of fact, he wasn't lovesick at all. Belle was just a lingering affection after mind-blowing sex.

Mind-blowing sex with an employee, the rational part of his brain screamed at him. Max had made a point never to get involved with his staff, and with the *Me Too* movement growing every day, he didn't need any of the bad publicity of being labeled as a sexual predator or rumors that he used his position to coerce a female staff member into having sex with him.

"Shit," what had he gotten himself into?

"Hey stranger," Max's voice startled Belle, causing her to drop her phone. The phone skidded across the carpet, landing by his expensive leather shoes. Her heart gave a panicked jolt when he knelt to pick it up. Luckily, he didn't read the message on the screen. Instead, he handed the phone back to her.

For most of the day, she had been in a heated conversation with Romero. He was still trying to convince Belle to come back and work for him. She had quit the escort business two weeks prior after she cremated her mother's body. There was no need to continue to work for him since the only reason she was doing it in the first place was because of her mother. She felt guilty for seeing a silver lining to her mother's death, but it wasn't like her mother would have wanted her to continue being paid for spending time with rich men, either.

Belle considered staying on as an escort for a few more months to build a cushy little nest egg for when she returned to college. After some thought, though, she realized that was exactly the kind of trap she didn't want to fall in. It had been almost two weeks since she quit, and Romero was still bothering her. What could she do to get rid of him? Standing before her was yet another complication in her life. He was smiling at her like she was the best thing he'd seen all day.

"Ma—I mean, Mr. Erickson. Good morning!" She pasted a smile on her face, forced with all of her teeth on display. It was the first time she'd seen him since their night together. When she'd returned from her leave, Max had left for a business trip to Tokyo. He had only been back for two days. This was his first day back in the office since his trip.

"Is this like your secret spot or something?" Max asked, leaning casually against the vending machine.

Belle flushed, shrinking back into the small space between the machine and the fern. Then she noticed three employees walk by, giving them curious looks. It made sense why they gave Max a wide berth, but she was certain gossip would soon spread that he was casually talking to a mere desk clerk.

"Something like that," she answered, smoothing down her wavy bangs as she examined Max from beneath her long lashes. He was dressed in a charcoal black suit this time, which showed off his narrow waist and clung to his broad shoulders. Belle had noticed that he liked to wear suits in shades of black and grey, which was too bad because he would look debonair in blue suits as well. "How are you doing, sir?" she asked, unable to think of anything else to say.

Max smirked at her use of "sir" but didn't comment on it.

"I'm doing fine. And you? How are you feeling? I wanted to be here when you came back to work. Unfortunately, I had urgent business to take care of. Are you working regular hours now?" he asked.

Belle toyed with the ends of her hair. She had splurged on a new haircut as a way of celebrating her new life. Her hair was now cut to her shoulders with bangs and caramel highlights. It was a way to pick up her spirits. She also decided to start wearing understated colors, pale-pink blouses, khaki skirts, and the like, at least for a while. Her theory was that, by wearing pastel-colored clothes, she could trick her mind into being happy. She didn't have any friends, so she had to find ways to keep her spirits up, or she knew depression would creep into her mind like a fog on a cold night.

"I'm fine, I guess. I still have hard days. I think you described them as a slap to the face, and it certainly feels like that," she chuckled. "Somehow, I still make it through the day. I'm thinking about enrolling in a marketing course," she mentioned as she beamed up at Max, her smile hopeful was full of innocence.

She was a walking paradox to Max, all light and pure goodness like a flower meadow in full bloom on a nice spring day. Though, there were moments when her expression became hard and dark, like a veteran coming back from the war.

"That's wonderful. When do you start? If you like, I could speak with the marketing team about interning with them for a while?" he offered, sounding more enthusiastic than Belle did.

She grimaced sheepishly. "Well, I haven't applied yet. I'm only studying marketing because that's what I studied before I had to drop out. I'm not sure if that's where my passion lies, you know?"

Someone called out Max's name before he could offer Belle any advice. He glared at the head of HR over his shoulder, causing the woman to stumble back on her heels. Belle shared a look with the startled woman, who offered an apologetic but curious glance at their exchange as she backed out of the room.

Max sighed heavily.

"Uh, I guess we both need to get back to work. My break is almost over. See you around, Mr. Erickson," Belle said, squeezing past him and walking down the corridor. She glanced over her shoulder once and saw that he was still standing where she left him, watching her with a mystified look on his face. Heat crept up her cheeks as she gave him a shy finger wave then hurried back to her desk.

As weeks passed by, Belle and Max continued with their little rendezvous by the vending machine. In those little moments, she learned things about Max, like how he was a nerd and turned into an adorable fanboy whenever he was talking about his passion for gaming and building his own

PC. He always had a twinkle in his eye when he talked about his work, especially the prototype modem and router Titan was working on to revolutionize the telecommunications industry. In his own words, "this would raise the stage even higher for the company."

Their newly-minted friendship garnered a lot of attention in the office and quickly became the hot topic of conversation during any break room gossip.

More than a few pointed questions came Belle's way from her supervisor and colleagues. It didn't matter how many times she told them they were just acquaintances—barely even friends—rumors still floated around. People started treating her differently, too. Some sucked up to her, and a few even treated her as though they'd been lifelong friends.

Then there were those people she called *the snakes*. People who silently judged her from a distance, observing her new status as the boss' fling with disdain and barely concealed envy. They were nice to her face, but it didn't take long for her to discover what they thought of her; calling her names behind her back seemed so juvenile, but honestly, Belle had heard worse.

She'd overheard three of the girls in the HR department accuse her of spreading her legs to move ahead in the company. They were re-applying their makeup in the ladies' bathroom while Belle was in one of the stalls. The horrified looks on their faces when she walked out and smirked at them cracked her up. She could barely contain her laughter as she walked out of the restroom. She'd brought the situation up to Max, and he'd shrugged it off with a less-than-pleased expression— his android face, she thought humorously.

"All I can tell you is to grow a thick skin. Society will always find some flaw to harp on about you, and if you dwell on it too much, you'll only play into their hands. The time and energy wasted on fretting over it could be better utilized on something more important. At the end of the day, all the naysayers are nothing but extras in your life; a protagonist doesn't concern him or herself with the cannon fodder," he told her in a bored tone.

"And the robot makes a reappearance. Does nothing ever bring you down?" Belle teased, poking lightly at his pecs and resisting the urge to cop a feel.

Before she could pull her hand away, Max snatched it, curling his long, thick fingers around her slim hand. Just thinking the words *long* and *thick* had desire pooling in her core. Embarrassingly, she could feel her lace panties growing damp by the second. They still hadn't talked about their one night together, and for the most part, Belle did a good job of pretending that it never happened.

Her time as an escort taught her to hide her feelings deep inside her heart, and so far, it worked. She was able to convince her colleagues she wasn't attracted to their CEO. Some believed her, but not many.

Yet, in times when he was so close that she could taste his breath, a girl had only so much self-control. She leaned in closer to him, inhaling his woodsy cologne.

Belle attempted to compose herself when she noticed someone approaching out of her peripheral vision. Someone was passing by the alcove where the vending machine was in. If anyone poked their head in…

Taking a deep breath, she muttered, "We're at work."

"I know," he hummed. "Have dinner with me tonight?" Max's head lowered toward hers, so if anyone walked by them, they could only assume they were kissing. His warm breath smelled like cigarettes, coffee, and mint gum; the three smells shouldn't blend well together, but to Belle, they smelled like heaven.

"What? Are you serious?" Belle giggled nervously, trying to tug her hand free, but Max wouldn't budge. "Isn't this against the rules or something?" she asked.

"Not when I'm the one making the rules. Besides, what's wrong with two friends grabbing a bite to eat after hours? I want to sit down and chat with you for more than ten minutes. If it happens to be over some good food and wine, and hopefully great music, then so be it. I'll pick you up at your house around seven tonight."

Belle's eyes narrowed as she stared at him. She pursed her lips and suggested, "How about you tell me the place and I meet you there instead? I don't think you coming to my house is a good idea." She flushed, remembering what he looked like naked and how good it felt to have him inside her.

Max gave her a crooked smirk, his eyes brimming with the same heated attraction she was feeling. "If you insist."

Belle took her time following her hostess to the table Max reserved for them. The Korean restaurant was fancier than what she'd expected, and she felt underdressed.

All the nice evening dresses that she owned were—she didn't want to say slutty—but they were very revealing. She also didn't want to wear anything she wore when she was with her clients to her first dinner date with Max, not that this was an official *date.* As he said, this was dinner between two friends. Innocent enough, but the line was beginning to blur rapidly, and she was losing sight of where it was drawn.

Still, she wished she'd put more effort into her appearance. She was wearing a simple red dress with a sweetheart neckline. The bodice clung to her upper body and flared out at the waist before stopping a few inches above her knees. Her petticoat jacket was nothing special. Neither were the black, red-bottomed pumps that she wore. In fact, they were a cheap knockoff of the real thing, and she was regretting wearing them as she took in Max's appearance.

Would he be embarrassed to see her so underdressed? Everyone else here looked so glamorous.

"Mr. Erickson, your guest has arrived," the petite Korean hostess announced. The lady gestured Belle to the table. Max stood with a smile.

Immediately, Belle thought what a magnificent sight he made in his black sweater vest and light blue shirt with each sleeve folded back to show off his muscular forearms. His hair was tousled this time like he'd just rolled out of bed.

"Belle, you look absolutely beautiful," he said before kissing her on the cheek. Her brain had to remind her heart not to skip a beat, or she'd faint. She didn't respond until after he pulled her chair out in a gentleman-like fashion.

"Oh please, compared to everyone else here, I look like I washed up on the seashore or something," she scoffed as Max took his seat. She let out a self-deprecating laugh that died when she saw Max's dark frown.

"Don't say that about yourself. You're gorgeous and kind, and amazingly compassionate. I feel as though I should carry a mirror to remind you of this," he spoke sharply, allowing for no argument. His tone and expression were so serious Belle was at a loss for words.

A warm sensation spread through her body, and she felt tipsy even though she hadn't drunk any alcohol yet. The only person who ever told her she was beautiful and meant it was her mother. Her past clients complimented her, but that was either when she was naked or after she'd stroked their egos in front of others.

It dawned on her how dangerous a game she was playing. If she wasn't careful, she was going to lose more than her head.

Breathe, Belle, she reminded herself.

Once they were settled, a waitress came for their orders. Belle deferred to Max. The only Asian cuisine she'd ever tasted was one of those instant ramen noodles and a bit of sushi, which she hadn't liked. He ordered spicy tofu bulgogi, four side dishes, and cold plum soju to go with it. Whatever those were.

She had never used chopsticks before, so Max had to coach her through it. Once she got the hang of using them, she was able to revel in all the new tastes on her plate.

"Can I ask you something?" She was looking down at the piece of beef she was picking up with her chopstick. Her brows furrowed in concentration, and so she missed the fond, almost loving smile on Max's face.

"Sure," he said, his smile growing wider when he watched the piece of beef plop back onto her bowl. Belle pouted in frustration. He picked the beef up with his chopsticks and pretended to give it to her, only to pull back and pluck it down his mouth.

Scowling at him, Belle asked, "How come you insist that everyone else call you Maxwell, but you want me to call you Max?" It had taken her a while to realize that she was the only one at the office who used the shortened form of his name. Her supervisor had once berated her for calling him Max, telling her that he preferred to be called by his full name or to address him as Mr. Erickson.

Something dark flickered in Max's blue eyes. He quickly smoothed out his expression.

"When I started Titan Telecom, I did so intending to start something meaningful," he began.

Belle's brow furrowed. "What do you mean?"

He leaned back in his chair. "When my parents were alive, they always called me Maxwell. My friends called me Max, but my father told me the importance of using my name. It was about more than your identity; it was about integrity, that which defines you. When I was growing up, I saw myself as two separate individuals. Maxwell started Titan Telecom. He's ruthless, cold, business savvy. What you would call a robot," he said with a grin.

She smirked. "And who's Max?"

He grew sullen for a moment before answering, "Max is who I want to be, who I can be when I'm alone. Maxwell is how my parents saw me, and I guess you could say I kept the name up to keep their memory alive. When they died, using my full name felt like the only connection I had to them, especially since my relatives sold off most of their belongings. Yet..." He paused and shared a meaningful look with her that took her breath away. "Max is how you make me feel when I'm with you. More than a robot... and maybe even human."

Belle swallowed hard as her heart raced. The depth of this man was never-ending, and she wanted to ask him so much more. What kind of people were his parents? What was he like as a child? She heard through office gossip he was orphaned at a young age and wasn't close to any other relatives.

"I guess Maxwell does sound more professional and intimidating for a man being dubbed as the second-coming of Steve Jobs. Maybe you should start rocking up to the office wearing black turtlenecks and washed-out blue jeans," she quipped.

Max huffed out something that wasn't quite a laugh but not quite a sigh either. He scratched the shell of his ear, something he did when he was flustered.

"It's kind of embarrassing to be called the second-coming of someone else and also a bit infuriating. I do want to leave behind a legacy like he has. You've heard about the 5G network, right?" he asked.

She nodded.

"We're about to be ushered into a new era of mobile networks and global connectivity that will change the world as we know it. I want Titan to be one of the companies leading the charge. I want the company to live up to its name, which is why I have my team working tirelessly around the clock and why I'm so intent on breaking into the Asian market. I want us to be the next Apple and Huawei. In fact, I want us to surpass them." He spoke so animatedly that Belle felt herself growing excited as she hung on his every word.

"That's why I'm so hard on everyone. I don't like working with slackers or people who are here just because they need a job. I want to be surrounded by people who are as passionate as I am. I want to be around people who are willing to unlock their full potential; otherwise, my efforts are wasted, and life is too short for me to have more regrets. Sorry, I'm rambling, aren't I?" he asked, a red tinge to his cheeks,

Belle folded her arms on the table and leaned forward. "I don't mind. Actually, I admire how passionate you are about everything. I hate to admit it, but I'm one of those people who shows up to work just because of the paycheck. I don't even know if I have a passion for anything. For the longest time, my main focus was caring for my mom, and now that she's gone, I'm kind of coasting along, waiting to see where the current leads me. So, I envy people like you who know what they want and go after it wholeheartedly. I'll be rooting for you, Max. I hope your vision comes true," she declared in an impassioned speech.

Max stared at Belle in stunned silence. It had been a while since someone sincerely wished him the best without having an ulterior motive. That is not to say that Belle didn't have an ulterior motive. Even if he was the one to invite her out for dinner, and he wasn't afraid to admit that he was smitten with her, there was a part of him that didn't trust people who were wary of the connection between them.

In a short space of time, Belle had become one of his closest friends. Yet, she knew next to nothing about him. He was still wavering between putting his trust in her hands and letting himself fall in love or cutting things off before things got too complicated. He'd meant it when he said Belle made him feel like the boy he used to be before his parents died— and how he was shuffled from one relative to another who couldn't be bothered to show a grieving child a bit of love and affection. Now that he was making millions, suddenly, everyone was quick to remind him that he shared their DNA.

Old friends he hadn't talked to in years started to crawl out of the woodwork and in need of a monetary favor or two. The women from his past were just as bad, scheming behind his back to lock him into a permanent commitment, which was why he avoided dating anyone for almost two years. And then there was Belle, with her guileless eyes and sweet smile, who never asked for anything and seemed to genuinely like him.

Ah, dammit! Could a person fall in love so quickly? Was it even love he felt, or was he confusing affection for something more?

"Max? Did I say something wrong? You look upset."

He forced his thoughts aside and saw that Belle looked a bit apprehensive. She was playing with the thin bracelet that hung around her wrist, not fully meeting his gaze.

"Uh... sorry about that. I had an epiphany about a problem the programming team has been working on, and my mind drifted. I tend to do that a lot, but I want you to know that I appreciate your well-wishes, and I hope that you find your passion as well."

"You're such a workaholic. You need to learn how to disconnect one of these days." She smiled at him, her shoulders sagging in relief. They continued eating, talking about their lives from the books Belle was reading to his latest obsession with the Red Dead Redemption game.

Their evening concluded without the spark of fireworks but was still as heated as the flame that ignited the wick.

Max stood outside Belle's house, watching that she reached her door safely. They had stood there together in silence, both wanting to continue the night in a more pleasurable fashion, but Belle seemed hesitant. He didn't want to push. Instead, Belle reached forward and kissed his cheek, her lips lingering with longing desire that he wished nothing more than to act on.

There was no denying a romantic relationship was brewing between them, but he told himself to take things slow. After all, Belle had just lost her mother, and it would be poor form for them to jump into anything without knowing for sure this was real.

He pocketed his hands and watched her ascend the stairs to her place before turning to walk back to his car. There was a moment during dinner where their feet began the old song and dance of playing footsie. Since then, he had a difficult time hiding his erection, especially as he watched her enjoy eating her chocolate mousse.

Even though they both restrained themselves, Max decided to remain home for the night. Spending some quality time with his hand, a long shower, and erotic dreams of Belle's naked body beneath his seemed like a good idea. He could settle for that.

CHAPTER 6

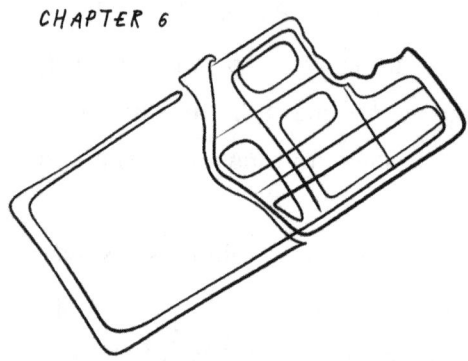

BELLE WAS TORN. She knew that she was starting to have feelings for Max—and much quicker than she had wanted to—but it was not something she was keen on admitting to yet. The two of them were like fire and ice, regardless of how well they got along.

Coming from such different backgrounds was a curse to any relationship, and she was self-aware enough to know that it was her, not Max, who was from the wrong side of the tracks. She didn't want to consider how he would react if he knew how she had earned her keep only a few months ago.

Belle shook her head, running a hand through her thick hair. It was not the time to ponder such pointless things here at work as she leaned back in her desk chair, rolling her shoulders after a particularly long stretch of data entry. It was only midmorning at the office, and everyone around her was still fully immersed in their screens, hurrying to finish their actual work before they engaged in their secondary job of discussing the office gossip.

If only they knew what kind of juicy gossip there *really* was.

After that first date, Max had asked Belle to go out with him again. She had told herself after the night at the restaurant that she was going to put some distance between them, knowing that any relationship between them could only end in cataclysmic heartbreak. When he had caught her in her secret vending machine hideout at work and asked her to come out with him again, she knew she should have said no. He had smiled at her for the brief moment that he waited for her reply, and that smile shone with the confidence, earnestness, and passion that she found so attractive in him.

The function of her mouth completely bypassed its usual thought process, and she accepted.

It had been months now, and she still couldn't force herself to put any distance between them. Whatever self-defense tactic she was hoping to accomplish with that thought process was clearly being overwhelmed by that smile. She felt like a roller coaster these days, dancing around happy and content one moment and the next devastated by the weight of her sorrows.

As she stood to take a short break and stretch her legs, her mind dwelled on the image of the man and his smile she was growing so fond of. Like many other girls, Belle had grown used to the urge that she had to compare herself to other women, but she had never imagined that she would be comparing herself to a man like Max.

She thought about what she had worn today—a fitted black skirt with a subtle, modern plaid and a tailored cream blouse to match. She imagined that she looked much like what the ideal office worker was meant to. She had perfected the look of business casual. She could pull her hair into the perfect, stylish buns and french twists. She wore heels to work, always three inches high so as not to be too low or too high. Her makeup was always done in muted, natural colors with the goal to enhance her features but not be distracting. But what most people didn't understand was that her perfect office worker outfits were just one of her many masks.

She knew, objectively, that she was beautiful, but that did not change the fact that she felt inadequate. Could she ever be a true match for Max? She mentally tried to go through a list of possible qualifications she might have for the position, desperately hoping that something would come to mind. Belle knew that she was somewhat intelligent, but she was far from one of those high-class ladies she saw in television dramas. Their grace was hard to mimic for someone like her: a college dropout with an unsavory, not-too-distant past. Those types of women were witty and clever, astute enough to know when to be quiet, great-mannered, and oozed intelligence and inward strength.

Those women moved up the chain at work by outwitting all of the competition and outworking everyone's expectations. She imagined that women like that were probably up on the fourteenth floor with Max right then. Compared to them, she had no idea what Max saw in her.

Belle turned to her secret vending machine in frustration, not quite ready to head back to her desk. Clearly, this thought process was going nowhere. If she kept thinking about the *what ifs* of their relationship, she would have to cancel. Belle knew deep down she had no chance of being accepted into his world, but that didn't mean she was ready to face that reality yet.

They may have been dating frequently now, but she couldn't help but feel like a charity case to Max. Her anxiety over their relationship had grown to the point of her feigning illness—even to herself—so that she did not have to deal with the thought of losing him.

How had she gotten so attached in such a short period of time? She looked back on all their dates, the times they had gone to fancy restaurants or had whispered conversations beside this very vending machine, and felt a tingly, sweet feeling itching up her throat. She wasn't stupid enough to not realize what it was.

She was falling. Hard.

And that was terrifying enough for her fear to quadruple in size.

She pulled out a bill from the hidden pocket in her skirt and punched in the code for a chocolate bar. It was far too early in the day to be succumbing to her sugar cravings, but today she couldn't help herself. Knowing she was in the same building as Max and having all these thoughts floating through her head was a dangerous combination. That, added on top of the feeling of profound loneliness that comes when a person is certain that there is no one on earth who really knows all the parts of you, Belle needed something to inject some joy into her system.

With Max, she felt joy, but she knew it wasn't something she should count on forever. Trying to be brave, Belle decided that the chocolate bar would have to do for today.

What if Max becomes bored of me? Belle thought suddenly, the ideas racing through her mind like a NASCAR driver.

Could she keep his attention long enough to convince him to fall in love with her too? Could he even love her at some point? Is that how love worked at all? She thought about all the time she had spent at her mother's sickbed or laying on a cheap motel mattress while a client fucked her numb and wondered what she might have been doing right now if her life had been different, if none of those things existed. Would she have fallen in love already, a long time ago? Would she have had some college sweetheart sweep her off her feet?

She thought about Max and found it hard to believe. In fact, even in that past reality, she couldn't imagine being as attracted to anyone like she was to Max.

Perhaps some people would be embarrassed with their lack of experience with love at her age, but that wasn't what she felt. Instead, she just felt ashamed of all the years of heartache and devastation that had prevented her from having those normal experiences.

One thing she knew for certain after working in such a twisted industry as an escort was that there were flaws not even make-up could fix. Anyone could make themselves look stunning if given enough time and money. What counted was hidden beneath the skin, the personality that shone through all the costumes. If a girl didn't have a decent personality, they were tossed to the side like a ragdoll after their partners had their fun. Being discarded after a man had his fun was an experience she was intimately familiar with.

Would that happen to Belle with Max, too? Would Max grow tired of her and toss her aside in the end?

Her musings were interrupted when she heard deep voices coming in her direction. Knowing that she was probably in too somber of a mood to have a friendly chat with any of her coworkers, Belle did her usual when she came to the secret vending machine and ducked around the side that was sheltered by the enormous palm plant.

She recognized Max's voice immediately and almost stepped back out to greet him before she realized that he wasn't alone. He was speaking to another man, the two sounding casual and comfortable with each other.

She was unintentionally eavesdropping for all intents and purposes, but Belle suddenly didn't know how to step back out from her hidden corner now without looking like a complete weirdo. Since Max wasn't alone, she hoped that they'd pass by her, leaving her unnoticed. At the most, they'd see her at the last second and assume she was just another employee taking a break in a quiet spot.

Instead, the two men stopped directly in front of the machine.

"So, no one said anything about it then?" the other man's voice said. Belle squinted her eyes, thinking. Did she recognize that voice?

"Of course not," Max replied. "You know Ana and I aren't like that."

"Riiiight," the man drawled sarcastically. "You're just *friends*."

"Don't be an ass, Grayson," Max said quietly, "You of all people know what's really going on."

Belle's stomach clenched at the topic of their conversation. Who was Ana? And was something "going on" between them? If it was possible, Belle's mood dropped even further, humiliation starting to mix in with the loneliness.

But to her surprise, the man with Max capitulated immediately to his request.

"You're right. Sorry," the man said, "I was just trying to get a rise out of you. But, wow! I mean, just—wow. Is this really how things are going for you now? Are your feelings getting so involved that I can't even make *jokes* about Ana anymore?"

Max sighed, "Don't make me say it."

The man barked out a laugh, clearly enjoying Max's discomfort. Belle started to feel uncomfortable hiding behind the vending machine, listening to what was clearly a private conversation—even if the conversation was something that she desperately wanted to hear. What kind of feelings was Max having? And more importantly, about who?

"Well, I'm glad," the man said, sobering, "This has been going on long enough that I'm glad you finally took a shot at it. Sheesh, how long has it been anyway? Where is *she* at? Is she right there with you?"

She? Belle's thoughts raced, imagining some other unnamed female. After all, Belle didn't know what Max and she *were*—an occasional date? Friends? A one-night stand turned casual romantic partner? If there was some other woman that Belle didn't know about, Max technically wouldn't be cheating or breaking any rules at all. That didn't mean it would hurt any less for Belle, though.

She almost couldn't let herself imagine that they were dating exclusively, that the woman the two men in front of her were talking about might be Belle herself. She was sure the likelihood of that was slim and letting herself really imagine it would just be too high of a cloud for her to fall from. There was no way, not after losing her mother so recently, that she could lose someone else she cared about and still have her heart survive the separation.

All at once, Belle realized that not only should she not be eavesdropping on their conversation, but that she didn't want to be. She didn't know what they would say next, and today in particular, she didn't know if she could handle whatever it would be without ending up in a heap of self-hating tears.

"I'm not sure," Max started to say, "It seems like she's— Oh! H-Hello!"

Max's eyes were wide, and he was so caught off guard that he took an uncharacteristic, wobbly step backward.

"Be—Ms. Aston!" he said again, seeming to be trying to get his bearings, "I'm just—this is my business partner, Gr—"

"Excuse me, Mr. Erickson," Belle said politely. "I was just having a short break and didn't want to be rude and not announce myself while you had a personal conversation."

"Oh. Oh, well—that's okay," Max stuttered.
What was going on? Belle had never seen Max so flustered before, certainly never so much so that he stuttered. The collected, professional Max Erickson was not a man who tripped over his words.

Belle glanced momentarily over at the man Max had been talking to. She was only able to take in his dark grey wool suit before she was captured by the smile that was spreading across his face and the quiet chuckles that he was making. He reached a hand up to cover his mouth, apparently to hide his reaction. Belle didn't know whether she was offended or not. Was he mocking her for something? Or was he amused about Max's unusual behavior, like Belle was?

"Well," the man started to say to Belle, "I have been waiting a long, long time to—"

"Grayson was just leaving," Max interrupted, glaring at the man.

The man tipped his head to the side in amusement. "Really?" he said to Max.

"Really," Max seethed back, clearly the butt of a joke that Belle wasn't getting.

Regardless, Belle couldn't help grinning at Max's discomfort, too, and she turned to the man to share a tiny smile with him before he tipped his chin at her and then turned to leave. "Until next time Ms. Belle," the man said.

He put his hands into the pockets of his suit pants and strolled around the corner, leaving Max and Belle alone.

"I'm sorry for interrupting," Belle said quietly, "I was just taking a minute away from my desk."

Max sighed and smiled, finally turning his body all the way to face her. "That's alright, Belle."

"There is almost never anyone in this hallway," she reminded him, trying to defend herself for the eavesdropping that she still felt bad about.

He let out a small chuckle, then met her eye and raised one eyebrow, "Yes. I'm *very* aware that you're the only one who comes through this hallway."

He stepped forward, getting far closer to her than he ever had at work before. Belle didn't miss the emphasis on the word 'very,' and a flutter had run through her stomach when he said it. Max reached a hand up to brush along her hairline as though he were going to push a strand behind her ear.

"Have my bangs come loose again?" Belle asked, moving her hand up to check the spot he had just brushed.

Max smiled and grabbed her hand, pulling it away from her forehead and closer to him.

"No, it hasn't," Max said quietly, the sound of his smooth, powerful voice sent a whole new surge of excitement through Belle's body.

He gazed down at her hand, and Belle followed, watching too as he turned it over, unfurled each finger, and ran his thumb across her exposed palm. After a moment of charged silence, Max brought her hand up slowly and, ever so carefully, placed a kiss in the center of her palm. When his lips touched her skin, it was as if a match had been lit at that place on her hand, the flames slowly igniting as they traveled up her arm.

Max pulled up just slightly and then turned his eyes up to meet Belle's. A small, gentle smile covered his lips, and he never looked away as he stood straight again and slowly lowered Belle's hand back down to her side.

Belle didn't know what to say. She had no idea how to read the expression on his face, and she was suddenly overwhelmed with the desire to never to let go of his hand. But knowing they were at work, and that she didn't want to let anyone see her getting this close to the boss, Belle pushed her feelings down and tried to put on a professional expression. She clasped her hands together in front of her.

"I'd better get back to work," Belle said, embarrassed that her voice was almost a whisper. She cleared her throat before she spoke again. "I still have a lot to do today."

Max nodded, his smile widening, "Then I won't keep you." He gestured with his hand in the direction of the hallway that led back to her desk. "I apologize for cutting your break short."

Belle shook her head and waved his comment away with a hand, the universal sign to say that it was no problem. She turned in the direction of her desk and began walking.

"Enjoy the rest of your day, Mr. Erickson," Belle called over her shoulder and then hurried down the hallway and back to her desk.

It wasn't until later, as she played the conversation between Max and his friend over and over in her head, that she realized the man had called her by name when neither Max nor she had given it.

But that fact was forgotten when she returned to her desk later in the afternoon. After having to deliver papers to another team member on a different floor, a chocolate bar was sitting on her desk. It was the exact same kind she had been eating when she'd unintentionally eavesdropped on Max this morning. There was a note attached to it, written on a blue sticky note.

To make up for cutting your break short this morning.

CHAPTER 7

"YOU WOULD TELL ME if something was wrong, right?" Max asked from the opposite side of the limousine.

They were on their way to an artist's gallery opening. Or a pre-gallery opening, as Max had informed her. It was a private party held separately from the official event that would take place in a few weeks, the kind of exclusive evening that Belle stressed over endlessly, worrying about how obvious it was that she didn't fit in.

After she heard Max and his friend talking at work a couple of weeks ago, Belle felt unsure how to view this thing that was developing between her and Max. Had the two men been talking about another woman? Then how was Max able to be so sweet and caring to her afterward? She remembered the gentle kiss on the center of her palm he had given. She curled her fingers into a loose fist as though she could hold that beautiful feeling there.

What if it was just to distract me? Belle thought. What if he had been talking about someone else but wanted to continue things with me? What if the kiss was just a diversion from his earlier conversation?

Belle uncurled her fingers and let the feeling dissolve into the air. She had to be cautious around him, she knew. She was falling so hard. So fast.

Belle nodded in response to Max's question and put on a bright mask, smiling wide to convince him that she was fine.

"Yes, of course," she replied, "Does something look wrong?"

Oh no. Did this dress look as cheap as it actually had been since she'd only been able to afford something from the discount rack at Nordstrom?

"You've been quiet tonight," Max said, studying her face carefully, "If you don't want to go, we can go back to your house. Have a night in?"

"I'm fine." She shot him a smile and put on a cheerful mask, "Just a little tired. But I'm still excited to be with you tonight."

Max reached his hand over the seat between them and grabbed on to Belle's, tangling their fingers together and giving a small squeeze. He gave her a small, sincere smile before he nodded in acquiescence and turned to gaze out the window while they drove.

As attentive as Max was—and he certainly was that—his words were like knives, digging into Belle's heart. Was it so blatant that she didn't want to go out? Was she so obviously a misfit for Max's usual, elegant company?

Belle had spent the last two hours doing her hair and make-up and thinking about all the reasons why she didn't want to go to this event tonight. It was the kind of posh outing that she would have been paid to attend a year ago, clutching the arm of a man who was richer than he was kind. The other people there would be sophisticated, educated, wealthy, a demographic so well defined that there might as well be a sign hanging around their necks that said, *"Belle, are you sure you belong here?"*

She knew the answer to that question, and yet the man sitting beside her, gently holding her hand, was making it hard for her to say no even though, for his sake, she knew she probably should.

She thought about the way Max had looked when he'd arrived to pick her up for the evening.

When she had come down the hallway to greet him, Max had already entered and was standing by the front door, gazing at the photographs on the wall and looking like he'd stepped out of the pages of a magazine. He was wearing a black suit and a blood-red shirt. Black certainly suited him, bringing out the golden undertones in his skin and the vibrancy in his eyes. It had another side effect, though, of making him look infinitely more intimidating and unattainable.

Since he hadn't noticed Belle yet, she took a moment to study him in detail, something she rarely could get away with at work. He was fidgeting with the cufflink on his sleeve, making him look nervous, as though he might be as eager to see her as she was to see him. Despite his commanding presence at work and the way he glowed with power and authority, Belle had been surprised in the month since they'd started spending time together, that in private, he often resembled a cute puppy. She softened even more toward him as she thought about it. In moments like this, it was easier to forget their differences.

Since they entered the limousine that he had rented for the night, though, his endearing fidgeting had eased, and his collected CEO face had taken over as he gazed out of the window quietly, probably thinking about all of the people he needed to talk to that night.

The rest of the car ride to the gallery passed in silence. Soft music vibrated from the front speakers, lulling Belle to finally relax. So many of her thoughts lately revolved around how unsuited she was for the role of Max's romantic partner. She had been trying to push those thoughts aside all evening, instead focusing on the fact that she was going on a date with an incredible man who seemed to genuinely care that she had a good time tonight.

Her heart, though, refused to calm down. How was she supposed to put those fears out of her mind anyway? She was an ex-escort sitting in a limo next to Maxwell Erickson, the best man she'd ever known. The moment she stepped out of the car, though, knew she was being foolishly naive to try and convince herself that her fears didn't matter. People were crowding the entrance, a few of them even trying to press through the stocky security men guarding the door.

Max had called this a small event. This was small? She looked at the glamorous dresses of the crowd and couldn't help but wonder what the people who were actually invited to the event were wearing. She swallowed hard.

"Ah, looks like we arrived just in time," Max said, leading Belle right to the front of the line. There was no questioning of their names as the bouncer nodded at them, and they brushed by him without a backward glance. Was he such an important figure that he did not have to prove who he was?

A woman attempted to slip in front of them, dressed in a cheap crimson dress that resembled Belle's too much for her liking.

"Excuse me, but I've been waiting for far longer than them! I am on the guest list; just check my name!" the woman exclaimed.

Max snorted an uncharacteristic sound that Belle had not expected from him. It wasn't the blatant derision she had heard so many times in the past from the men she'd worked with, but it was a noise of discomfort and awkwardness—maybe even annoyance.

Unfortunately, she recognized the woman's desperation all too well.

Scarlet hair in a messy bun, deep cleavage that appeared just slightly too crass at such events as this, clothes that were made to resemble famous brands but were made from scratchy, synthetic material: her appearance screamed escort from top to bottom. Belle went through something similar a couple of times.

Some clients liked to embarrass their escorts before rushing in to save them. It was a disgusting practice that had made her skin crawl, but there were a lot of men who enjoyed playing hero.

Shaking her head to clear it of the past, Belle focused on her date. For once, she was not there to be arm-candy. It was still difficult to wrap her mind around it even though the two of them had been seeing each other frequently for a while now. Belle knew that it was not a good idea for her mind to focus on bad memories. Still, she couldn't help but be confused by the 180-degree flip in her situation now. What were Max and her to each other anyway?

The crowd cheered behind the fences, making her feel that she was more than a clerk at some tech company.

He wasn't paying her for her company, and even though she knew that she was supposed to have more self-respect than that, the lack of this evening being a business transactional one was enough to make her feel special. He never gave her a play-by-play for a role she needed to fulfill for the evening, nor did she need to spend hours rehearsing to make sure she fit the part. This was supposed to be fun, the two of them browsing paintings, snacking on overpriced food she more than likely wouldn't be able to pronounce correctly.

Belle released a soft sigh. *It's common courtesy, not my training,* she though to herself.

"Do you know her?" she asked about the red-headed woman after a moment of silence. Max seemed entirely indifferent as the woman was dragged away by security, but she could hear the noise he'd made before echoing through her head. Belle winced, hit with a pang of sympathy for the woman. The poor woman was almost too horrible to watch. She recalled something similar happening to her when she first started working as an escort.

"No," Max admitted, clearly unaware of Belle's inner turmoil, "But I do pity her."

He pulled her closer. "Come with me. There's a painting I want to show you."

Pity, right. That didn't make her feel better.

But at least he hadn't shown contemptuous disgust like others around them had. She didn't know how to feel about his reaction, and between feeling defensive of the woman and the same pitying sadness that Max seemed to feel, her heart settled far away from any thoughts of the woman entirely. The whole encounter just reminded her of how different Max and she really were.

The exhibition was tastefully decorated with shades of blues. Gold table cloths and fabric napkins covered bar height tables around the enormous room. It was all the things one would associate with an event like this, and it was far different from what she was used to. Modern art sculptures broke up the elegant, traditional décor, creating a curious atmosphere. Belle had to admit it was strange, but the crowd seemed to enjoy it.

As they entered the crowd of party-goers, Max placed her hand in the crook of his elbow. It was a courteous gesture, but by the sudden onslaught of heads that turned their way, she couldn't help but feel it was a possessive one too. Blending in was something an escort was supposed to be good at, right? Why then did she feel like everyone was watching her? She knew it must be her imagination. Why, in an entire gallery full of art, would she be the center of everyone's attention?

"I feel bad for her, too," Belle said as she eyed one of the enormous paintings that hung on an otherwise empty grey wall. Her sudden change of topic caused Max to question what she meant. "The woman outside," she elaborated, "I feel bad for her, too."

He didn't respond, his mind obviously having moved so far beyond the incident that he didn't even seem to register what she had said. He pointed to the painting before them. The art itself was nothing more than an empty canvas, with only five brilliant red brushstrokes adorning it. Belle's eyes narrowed as she tried to make heads or tails of why it was so adored.

"You don't seem overly fond of this one," Max whispered, giving her a devious grin. Her cheeks flushed.

"I don't understand it," she admitted.

"Ah, I don't doubt that most people here feel the same." He drew her closer, his fingers brushing a flyaway piece of hair from her eyes to behind her ears. She shivered. "Sometimes, the price tag doesn't truly reflect an item's value."

Belle nodded, unsure of what he meant. They paused as they pretended to take in the silly piece, and then the two of them continued their tour of the exhibition. After that less than impressive first impression, Belle was surprised to see that some of the items were far more interesting. There was a gorgeous dress created from hand-dyed silk that hung from the ceiling in the middle of the room. It seemed to attract plenty of attention.

"That is one of the main attractions tonight. But you'll hear more about it later," Max explained as the pair stepped closer to the dress. Belle imagined herself wearing the dress—could almost feel how the vibrant silks would smooth across her skin. She smiled at the mental image.

"It's stunning!"

Her face was turned away, entranced by the artwork, but her genuine awe didn't go unnoticed by Max.

"It is," he said, clearing his throat, "however, I bet it would be uncomfortable to wear."

Belle smiled again at his pragmatism. He was right. Even a taller woman would have swum in the abundance of material. The dress bodice was a deep scarlet that slowly bled into a bright yellow skirt. It was named "The Kimono," a title that Belle found on a clear plexiglass stand directly underneath the display. All around the dress, small cut-out birds flew while a brilliantly painted gold and red sun beamed from behind it. It was both a garment that could be worn and a living piece of artwork, too exquisite to touch.

"I bet it would be," Belle admitted, " But I still wouldn't mind trying it on."

The ornate gold jewelry that accompanied the dress caught Belle's attention. A sigh escaped her as she imagined what it would feel like to wear something so breathtaking.

"Ana, hello!" Max exclaimed, and Belle wrenched her head away from the dress to watch as a stunning blonde walked right up to Max, placed her hands on each of his shoulders, and kissed him on the cheek as though they were high society socialites. On second thought, Belle realized that was probably precisely who they were.

A flood of jealousy filled her vision. Who the hell was this?

"Maxy!" she said in a voice that was surprisingly low and smooth, "You brought someone with you! Hello, darling, I'm Anastasia Berkley, Max's friend from college. It is such a pleasure to meet a date of Max's that isn't actively draping herself all over him."

She laughed at her own joke and then held out an elegant hand, perfectly manicured with red paint, for Belle to shake. *Wasn't actively draping themselves all over Max?* What did that mean? Was she annoyed because women were always throwing themselves at Max for his money or because being draped all over him was exactly what she wanted to be doing? Based on their friendly greeting, it could have been either.

"This is Belle," Max said, gazing down at Belle with a wide smile and then back at Anastasia with an equally happy expression.

Belle had always noticed how his demeanor changed when Max and she were together, how his shoulders would relax and his face would soften. She had felt special, thinking it was something that only she could bring out in him, but seeing him looking at Anastasia now, she wasn't so sure.

"It's nice to meet you, Ms. Berkley," Belle said politely with a slight dip of the chin. She swallowed nervously, unsure of how she was supposed to act around someone as elegantly stunning as this blonde-haired, curvy bombshell in front of her. One who apparently was on friendly enough terms with the man that Belle fervently hoped would officially be her boyfriend soon, as to call him by a cutesy nickname in public.

Maxy.

Belle was the only one who went so far as to call him by his first name at all, nonetheless: Maxy. How close did you have to be to Max for him to not even flinch when you called him something so familiar?

She was already jealous, but should she be feeling anything else? Worry? Suspicion?

Anastasia's smile widened as she addressed Max again.

"Have you seen 'The Bleeding' yet?" she whispered, leaning in as though she were about to convey a secret, "It's just a bunch of red paint strokes! I heard it's been priced at over two million!"

Max shook his head and chuckled. "We just came from there, didn't we, Belle?"

"Yes," Belle replied, trying to be gracious even though the words 'two million' were echoing through her head like a shotgun fired in a canyon. "Though it wasn't my favourite, there are certainly other pieces here I've enjoyed."

She thought of the silk dress and its sunset-themed splendor. *How much was that worth?* Belle wondered.

Anastasia let out a knowing laugh, "Your date is so polite, Max. She must not know yet how much I loathe modern art. Come on, you two. You must see the atrocity in the east ballroom. I think it is made entirely from cat hair and wax."

Max smiled politely but held firm when Anastasia wrapped her hands around his free arm and started to tug him in the direction she had indicated.

"I can't tonight, Ana," he said. "Belle and I have some associates to meet before we are free for the evening. Besides, even if I agreed with you, the sight of the three of us whispering and giggly would be bad press for the artist. Surely, you can't dislike modern art *that* much."

"Oh, but I do," Anastasia said firmly. "You agree with me, don't you, Belle?"

Belle wasn't sure what to say. She wasn't even sure what to think of the woman. Whatever she said, she quickly decided that it needed to end the conversation. At least, she'd be able to breathe then.

"I certainly agree with you about the painting. I'm sorry to have to decline the invitation to see the cat-haired atrocity."

Anastasia sighed theatrically and then smiled. "Oh, alright. You two go carry on with your boring networking then."

She waved her hand as though she were shooing them off, and then, with a laugh, she turned and waltzed away to the next artwork.

"Maxy?" Belle said, trying to sound as though she were teasing and not as though she were devastated that there was a woman who called him by a nickname when she'd never even considered that anyone could be so close with him to such an extent before.

Max chuckled and smoothed down the back of his hair, looking embarrassed.

"Yeah. We met for the first time when I was only nineteen. She's a bit of a character and refused to take me seriously no matter what I told her," he admitted.

"She seemed nice, though," Belle said, torturing herself. "Maybe she is a fun character."

"She is," Max agreed, "but I rarely get the chance to see her anymore with both of us being so busy these days."

His words conveyed a familiarity that made Belle uneasy. Did he wish he saw her more? Belle shook her head. If Max had wanted to come with Anastasia Berkley, he would have invited her as his date tonight, not Belle. She took a deep breath and reminded herself that it wasn't a crime for Max to have female friends and that not everyone longed to be his partner as much as she did. She told herself that, albeit still believing it was a different matter altogether.

She returned her gaze to the beautiful dress above them, letting the subject of the woman she'd just met drop.

"If that painting we just saw cost two million dollars, what do you think this is going for?" Belle asked Max. "I don't know that I've ever seen anything so beautiful."

When he didn't answer, Belle turned toward him and caught him gazing at her face, admiring her in a similar way to how she had just been admiring the artwork. Warmth suffused her body.

Max cleared his throat quietly and turned his gaze back out to the crowd.

"Let's go. I see some familiar faces over there," Max pointed out suddenly. Disappointed, Belle shot another fleeting look at the garment. She had hoped to find a way to sneak a photo of it, but with the glamourous crowd milling around them, she couldn't figure out how to do it without looking like a gawking tourist. She doubted that was the image Max would want hanging on his arm at an event like this.

As they walked, her eyes paused as she saw the woman who had been removed from the building half an hour before. A memory came flooding through her at the sight of the redhead hanging on the arm of a man double her age. The humiliating experience Belle had seen earlier reminded her of something similar that had happened to her as an escort. The memory was gone almost as quickly as it came, but in its place, left an ugly feeling behind, something icky that made it feel difficult to take a deep breath. She shook her head and tried to hold her chin up with feigned pride.

She had thought that she and Max would carry on through the crowd to meet whichever friends he had seen, but her heart sped up as Max led them directly toward the couple she had just been looking at.

The woman was now clutching the hand of a balding man who appeared to be twice her age. With Terminator-like vision, the woman scanned over Belle, assessing her for any possible rivalry. Belle had seen it all before. It was a practice that was too common in the escort business. She shot Belle a look of distaste, and it was at that moment that Belle recognized her.

The two of them used to work together.

Belle's heart leaped in her throat as the woman smirked in recognition, obviously amused that it had taken Belle a moment to realize who she was. Belle spared a nervous glance at Max, fearing that her secret was about to be exposed.

Of course, the man Max had to meet tonight just so happened to be Aqua's client, Bell thought, adrenaline flooding her system.

The group politely greeted each other, but Max and the man, a business associate it seemed, were fast to excuse themselves to have a very dull and uneventful chat about coding.

It was difficult for Belle not to ask Max to stay. She wanted to beg. Being left alone with her ex-coworker felt like a death sentence, but she knew that being a bother to her partner would have been even worse.

"Feel free to browse the studio if you wish. I'll catch up with you in a few minutes" Max gently squeezed Belle's hand before walking away, his eyes a clear, unexpected mirror to his thoughts. Was he bored by having to greet all these people he was familiar with?

She would have laughed at his poorly concealed expression, had she not been about to be left to fend for herself with the predatory animals.

"Belle, is that you?" Aqua—her stage name—asked. She eyed her up and down once more before placing a hand over her mouth to stifle a giggle. Her shock was a blatant act of mockery; it was easy to notice when one was used to seeing it.

Here we go, Belle thought with disdain.

She plastered a forced smile on her face that felt too big and showed most of her teeth. A polite expression to anyone watching; a snarl to the woman in front of her.

"Aqua!" They exchanged air kisses, and it provided Belle with a pungent whiff of the girl's perfume.

Holy shit, it made her want to cough. Maybe even gag.

It was important to stay professional even when one was encountering their nemesis. That was what separated high-class escorts from rookies who were still too young and too emotional to know how to move up in their field.

In the escort business, there was no room for emotions. Outside the consideration of your need to make a quick buck through a quick fuck, your personal thoughts were nothing more than a hindrance.

Aqua was the one who gave that advice to Belle when the two of them were still friends. Well, friends in the loose term. Belle had never really liked her, that was true, but that didn't mean they were enemies back then either.

"Ah, darling, I thought that you quit the industry?"

And here it was, the topic Belle dreaded. She knew that if she were to meet anyone from her past, they would bring it up. But of all the people she was bound to run into at some point, why did it have to be her? Aqua had a knack for knowing how to rub salt into invisible wounds and look pretty while doing so; one of the reasons why she was so popular among both pimps and clients. She emotionally crushed the competition until she appeared to be the only professional that was left.

Aqua was one of the top girls when Belle started. She was the example for all new escorts to strive to be, a beauty who happened to be great with her words. She was one of the best-paid escorts in the city as well, and for that alone, Belle had tried to emulate her techniques.

Her personality changed when men were not around. She was like a pet cat that knew how to act sweet in front of its owners and get all the treats it wanted, but once they were gone, her claws came out, and her hunter's instinct was unleashed. She was the perfect actress, which used to make Belle wonder why she came to work in the escort industry in the first place.

Belle had to wonder if she was any different from Aqua and the others now that she had quit being an escort? Did her boring desk job and her considerate almost-boyfriend make her better than any of them? Or on the inside, was she still exactly like them, and her time as an escort would forever haunt her? She might have "quit" the industry, but what did that mean for her as an individual? Experience and memories didn't exactly disappear into the ether just because she wanted them to.

"I did quit," Belle said, pushing her thoughts away, "for some time now." Belle pushed her thoughts away. It didn't matter who she had been when she knew Aqua before. She was trying to be someone different now, and trying had to count for something. She stood her ground, raising her head with pride.

Aqua's lips pulled into an ugly upward curve, forming a smirk. Her brow arched dubiously, her eyes flitting to Max and back as she came to some conclusion. The look made Belle wish she could repeatedly slam her head into the ground until the older woman didn't have the ability to look down on her anymore. That might have worked if they were at a bar, but for now, they were attending a posh art show, and that type of behaviour was frowned upon here. Remembering who she was trying to become, she rephrased the thought. That type of behaviour was unacceptable *anywhere*. If people knew her past, she would be looked down on everywhere she went. Everyone in this room would judge her. If she was ever going to move on from that life, she shouldn't be so affected by anyone's scorn. "Oh, did you? Then what are you doing here with that hunk of man? He certainly looks like he has it all, money, and looks enough for ten of your average clients. He doesn't look like a man who'd need our services, though." The older woman crossed her hands, her pose a clear challenge.

Aqua was in her mid-thirties, but she was still stunning. Her pay was good enough to afford the best skincare products on the market, something Belle could only dream of. Despite her cheap dress, the rest was expensive. It was always odd what she would choose to spend her money on, but it did make sense. A pretty face could pull off even the ugliest garments, after all, while the look of someone who'd been down forty miles on a bad road couldn't be gussied up, no matter a dress' price tag.

"He... uh," Belle stumbled, unsure of how much to convey, "Well, we're on a date."

Not that it concerns you, bitch, she desperately wanted to add.

"A date? You and him?" Aqua let out a sarcastic laugh, "You might be able to fool others, but I won't buy it. Come on, how much is he paying you? Do you fuck him at the end of your date or before? I bet he'd consider switching to someone more experienced."

Aqua smiled as if she were making small talk, but her lips spat poison directly into Belle's heart.

There is no way this stupid bitch is coming near Max, Belle thought as her face began to redden. She almost lost her temper at the thought of Aqua propositioning him; she was *so* close to raising her voice.

"It's a date," she growled. "He's not paying me. Do you think I would turn up in this old rag if a man like him was paying me?" Inwardly, she shook her head at herself for even speaking like that. She hated the iciness of her words, the way she *knew* her eyes screamed, *what else do you have?*

"He's giving you gifts, isn't he? Keeping you in a nice apartment? Bringing you to places like this? Oh, honey," she accused in condescending tones. An accusatory expression flashed across the red head's face making Belle want to scratch it right off her. Belle *knew* what she was going to say.

"You don't think that he's letting you tag along because he likes you, right? I warned you about falling into this trap."

The reason why Belle *despised* Aqua was that she had pretended to care about her when they first met. Belle, however, soon realized that her words were carefully chosen daggers aimed right at her opponent's heart. Belle had once, quite accidentally, stolen one of Aqua's clients. She would never have imagined Aqua doing such a thing at the time, but the man was someone whom Aqua had fancied for real. When he had asked for Belle one night instead of her, Belle hadn't even realized that the older woman knew him, notwithstanding that he had been with her for years, showering her with affection and gifts, letting her live (when his wife wasn't there, of course) in his second home on the lake, or that Aqua had committed the unpardonable sin of having developed feelings for her client. Belle's mom had just suffered a collapsed lung, and the emergency surgery to repair it meant that Belle would take on any client that asked for her. Emotions had no place in the business, after all.

Since then, Aqua had been like a feral animal ready to crush Belle whenever she had an opportunity. The situation couldn't—under any definition—ever be imagined to be Belle's fault. They both knew it, but jealousy bred hatred in their profession, and the two of them were just its latest victims.

"Just stop, Aqua."

Belle was trying to shut the conversation down before things got heated, but deep down, her soul was already hurting. Aqua was the personification of her demons, and her claws had hit its mark.

Just then, Max appeared beside her, guilt flickering in his gaze. Was he upset for leaving his date with such a woman? Did he see how uncomfortable Aqua was making Belle? She closed her eyes and took a breath to bring herself back to reality. The guilty expression on Max's face was probably just a courtesy at having abandoned her while they were on a date, nothing more.

"Well, we are done, ladies." He plastered on a charming grin as Belle leaned against his side, comforted despite herself. Aqua rose an intricately drawn brow, her hand now held by the older gentleman.

The differences between the two couples were apparent. While Max shielded Belle, almost as if to hide her from the public eye, Aqua was proudly shown off.

Perfect

A thought suddenly threw her off guard, blazing through her mind like a wildfire.

Is he ashamed of me? Belle worried, her thoughts swallowed by her phantom tears.

"Just in time!" Aqua sang, gazing up at her companion with a seductive pout and pushing her breasts into his arm, "You promised that the champagne here would be the best I'd ever had, and we've yet to have a single glass. Come on."

They all said their polite goodbyes and Max placed his hand at the small of Belle's back as he drew her away, headed in the direction of a nearby exit.

"I knew it. You're unwell," Max whispered as he embraced her, putting his arm entirely around her waist. He squeezed her gently into his side as he whisked her out of the crowded room and onto a garden behind the art studio. "How about we find some fresh air?"

Belle knew she was supposed to say she was fine. It was important for him to be mingling with his business partners and friends, but her selfish desire to be alone with him won over. Max wasn't a client after all, and she wasn't the paid escort whose feelings he could ignore. Maybe disappearing from the studio would be a relief for the both of them.

"I might need a minute. It's a bit stuffy in there," she admitted, finding it easier than she had thought to be honest.

Aqua's taunting gaze followed her as they entered the garden, her eyes searing through her back. She could almost feel the contempt of it stinging her skin.

Outside was less spectacular than the exhibition room. From what Belle had heard from Max on the drive here, the garden was where the main attractions of the exhibit were meant to be displayed. However, when the weather had quickly turned chilly, the organizers worried the cold would cause damage to some of the art pieces. They'd rearranged the show indoors, leaving the simple gardens to be the quiet haven they now were in.

Max looked at Belle, concern glazing his eyes as he led her to a nearby bench. The garden was lit by fairy lights adorning the lamp posts that surrounded the sitting areas. Everything in the garden was in pristine condition. There were even two waiters waiting outside on any guests who wished to admire the gardens, though few seemed to have ventured this far yet.

"Would you like a bottle of water?" Max tipped her chin up with a finger, observing her face for any clear indication as to what could be wrong. She couldn't help but shudder and lean into his touch with a soft sigh, relieved to be alone with him and away from prying eyes.

"Yes, please," she replied.

She could have pretended to be ill and talked him into leaving with her, but she knew how important this gallery opening was to him. It was evident to her that though he had brought her here as an opportunity for them to spend time together, he was also in a prime environment to be networking, taking every advantage he could to introduce Titan to anyone and everyone he met. So she quelled her turmoil enough to persevere. She never wanted to be someone that would hold

Max back from the remarkable future she could see in front of him.

"This is pretty boring, huh?" Max joked with a grin. He thought she was bored! She wished she could laugh along, admitting to how out of place she felt, and how she wished they could be watching a movie together instead, her in a sweatshirt and leggings and him in jeans and a T-shirt.

But admitting how she was actually feeling was opening up the opportunity for too many other questions that she couldn't let him ask, and so instead, her heartache looked, from the outside, like boredom.

She could work with that. After all, the only time she had ever come to functions like this in the past was when her pockets were being filled. There was no denying it was a chore having to deal with people who thought of themselves as better than her.

She shrugged. "Only a little," she teased. It took them a minute to move. They stood as the waiter approached them to offer various beverages. "Maybe if I had a drink, I'd feel less...." She trailed off when the knowing look on Max's face caught her off guard. She stopped her sentence, shocked at the way he was looking at her as though he knew everything and understood her perfectly. Her heart hammered in her chest as their eyes met.

"It doesn't help. Trust me," he said quietly. He grabbed two bottles of water and handed one to her, nodding to the waiter, who was swift to scamper away. "Don't worry. We only need to stay for a little longer."

"Shouldn't you stay, though? Until, like, midnight at least? It's not even eleven. I mean, don't they expect that from you?" Belle's honest question caused him to laugh.

"No, not tonight, Cinderella." He ran a hand down her side, curving it around her hip, where it sat with an electric charge. "You look stunning tonight, by the way."

"Thank you," Belle muttered, still embarrassed she couldn't afford a dress like the other women attending the party. The breeze picked up, causing her to shiver. "This look doesn't do a good job at covering me up, though. I should have brought a bolero or a scarf. Something."

"Let's go back inside, then. The quicker we greet the rest of the guests, the faster we can leave," Max said.

Belle nodded. She hoped it was not overly obvious how eager she was to leave.

The room was different when they came back in. The dark walls of the gallery were now lit with the images of candles projected onto the artwork. Even the deep-blue rug seemed to glimmer in the candlelight. The gallery had a feeling in it now like they had stepped into a twisted fairy tale.

How did they do that? Belle pondered for a moment, mesmerized by the sudden change. She quickly glanced back at Max, who didn't seem at all surprised. Maybe such magical tricks were commonplace for him as his world.

He scanned the room, searching for someone. "Oh, there he is! Belle, I need to speak with that man over there. After I'm finished, we can leave, okay?" He gestured to a gentleman across the room. "Do you mind?"

Belle smiled and shook her head. "Of course not," she said, "Go ahead."

He guided her over to a small sculpture of something decidedly duck-shaped and then turned to speak to the man he had pointed out before. Belle was surprised when the man turned around to face them, and she recognized him as the man from the other day at the office, the one who'd teased Max while she hid behind the vending machine. The man wasn't far from where she stood now, and when Max walked the short distance over to him, the pair of men greeted each other warmly with a one-armed hug and then a more formal handshake.

"Grayson," Max said, his tone of voice more genuinely pleased than it had been all night, "This is Belle, my date. You might remember her from the office a couple of weeks ago when we... ran into her. Belle, this is Grayson Sinclair, my close friend and business partner."

The man bowed his head slightly. "A pleasure," he murmured in a husky voice.

He took her hand in his and leaned down to kiss it. Her eyes grew wide when his lips barely brushed her skin. It was such an old-fashioned greeting that she couldn't decide if he was making an unexpected attempt to be chivalrous or if it was the seedy gesture of a man used to getting what he wanted from a woman. She'd seen it used in the latter way more than enough that it was hard not to consider it a possibility. Suddenly, her hand was seized by another. Max tugged her back into the safety of his arms, their difference in height meaning that she fit perfectly tucked into his side.

"Possessive around this one, aren't you?" Grayson accused playfully.

This one? Belle questioned, wondering how many women had Max dated before? Were there so many they had to be referred to with such a general moniker as "this one"? Did Max attend events like these with many different women? It was not her right to ask, but doubts were once again clouding her mind, making her wonder how much more suited those women might have been to his life. Had he known about her past, would she have been the one he would have picked to attend this glamorous affair with?

She doubted it.

"Grayson," Max scolded with a scowl that was half-joking, half-serious.

The man, Grayson, held up his hands as if in surrender. "Only making an observation," he defended himself with a laugh.

Ignoring his friend, Grayson turned toward Belle.

"It's a pleasure to meet you, Belle. Officially," he said. "I am usually the boorish one out of Max and me, but if his possessive hand snatching is any indication then I'd be so very pleased if you thought the opposite."

Max rolled his eyes but was smiling along with Grayson, a dynamic that seemed to be the norm between the two men. Putting together in her mind the image of this brief exchange as well as the moments she had seen previously of the two men interacting at the office, Belle was able to realize something: Max and Grayson were friends.

Actual friends.

They were not the type of friends that everyone else at this party seemed to be, a kind of half-friend that you treated with faux politeness in the hopes that your good manners would pay off in the form of a profitable business transaction one day. Whatever friendship existed between these two men was genuine, and Belle immediately breathed a sigh of relief. If he was Max's friend, then she trusted her date's judgment enough to know that Grayson must be a good guy.

"You're right," Belle teased, taking a gamble and playing along with the man. "I thought I was the only one who noticed how awful he was being. I mean, did you *see* how he has been treating everyone this evening?"

Grayson laughed at the obvious joke. Max was nothing if not utterly polite to his business associates.

"Alright, alright," Max said, curving his body between Belle and Grayson in a way that could only be described as, well—possessive.

"I knew you were going to be here tonight, Grayson, but I didn't think I'd have to protect myself from you *and* my date ganging up on me."

Max smiled down at Belle to let her know that he was also teasing, and seeing this new side of him made something pang inside of Belle's chest. He'd been playful with her before, but nothing so obvious. Max was including her in a joke with his friend, and somehow that made Belle feel more special than even the crowd of jealous onlookers at the entrance had.

She smiled back at him tentatively, trying not to let it show how suddenly shy her own thoughts were making her feel.

Grayson and Max chatted for several minutes after that, the topics of business, art, and even politics all coming up in their casual conversation. Max made sure to include Belle in their conversations, ensuring he never let her feel abandoned or ignored. When Grayson announced that he had a few more people to speak with before he could leave for the night, Belle was surprised to find that she had enjoyed the short interaction immensely. It was so hard for her to trust people in general that she hadn't realized how much she missed such basic human connection as having a conversation with a friend.

Thoughts of friends put her earlier interaction with Aqua into stark contrast with this one. Here she was playing along with one of Max's friends to tease the charming, collected man into feeling comfortable enough to play along right back, when only a few moments before she had been panicked about Max finding out that Aqua and her used to attend evenings like this on the arms of men who were paying to fuck them later. What if he had noticed how casual Aqua was being with Belle before? What if he'd asked if they knew each other and Aqua, always eager for a chance to hurt Belle, had told him exactly how they were associated? Did Belle really think she could fit into this life, talking and enjoying herself at pre-art gallery openings as though this was her norm?

The rest of the evening flew by. After a short speech by the gallery's founder was given, Max and she were finally able to leave. Belle clapped politely along with the crowd, but her mind remained for the rest of the night, elsewhere. Max had attempted to sneak away from the party immediately after they were done talking to Grayson, but a greying older woman caught them on their way to the exit saying how desperately she needed them in the audience.

Maybe, if things were different, Belle would have found it amusing how shamelessly she seemed to have been flirting with Max, but by the time the event was finally over, and they were on their way to her home, the only thing she felt was completely numb. Allowing her thoughts to gain the better of her was a mistake she still made every single day. Every morning she'd wake up, grieve for her lost mother, and then feel guilty for now being able to never have to fuck a man for money again. It was a jumble of emotions and thoughts she could never seem to unravel, unravel, and so, on days like today, no matter how many times she promised herself that she was going to stop thinking about her past as a dark stain on her identity, the shame would creep back in.

Max remained silent during the car ride back to her house, an uncomfortable contrast to their ride here at the beginning of the night. At first, she thought he was just taking a breather, unwinding from the hectic environment of having to put on a perfect mask while networking under the guise of being friends. But his silence hadn't ended, and the entire twenty-minute drive spanned on without a word. He didn't even ask if he could come up for a drink. Belle didn't even bother offering.

The night went unexpectedly, and she wasn't sure if she could handle another moment in his presence without falling to pieces over her insecurities.

She felt regret creep up her spine as she locked the door to her house. She fell back against it and kicked off her heels. She should have known better than to make such a fool out of herself tonight, becoming flustered over her interaction with Aqua and then forgetting that it had happened at all when she met Max's friend. She didn't want to be alone at that moment; her thoughts would be vicious company tonight. Of course, she could have called Max and pleaded for him to turn around and be with her. They could talk and maybe clear up what was between them. He would be confused, not understanding why she had withdrawn so completely at the end of the night, and she would share some of her fears with him—though of course, not the ones that really kept her from sleeping at night. There was also the appealing thought of having another fun night between the sheets with him.

"No, he doesn't need to see me like this," she muttered to herself. Maybe, based on the silence she hadn't been able to identify the source for, he wouldn't have come at all.

Belle had seen the difference between the two of them before, but she'd tried to ignore it. She genuinely liked Max— maybe even too much—and could not have cared less about his money. Yet, on the silent drive back as Max gazed out of the window and away from her, she still felt like nothing but a cute face to show off, regardless of whether it was the truth or not. Still, maybe she could pretend for a while. She desperately wanted to feel like she mattered to at least one person. Why hadn't he spoken to her again after they'd talked to Grayson, then? Why had she held back tears as she silently couldn't help but make the connection between that drive and all the other similar ones she had taken with clients, after an event, before they had their fun?

Was a *single man* worth risking her *dignity* for?

Even if he was, Belle didn't trust herself enough to make the judgement anymore. After all these years, the only thing she was sure she knew how to do was protect herself.

CHAPTER 8

"OKAY, BELLE, JUST PRESS SEND. Stop being a baby about it. Just do it," she muttered to herself, rubbing her eyebrows in annoyance. She had finished filling out an application for a local community college. She had ambitions of pursuing a double major in marketing and graphic design, which offered her a promising future—if it weren't for the crippling fear of rejection that was now choking her. For the past thirty minutes, she'd been editing and re-editing her application and agonizing over whether to send it.

It was now after two in the afternoon, and she was still in her PJs. Her armpits and breath could have wilted the nose hairs off anyone within an arm's length of her. She was surrounded by an empty bag of Doritos, a half-eaten slice of pizza, and three energy bars. The perfect balance for a healthy breakfast. Today was her first day off in weeks, and she was supposed to use it to catch up on chores, like tackling a heap of dirty laundry in her room, but instead, she was here, on her couch, smelling terrible and stressing over an application she hadn't even sent yet. There was no way she would be able to get to anything else until she just hit that button. "Wish me luck, mom," she said, looking at the golden urn with her mom's ashes on the mantle of the fireplace. Her disheveled state was reflected from the black TV mounted above, and Belle grimaced. She took three deep breaths, closed her eyes, and pressed send. Belle leaped up and declared, "Fuck! Okay, there's no taking it back now!"

She went to switch off the laptop when a notification popped up. In what could easily be misconstrued as a stalker move, she had put out a Google alert on all things Max and Titan related, just to see how he was progressing with his big dreams and, of course, to stare at his pictures when the real thing was unavailable.

They went out four more times since the gallery opening five weeks ago. Neither of them had mentioned the strange silence that had ended that night. There had been no formalities made between them. They hadn't even gotten beyond second base yet. Max also never stayed the night again. They still hadn't discussed their relationship at all, and Belle had no idea whether they were exclusively dating or if Max was leading her on.

Based on what she considered to be a hefty dose of life experience, she believed the latter was the correct assumption. She couldn't muster up the energy to feel angry with him, especially when he belonged with a woman like the one who was standing by his side in the picture that accompanied the byline from the alert she'd just received.

Anastasia Berkeley and Maxwell Erickson at a celebratory and retirement gala to honor the former's father, Henry Berkeley, and his contribution to the pharmaceutical industry.

She skimmed over the article to see if they said anything that alluded to them being romantically involved, but aside from a short mention of Anastasia and Max being old university acquaintances, there was nothing about a romantic involvement. That didn't mean they weren't secretly dating or if they had dated in the past. And even though it wasn't explicitly stated in the article, whoever the author was sure had tried their hardest to make it sound like there could be some possible future involvement between the two. She might have been grasping at straws to make a connection, but Belle wasn't.

Looking at them side by side, they made a handsome couple. It was the exact same thought she'd had when she'd met Anastasia at the gallery opening, and here it was, back again as she looked at the photo on her screen. Max in a tuxedo, his hair gelled back with his movie-star good looks, and Anastasia, who looked like Jessica Rabbit came to life but with platinum blonde hair. Belle had never seen Max smile that widely with anyone else but her. Frustratingly, Max had asked Belle if she would like to come with him to this exact gala, another formal event where she would be underdressed and underqualified to be his date. Now she was obsessing over a photograph of him there. If she hadn't declined to accompany him—mainly because of her stupid insecurity—she would have been the one in the picture by his side.

And more than likely, the media and even that exact author would have torn her to shreds.

Jealousy coated her mouth, making it hard to swallow. It was a similar sensation to how her body reacted before she threw up. It also tasted like bitter oranges and marmalade, the jam she smeared on her toast earlier that morning. She obsessed over the picture for over an hour, nit-picking and trying to look for one tiny imperfection in Anastasia Berkeley's flawless image yet finding none. She could have attributed it to the magic of makeup and photo-retouching, but she couldn't. It had been the same the last time she'd seen Anastasia.

A girl like her probably hadn't known a single day of suffering in her entire life. And she probably would never know what it was like to be stuck between a rock and a hard place where the only choices you had were as bad as the other. Maybe she had skeletons in her closet, maybe there was something in her personality that left something to be desired, but there was no way she'd been so close to drowning in doubt, forced to watch her only family die in agony, that she'd had to lie naked on her back, as a man paid her to take something she didn't want to give.

Anastasia looked pure with her flawless golden skin, a princess with a pedigree that matched a man of Max's stature. Even if Anastasia had had lovers before, they had been of her choosing, and she'd been with them out of love, not because of desperation.

Max was the only man she'd ever given herself to freely. Belle was a virgin when she became an escort, and when the small salary she got from working at Titan hadn't been able to pay for her mother's medicine and buy groceries as well, she was desperate enough not to hesitate to sell her virginity to the highest bidder when Romero suggested it.

She had puked over and over that night, feeling disgusted with herself, disenchanted with life, and stuck at the bottom of a well of hopelessness. Not only that, but her client had not been a gentle lover. Belle knew that some girls bled when they had sex for the first time, but she'd never imagined it would be as bloody and excruciatingly painful as the way her client left her.

Romero was pissed when he found her bent over a toilet bowl, all pale and bloody. After her experience, he banned that particular client from his establishment. Not that it mattered to Belle. The damage had been done. She lied to her mother about why she was in pain for the four days it took her to be able to walk normally again, telling her that her period pains were extra painful that month.

At the time, her mother was so sick she didn't realize that it wasn't around the time of the month when Belle usually got her period; her mother had encouraged Belle to keep track of when she had her period, so they both had a pretty good idea of what her calendar looked like.

It took her weeks before she was desperate enough to sleep with another client. The next time she was with a client, she'd lay there like a dead log as the man grunted like a pig on top of her. She quickly learned how to disconnect from the act after that, and before Max, Belle didn't believe she would ever enjoy sex the way it was meant to be enjoyed. Romero had to pull her aside and give her advice. Her inexperience was an issue, and Belle had taken it upon herself to sleep with Romero for the experience until it was no longer a problem. At least, that's what she told herself. Looking back on the way Romero had suggested it, Belle realized that it had probably been just as little her own choice as it had been with any of the clients. If someone had asked her if the experience with him was better or enjoyable, she couldn't have answered honestly. It was such a blur that all the nights with all the different men had blended together in her mind.

Max shattered her expectations and left her wanting more, except now he didn't seem to be interested in taking things further than kissing—heavily, if she was lucky. Maybe he sensed that she was damaged goods and was working up the nerve to dump her. They weren't exclusively dating in the first place. Were they even dating at all?

Suddenly a slimy and dirty feeling fell over her. And it had nothing to do with not taking a shower yet today.

She needed to leave the confines of her house and do something that would keep her thoughts distracted. Determined not to wallow, she jumped into the shower, scrubbing extra hard until her skin was pink and raw. She dressed in tight black jeans, boots that came up to her calves, and a cream oversized knit sweater. It was only October, but there was no mistaking that winter was well on its way. She completed the look with a beanie and grabbed her wallet and phone.

Maybe she would walk around the block and stop by that new cupcake place that opened a few weeks prior. She hadn't been there yet, but she'd seen it pop up on her Facebook and Instagram feed. Apparently, they served more than cupcakes even though the bakery was literally named *That Cupcake Place*.

Outside, the lush greens of summer were fading, and the air was growing cool.

Autumn was her favorite season of the year. She loved when the leaves turned from green into vibrant reds, rich oranges, warm mustard yellows. She also loved the clothing, and of course, it signaled that Halloween was near, the holiday that she adored so much, it was bordering on being a guilty pleasure she had to hide her enthusiasm about around more sane people. Halloween was two weeks away, but some of the houses in the neighborhood were already decked out in their scary decorations.

She and her mother used to go all out on Halloween with the candy and decorations as well as wearing elaborate costumes. When she was younger, her mother would take her trick-or-treating down the block before they came back home, where Belle helped her give out candy. Last year, she made jack-o-lanterns herself, and in the evening, she'd set out two chairs on the porch so that she and her mom could watch other kids collecting candy.

She didn't think she'd be doing anything to celebrate this year. Maybe she'd binge on some popular television series she hadn't seen yet and get drunk on cheap wine and Turkish Delights.

Now that sounded like a nice evening in.

She walked into the bakery, admiring the brilliant use of bright colors and the quirky design of the place when her phone rang. As usual, her heartbeat went out of whack when she saw that it was Max calling. If she weren't deathly scared of hospitals, she would have gone to see a doctor about her developing an arrhythmia.

"Max, hey," she greeted and internally cringing when her voice came out extra chipper and high-pitched. Clearing her throat, she asked, "What's up?" And she stepped into a line that was seven people long.

"Nothing much. What are you doing right now?" Belle heard sounds as if someone was opening and slamming doors closed. Max sounded a bit distracted.

"Buying cupcakes. What about you?" she asked, moving forward as the next customer stepped up to the counter.

Max groaned and let out what sounded like a sigh. "You haven't eaten any yet, have you?" He sounded disappointed, and Belle wondered what was wrong with him.

"No, I'm still waiting in line," she told him.

"Great. Good. Excellent!" Max said enthusiastically. Belle frowned at his strange behavior.

"Actually, I called you because I got my hands on some truffles, and I wanted to cook dinner for you. At my house. Tonight. Could you—would you mind coming over?" He sounded adorably shy and flustered, sending her heart into overdrive once again.

"You can cook?" she asked, unable to keep the shock from her voice.

"I'm decent enough. I won't give you food poisoning or anything," he said in a wry tone. "So, will you come over, or are you going to reject me two nights in a row?"

Belle bit her lip as they tugged into a delighted smile. "I'll come over, but I don't know your address."

"Actually, why don't I pick you up from your place in— let me see, two hours?"

"Okay then, it's a date."

She was wearing a big smile when she stepped up to the bakery counter. Surely one cupcake wouldn't ruin her appetite.

"Hello there, what can I get you?" A curvy redhead with crystal blue eyes smiled at Belle from behind the counter. Her hair was pulled up in a bun, and she had on a polka-dotted blue bandana, tied in a bowtie around her head with her curled fringe peeking out. Her face was round and plump like she'd yet to lose some of her baby fat, and she had a smattering of freckles down the bridge of her nose and cheeks. Her eyes were ringed with a thick coat of winged eyeliner that made them pop.

The fifties hairdo contrasted with the jewel green, cropped sweater she wore and the high waist jeans, but she made the look work. There was a silver-plated name tag above her right boob, which read *Chloe Martin, CEO*.

She looked to be around Belle's age and already knew what she wanted in life. Max was only twenty-six, and he already had a multimillion dollar company.

She felt like a complete failure compared to them.

"Um, what would you recommend?" she asked Chloe, trying to keep her voice positive while looking at the array of sweet confectioneries on the glass counter.

"Hmm, let's see," Chloe said, tapping at her lips thoughtfully. "You look like you could use some loosening up. Have you ever tried alcohol-infused cupcakes, sweetie?" Belle arched her brows at the endearment. "Nope, but I have a date in a few hours. I don't want to show up nine sheets to the wind."

"I think you mean seven sheets to the wind, but who cares?" Chloe laughed, showing off an overbite on her upper teeth. "Don't worry. You can just try one. It won't make you drunk, but maybe it will calm your nerves."

She gestured to a display. "I call these drunken cupcakes. They're chocolate cupcakes with a shot of Irish Cream. A Martin family recipe passed on from mother to daughter. At least that's what I tell everyone, but between you and me," Chloe whispered conspiratorially, leaning over the counter.

Belle mirrored her movements and leaned over as well. "I found the recipe on the internet, and I whip up a batch or two whenever there's a family event. They're great for making people mellow out!" Chloe threw her head back and laughed.

It was such an effervescent sound that made Belle smile. "Okay, I'll take one for now."

"Excellent choice," Chloe exclaimed, packing up the cupcake in a cute, frilly box before turning to ring her up. "Feel free to come back for more and tell me how your date goes. I've been single so long that I live vicariously through other people."

"Uh, sure. I'm Belle, by the way," she said, stretching out her hand. Chloe's handshake was hard, firm, and very warm. "I'm Chloe, but you already knew that. Good luck on your date, Tinkerbell." Chloe winked at her. She frowned when Belle went slack-jawed.

"Sorry, love. Did I say something wrong?"

"N-no. It's just... well, that's what my mom used to call me." Belle swallowed hard and pasted on a smile of thanks. "Anyway, see you around, Chloe, and thanks for this." She held up the tiny box.

When she left the bakery and made her way back home, she was in a daze, like someone had taken a hammer to her heart and pounded it to a pulp.

"So, this is my place," Max declared as he led Belle inside. He lived in a warehouse loft apartment, exposed brick covering one wall. The property wasn't exactly what she expected; it was a simple two-story building owned by the man she had met at the art exhibition, his friend (and later, as she discovered) lawyer, Grayson Sinclair, who just so happened to invest in real estate properties as a sort of hobby.

Belle could only imagine having enough money that buying and selling property could be a part-time hobby.

Belle could feel his nervous eyes on her as she pivoted on her heels, her eyes wide as she drank in every detail. He seemed to grow more anxious the longer she went without saying anything.

The loft was basically one giant room, except for the wall that hid the shower and toilet from view. There was another small room he used as his walk-in closet. It was an open floor plan that showed the entire apartment off, and with the natural lighting from the numerous windows, it looked gorgeously rustic and simple; not something one would imagine a multi-billionaire living in of their own choice.

Where was the glorious penthouse with floor-to-ceiling windows and marble flooring, or the large fireplace that would amount as a centerpiece to tie the décor together?

Max had unexpected depths that Belle kept being surprised by, never quite fitting into the box she tried to label him under.

He'd placed his queen-sized bed a few feet away from the bathroom, the area closed off from the rest of the living space by a curtain that was hung high up on what appeared to be metal shower hangers.

The kitchen came fully outfitted with an island dinner table that separated it from the living room. The cabinets and stove were built into the walls, with a large hood hanging above the stove.

The rest of the house was one large living area. A sectional couch faced a giant flat-screen TV mounted on the wall and surrounded by an entertainment center occupied by his state-of-the-art sound system and gaming consoles.

There was the area he'd carved out for his gaming PC with four different monitors placed next to each other on a desk. That included another sound system as well and his ergonomic chair. A bookcase completed the picture, but it had tons of games and his headphone collection instead of books.

"This is like the ultimate bachelor pad," Belle commented as she walked over to his gaming setup. "I bet there are hundreds of teenage boys who'd sell both their kidneys for all this. I don't know why I'm surprised you're such a minimalist, but this place suits you." She wandered around freely. "I like the open space, especially the huge windows that let in all the light during the day. I'd worry about someone looking up and seeing me naked, though." She looked pointedly at the other set of windows by the bedroom.

"The windows are treated so that no one can see inside, so even if I were to pin you up against them and fuck you, the people walking down the streets wouldn't have a single clue," Max told her, his voice husky and full of need.

"Oh," Belle replied dumbly, her mind suddenly blank of all thoughts except the image of Max and her against the wall, him pounding into her with relentless vigor.

An ache bloomed between her thighs, and she pressed them together, biting down on her lip when she felt the phantom caress of his lips against hers.

She blinked, and Max was in her personal space, tugging her lip free from her teeth and pressing their bodies together so that she felt his aroused cock poking at her abdomen through his pants.

"You shouldn't look at me like that, Belle. At least not until I've fed you, and I know for sure that you have the energy for what I want to do to you." His voice was like smooth whiskey and had her toes curling and her body experiencing hot flashes.

Holy shit, Belle thought. *Is this finally happening?*

After spending the morning wondering what was going on between them and figuring that he was already halfway out the door of whatever semi-relationship they seemed to be in, this wasn't what she expected the night to be.

He bent down to kiss her, but before their lips connected, Belle stopped him with her hand over his mouth. There was something they needed to discuss first.

He raised a brow at her in question. "Something wrong?" he asked, his soft lips brushing against her fingers.

"Yes—no, I mean…" She trailed off and sighed. "We need to talk—about us," she explained, taking her fingers from his mouth and wrapping her arms around herself. "We've been out on a few dates, and you know, kissed more than a few times." Her face felt like it was on fire, and she was too embarrassed to look Max in the eye. She kept curling and uncurling her toes. "But we've never talked about if we're exclusive or if you want to see other people."

He stared down at her for a long moment before saying, "I don't share what's mine, Belle. I won't be responsible for my actions if some fucker lays their hands on you. Feel free to repeat my warning."

Belle rolled her eyes at his response, but her heart leaped for joy, and she allowed him to kiss her.

They moved to the kitchen, where she had a fun time helping him prepare the pasta and truffles that they had for dinner. Conversation flowed as freely as the white wine she drank. She usually preferred red, but Max convinced her to give it a try. Belle got lost in the domestic atmosphere of the night as she and Max cleaned up together before they watched a movie. There was more kissing than actual movie watching, though, and popcorn scattered all over the couch and floor when the bowl tipped over.

"Oops," Belle giggled. She was a little buzzed, but she suspected that her giddiness was more due to Max's excellent kissing than the wine. "I think that's my sign to get back home. It's getting pretty late."

She wasn't ready to leave the warmth of Max's embrace, so when he asked her to stay the night—looking at her with desire and longing in his eyes—Belle didn't even pretend to think about it.

He picked her up and crossed the open space loft to his bed. His lips were already on hers before her feet touched the floor. They made quick work of their clothes, and in a show of extraordinary upper-body strength, Max picked her up again, hoisting her legs over his shoulders so that her pussy was right by his mouth.

Belle struggled for a second, not used to being so high up, but soon her protests dwindled to moans of encouragement.

His breath came out in hot bursts. He ran his hands over her thighs and then leaned down to lick along her wet slit. She shuddered, a soft sound leaving her at the sensation. Max decided he quite liked her noises and found himself determined to bring out more of it.

He made a move, pressing them both to the wall, so he had the support needed for what he did next. With his tongue buried inside her, he eased a hand away from her bottom to brush at her hard nub. Belle squealed, her legs tightening on his shoulders, and he pulled his mouth away so he could nip at the inside of her thighs.

She wanted to roll her hips, but her position prevented her from moving much, so she pushed his head away, causing him to growl in protest. He caught on to what she wanted quickly, though, and lowered her down so he could deposit her onto the bed. From there, she was able to do just that, her hips rolling and pressing them against him as he delved back below.

He hummed against her, the vibrations shooting right through her core, and she wailed out his name.

She was teetering on the edge of her second orgasm, barely having finished the first one, as he fingered her and thumbed her clit expertly.

Max was relentless. This wasn't like the last time they had been together when she was freshly mourning and needed a tender touch. This was his forte.

He stretched her walls by spreading his fingers and then crooked them, pointedly dragging them against that little bundle of nerves inside of her, over and over, pushing her up and up that slippery slope.

He gave her no time to catch her breath. Max ground the flat of his palm against her clit and twisted. Her whole body jerked, hips rocking against his hand.

"There we go," he all but cooed. "Just like that, princess."

His words must have struck a chord—or maybe she really was already at that point. Belle's whole body jerked, muscles going tight as she came for a second time, letting out a shout that could have rattled the windows.

"Jesus!" Belle exhaled, out of breath, and hands still clutching at the sheets. "I don't think I've ever come that hard before. My legs are still trembling."

Max straddled her, a smug look on his face. "Bet you five bucks I can top that," he teased. He lowered on his haunches to kiss her.

Belle stopped him with a hand on his sweaty chest.

"It's my turn now," she told him, giving him a saucy smirk. Max arched a brow but didn't protest when she made him lay down on his back. She ran her hands down his abs, the muscles flinching and quivering beneath her touch. Looking up at him from beneath her lashes, she began kissing her way down his body, following the light spattering of hair she called the goody-trail, a direct descent to his cock.

Belle was better at this than he would have expected. She dragged her tongue along the length of his shaft, mouthing at the side of it before licking, almost gently, at the head.

Max had a lot of girth to cover. She gave it her best shot, though, wringing her hand over the thickness of his shaft and pressing her thumb up against the underside of its head. Heat flooded him, his chest tight at the look on her face when she took him into her mouth in earnest, only to pull back and press the flat of her tongue against him.

When she took him back into her mouth, the head of his cock bumped against the back of her throat in her zealous effort to outdo him. Wet heat engulfed him and Belle breathed in harder through her nose before venturing to take him in deeper, the tight confines of her throat pressing against Max from all sides.

She swallowed with a noisy gag. That was all it took for Max to lose his careful grasp of control. He tangled his fingers in her hair, pinning her in place and pushing in as deep as he could. He rolled his hips, grinding himself into her until she was gagging in earnest. Her face had gone red, tears brimming in the corners of her eyes. But that wasn't what made him pause.

No, it was the way that pleasure had turned into a fire in his spine—an imminent sign that he was nearing his limit. Not wanting things to end yet, he pushed her roughly backward. Belle let out a sound of disappointment but perked up when she saw him take out a condom from one of the drawers. He quickly rolled the latex down his length. Standing at the foot of his bed, he dragged Belle by her ankles toward him until her legs were dangling over the bed.

"Hands and knees. Now," barked Max, his voice gruff.

To his surprise and joy, she listened. Belle rolled into the directed position, her ass in the air and her head down. He rubbed each cheek delicately, palming her for a moment before slipping one hand down and shoving two fingers into her.

With all of the fun that they'd already had, there wasn't anything that Max had to do. She was stretched and wet.

"Good girl," he rumbled. "Just like that. Oh, I'm going to fuck you so good, sweetheart. Going to make you forget about everything else."

Everything and everyone, she thought with satisfaction.

Max didn't have to try and control himself, not like the last time. He curled his hands around Belle's hips, holding her steady and rolling his hips a few times, letting his cock rub against her. When he was certain that she wasn't expecting it, Max adjusted himself and plunged into her waiting cunt.

There was no pause this time. He was lost in the heat of the moment and the thrill of having Belle at his mercy. He set up a hard, fast pace, not bothering to give her time to adjust. She wailed in response.

"Just like that," he grunted. Max curled over her back, deepening his thrusts. He pressed a hand against the back of Belle's neck, pinning her against the mattress. She was utterly at his mercy, and judging from the sounds that kept falling from her, she loved that.

With every thrust, Max's thick length hit that sweet spot deep inside her that had her screaming out and her muscles clenching against his cock. She did not expect the veracity with which he fucked her, especially when he'd been so gentle last time, but now he was like a possessed man.

He pinned her, chasing his own high. There was no way for her to get a hand down between her legs, but that didn't matter. The slapping of skin against skin filled the room.

"You like that?" he growled into her ear, biting lightly on her ear lobe.

"Yes," whined Belle. "Please, please, Max! I'm so close; I'm so close!"

He growled in her ear, biting the side of her neck. He pushed in deep, cum flooding the tight confines of the condom he was wearing. Then, while he was still inside of her, he reached down and roughly rubbed at her clit until she found her release.

She had no idea how long they lay in each other's arms, trying to catch their breath. Max was still inside her and hadn't wholly softened yet. He groaned when Belle began to undulate against him.

"If we're doing this again, I need to put on another condom," he said, reluctantly pulling out of her warmth.

"Dammit!" He suddenly cursed, his blood freezing in his veins.

"What's wrong?" Belle sat up quickly, using her elbows to support her weight. Her skin was flushed and glistening with sweat from their exertions, her bangs sticking to her forehead.

He considered not telling her but rid himself of that thought as soon as it entered his brain that it would be cruel to lie. He took a breath and smoothed out his expression, making sure not to betray the panic he was feeling.

"The, um…" he cleared his throat. "The condom broke," he told her in as neutral a voice as he could muster. Belle blinked at him twice, looking at him as if he'd spoken a foreign language.

When the words sunk in, her eyes went wide, and her cheeks flushed an even deeper shade of red.

"It's just that we started seeing each other, you know, and we both have a lot going on at the moment. A baby would just… Fuck, you're only twenty-three," Max finished lamely, still kneeling on the bed, staring down at the damned condom and feeling ashamed.

How had he bungled up so bad? He hadn't even checked to see if they were still safe to use. It had been a while since he brought a lover back to his place.

"Oh. Oh!" She scrambled off the bed, clenching the sheets to her body and tripping over the bedding. "There's no need to worry. I, um... I'm on the pill, so we're good on that front. And I'm clean as a whistle, no infections—"

"So am I, clean as a whistle," Max rushed to say as he got to his feet as well, the faulty condom dangling from his fingers. When he saw that he was still holding up, he quickly hid his hands behind his back.

"Good, good. I wanted you to know that you don't have to worry about being shackled to me or anything like that," Belle chuckled weakly as she swiped her bangs to the side. She swallowed down the dejected feeling that was tinged with bitterness.

Of course, she wasn't the type of woman Max would want to have a child with. She knew that, and yet for a moment, a tiny inconsequential moment before the panic descended, she had entertained the thought of having Max's child.

The reality knocked her on her ass. She wasn't anywhere near ready to raise a child when she still felt like one.

CHAPTER 9

"WELL, DON'T KEEP ME IN SUSPENSE. Are they any good?" Chloe asked impatiently as Belle swallowed down the last bite of lemon cupcakes she wanted to serve at the bakery.

"I don't know why you keep asking for my opinion when you know I love all things sweet. And I'm already biased because everything you make is amazing!" Belle replied, licking the icing off her fingers.

"You only say that cause I give you free goods," Chloe said with a roll of her eyes. They were in the backroom of her bakery, where they hung out every morning before the shop opened up.

Belle had been pleasantly surprised how quickly they struck up a friendship in the weeks since they'd met. The two of them had bonded over their grief, Chloe having lost her grandmother a few months before Belle lost her mother. She could talk to her about things she would otherwise have trouble bringing up with Max. Having them both in her life now caused the piercing claws of loneliness to only appear every once in a while, and the pain of it wasn't as suffocating as it used to be.

"Do you think they're good enough to sell, though? Maybe I need to tweak the recipe some more. They tasted bland to me," Chloe probed as she took another bite for good measure. She was a perfectionist when it came to baking and running her business. She inherited a significant amount of money from her grandmother, which gave her the courage she needed to quit med school and follow her dreams of owning a cute little bakery, much to her family's chagrin.

Chloe was determined to see her endeavors succeed if only to prove her parents and brothers wrong.

"You know they are. Stop fishing for compliments," Belle teased. She checked the time on her phone and saw that she needed to leave soon if she wanted to beat the morning traffic and get to work on time. Which reminded her, "Hey Chloe, you know of a place that sells used cars for a reasonable price?" If she was going to start attending classes and commuting between college and Titan, having a car seemed like the cheaper option than a bus fare.

"My brother might know a guy. I'll ask him," Chloe replied as she got up and started clearing up the dishes from the table. Belle stood as well, getting ready to leave when a wave of dizziness had her sitting back down.

Her *oomph* caught Chloe's attention, and the woman rushed to her side in concern. "You okay? What's wrong?"

It took a few moments for the room to stop spinning and for the queasy feeling to abate.

"Yeah. I think I should lay off the cupcakes for a while. I haven't been feeling well for the past few days." With the support of the table, Belle stood and took a deep breath through her nose and out her mouth. It took a few more moments for her vertigo to settle before she was capable of grabbing her coat and gloves.

"Maybe you should take a sick day. You look a bit pale."

In the reflection of the glass, Belle caught her appearance and admitted her cheeks were more gray than usual. Behind her, Chloe had her hands splayed and ready to catch Belle if she swayed on her feet again.

She waved her friend away. "I don't want to give my supervisor more reasons to hate me."

Chloe scoffed. "Bitch, you're dating the big boss. Your asshat of a supervisor can't touch you."

Belle shook her head and hugged her friend goodbye. Dating Max was precisely why she had to work harder than everyone else. It was the only way to prove that she wasn't at Titan *because* of him.

Three weeks later, Belle found herself hunched over the toilets, tossing up the egg rolls she'd had on her lunch break. She made a mental note to pick up something on the way home for her stomach. She wouldn't be surprised if the sushi she and Max had a few days prior may be the cause for her sickness.

The last few days had been dragging because she felt sick as a dog and extremely fatigued. At least it was a Friday, and she didn't have to come in to work tomorrow; she could veg out on the couch all weekend until she felt better.

She was a bit disheartened, though, since she wanted to invite Max over and make him dinner but, with another wave of nausea hitting her, she cast that thought aside.

The journey back to her desk felt twice as long. She trudged along on heavy feet, keeping close to the walls so that she could use them to hold herself up. Perhaps she could ask to knock off early; anyone who looked at her would be able to tell straight away she was on the verge of keeling over. Belle squeezed past the group of other clerks, circling someone's desk, and plopped down onto her seat. She made no move to go back to work and absently listened to the excited chatter as she scrolled through her Facebook feed.

As she sat, reading over her high school friends' Facebook feeds, she noticed that yet another of her friends had a baby. She rolled her eyes, finding it ridiculous that so many of her friends were having children. Then it dawned on her... she hadn't had her period in some time. She opened her period tracker app, noticing that she was now over two weeks late.

Behind her, in one cubicle over, the ladies in HR congregated, gushing about a baby shower she had attended last week. They were going on about gender reveal parties and whatnot.

Time slowed then, and the room narrowed, tilted, and swayed like a ship amid waves. Saliva filled her mouth, and her skin felt clammy, sweaty, and hot. Belle startled everyone as she blindly ran back to the restroom, hand cupped over her mouth. She burst through the doors just in time as bile crept up her throat, and she vomited into the nearest sink and kept doing so until she was dry heaving and her throat felt raw.

"No, no, no! This can't be happening. I can't be pa-pa—" She vomited again. This couldn't possibly be happening to her. Not when she was about to start classes again. And what about Max?

If she was pregnant, would Max even believe the baby was his, or maybe he'd think she was trying to trap him? Especially after she had reassured him that she was on the pill. How on earth did this happen? Should she tell him? She couldn't exactly keep it a secret, not when she worked at his company. First off, she needed to know for sure.

She hurried back to her desk, grabbing her things, then went to her supervisor to ask for the rest of the day off. She only had an hour left in the day, but she had to know for certain.

On the way home, she stopped at a local drug store and grabbed the first pregnancy test she came to. She only hoped it was the right one. As soon as she opened the door, she ran to the restroom with the test in hand.

Her hands shook as she unwrapped the test from its box. Carefully, she read over the instructions, then peed on the stick. Five minutes felt like an eternity as she waited to see if the stick had one line or two. The lines began to form.

One clear sign appeared, and she felt herself breathe a sigh of relief, but that was cut short as the second line formed. Shocked, Belle slipped down the counter to a seat on the floor as she stared at the stick. She was going to be a mother... a mother to Max's child. How was she going to tell him?

She managed to avoid seeing Max for the entire weekend, making up random excuses that sounded lame even to her ears. The prudent thing would have been to go see a doctor, but the mere thought of it made her feel even sicker. So, she kept putting it off until the following week.

On Wednesday, Max cornered her at her desk. "Why have you been avoiding me?" Max asked Belle in quiet, clipped tone, not wanting to draw attention to them. It proved to be useless because people stared anyway. Even after he glared at them, they were back to staring the second his back was turned.

Belle was slumped over her desk and slowly raised her head, a stricken look in her dull, red-rimmed eyes. All feelings regarding Belle ghosting him were promptly shot down when he saw her gaunt state.

"Jesus Christ, Belle! You look pale. Are you feeling ill again?" he asked, feeling her temperature at her forehead with the back of his hand. She didn't seem to be running a fever, but that didn't mean there was nothing wrong.

She opened her mouth to speak and immediately covered her mouth as she ran past him. Max followed her to the ladies' room and found her bent over the toilet, retching rather violently.

"Fuck it," he cursed when she slumped down on the floor. "I'm taking you to the hospital," he declared as he picked her up, bridal style. Alarm flared in her eyes, and he knew what she would say before she spoke, so Max cut her off. "Don't you dare say no. I just saw you throw your guts up, so we're going to see a doctor."

"It's just a stomach bug. I'll be fine. No hospitals!" she argued, struggling weakly in his arms.

"There's nothing to be afraid of. I'll be by your side the entire time."

Tears welled in her eyes, and so many emotions flickered across her face in a short time, he couldn't read them all. Seeing that she couldn't win the argument, Belle closed her mouth, her lips cracked and in a thin line.

The drive to the hospital was filled with silence. Belle was aware of Max sending her worried looks every couple of minutes. She knew she should warn him before he was blindsided, but it was all she could do to keep her breathing steady. She felt like a python had wrapped itself around her throat, barring her from speaking. Her nails bit into her palms, threatening to draw blood if they dug any deeper. The closer they got to the hospital, the closer she came to losing her nerve.

A small whimper escaped her when they arrived. Max kept murmuring reassurances that only heightened her guilt and panic. She felt like an inmate being led to her execution as he led her past the doors of the hospital.

He wanted to carry her, but she protested that she could walk. He threatened to put her in a wheelchair at the first sign of a fainting spell, and she really didn't want that. Still, she pushed him away, rather weakly, and stood on her own. Her stomach immediately revolted when she smelled the disinfectant that clung to hospitals.

Max led her into the waiting room, where there were dozens of people waiting. The thought of waiting amongst them had her imagining using that time to come up with an excuse to leave, but her hopes were dashed when Max called out to someone.

"Richardson, over here!"

Belle raised her eyes to see a dark woman in a white coat make her way toward them,

"Erickson, it's been a minute! How have you been?" Dr. Richardson asked. Max let go of Belle's hand to pull the tall woman into a hug. Jealousy reared its ugly little head, but Belle pushed the nasty feeling down when the doctor pulled away from Max and gave Belle a warm smile.

"So, what can I do for you?" Dr. Richardson asked.

Max cleared his throat, looking a bit sheepish. "I was hoping you would allow us to bypass all this and let us see a physician."

"Max..."

"Please, Sarah, my fiancée is ill, and you owe me a favor."

Belle felt as surprised as the doctor looked towards her at the mention of the word fiancée. She was too focused on not throwing up to say anything, though, so she watched the silent exchange of meaningful looks between the two.

The doctor let out an exaggerated sigh and led them to a private examination room, promising to be back with her attending physician.

"This will all be over soon, and then we'll go home," Max said reassuringly while rubbing soothing circles on her back.

Belle gave him a wan smile, trying to block out memories of her mother lying unconscious in a sterile room like the one they currently stood in.

An older woman walked in with Dr. Richardson following close behind. "Afternoon, everyone. I'm Dr. Gupta. What seems to be the problem?"

Max looked to Belle to explain what was wrong. She tried, but the words lodged in her throat. It took a few tries to speak, and Belle could see from the knowing glint in their eyes that Dr. Gupta and Richardson had a hunch, especially after they asked very pointed questions regarding her menstrual cycle.

"When did these symptoms start?"

Licking her lips, Belle answered, "A few weeks ago, but it's steadily gotten worse and more consistent this last week."

Max frowned. "Why didn't you say anything to me?"

She shrugged. "I didn't want to worry you."

"Jesus, Belle! You need to tell me these things so I can help take care of you!"

"I know, I'm sorry."

"Okay," Dr. Gupta began. "We'll take some blood and run some tests. I'll have one of the nurses come in, and we'll have some answers soon."

"What do you think it could be?" He asked as he ran a soothing hand over the back of Belle's head.

Dr. Gupta sighed. "It's difficult to tell. Could be food poisoning, gastroenteritis, a sinus infection…" She trailed off. "Or you could be pregnant."

"Pregnant?" Max's eyes widened.

"It's possible. You said it's been a while since your last period. You are sexually active, right?"

The pair nodded.

"We use condoms, though, and I'm on birth control," Belle tried to interject, scared to admit what it really could be.

"Well, safe sex is still sex, so it wouldn't hurt to double-check. After all, nothing offers complete protection." She smiled at them and left with the promise that a nurse would be with them soon.

A tense silence grew between them. Belle laid back on the bed when another wave of dizziness overcame her. She saw out of her peripheral vision Max pacing, his face tense and in deep thought.

Before she could address him, a nurse came in with a tray of vials and needles. She greeted the couple and set to work, wrapping a tourniquet around Belle's arm and feeling for a vein. The whole process was done and over in a matter of two minutes, and they were left to themselves once more.

The clock on the wall ticked rhythmically, and it helped to fill the dead silence. Despite her fear of hospitals, the coolness of the room helped to settle her stomach. She rolled onto her side, facing the doorway with Max behind her.

"Are you feeling sick again?" he asked.

"No," Belle murmured. "Just tired."

"You'd tell me if you were, though, right?"

"Yeah." She sniffed. She was on the verge of tears. They only had a short time together, and she could already feel them drifting further apart.

"Max?"

"Hmm?" His acknowledgment was a distracted one, and she couldn't take it if he thought she cheated.

"If I am pregnant," she began with a deep sigh. "It's yours."

"Belle…"

She shook her head, but that was a mistake. Wildly, she gestured for a bin, and Max rushed to hand her one of the pink basins that were left behind. She dry heaved, her stomach having nothing more to give.

Max lovingly wiped her mouth with a damp paper towel, and Belle laid back, completely exhausted. Soon, Dr. Gupta returned with Dr. Richardson, and the look on their faces confirmed what Belle feared.

"Well, Belle, looks like you'll be feeling this for a few more weeks," the good doctor said with a bright smile. "You're pregnant! The next step would be to schedule an ultrasound and begin prenatal vitamins, but we can help set all that up for you. Do you have a gynecologist you prefer to see?"

The words faded as the floor opened up to swallow her. Max was dead silent, and she was terrified to see his reaction.

"Max?" Dr. Richardson called out to him, and the two medical professionals shared a wary look.

Belle's heartbeat sounded like a timer, counting down the seconds to Max's enraged explosion and the accusations that would follow. "I've suspected for a while now, but I was terrified of how you would react to the news, so I kept putting off telling you," she whispered in a rush.

The accusations never came.

Instead, Max started laughing and placed a short bruising kiss on her lips. She cringed away because she still had the smell of puke on her breath, but Max was too excited to notice, which stumped her because she hadn't expected him to be this ecstatic.

"I'm going to be a father!" Max beamed, grasping her hands between his. His cornflower blue eyes were radiant, but there was a hidden terror behind them too.

"I promise I'm not angry, Belle. This is the best news ever! Unless, of course, you don't *want* to have the baby?" Max asked, sounding a bit sick.

Belle sat on the edge of the bed in silence, unsure of what to say. She hadn't thought about being anyone's mother, let alone having a committed relationship. Everything was happening so quickly; she wasn't sure what to think.

"Do you not want to keep the baby, Belle? Ultimately, this is your choice, and I'd never force you to have the baby if you're not ready. But please know that I would do everything in my power to see that the two of you are loved and well cared for. I know that he or she is about the size of a bean right now...." he said, placing his hand on Belle's flat stomach.

Belle's heart leaped with hope when he placed his hand over hers.

"But I already love this baby more than anything in the world." He wanted to add that he loved her, too, but held back.

"You're not angry with me? You're not going to accuse me of trying to trap you? I love you, Max, but I couldn't stand it if you ended up resenting me and our child years down the line," Belle declared with a tremor in her voice.

She could tell that her words wounded him, but her confession seemed to soften the blow. She didn't even realize she'd told Max that she loved him. A smile crept across his lips as he kissed her. He softly murmured against her lips. "I love you too. Marry me, Belle. Marry me, and let's start this new chapter of our lives together."

Belle spluttered a string of incoherent sounds. Before Max could encourage a straight answer out of her, Dr. Gupta cleared her throat, shocking Max out of his elated state; he had entirely forgotten that the doctors were still present.

"I thought you were already engaged, but you are proposing again?" Dr. Gupta's brows were creased in confusion

"Uh… well, why don't we give the couple some time alone?" Dr. Richardson cut in, ushering her supervisor out of the room. Max flashed her a grateful smile and got a glare in return. "You owe me an explanation," she mouthed as they left.

All of the air escaped Belle's lungs. Max wanted to marry her, but for all the wrong reasons. *However, he did say that he loves you,* the angel on her shoulder reminded Belle.

Only because he knocked you up, scoffed the devil on the other shoulder.

"I can't marry you, Max," she said, breaking both their hearts. She couldn't let him make this mistake. He was caught up in the moment, but years or even months from now, he would realize that this was not what he wanted, that *she* was not what he wanted. In the end, Max would hate her. And what if he found out about her past? What if his resentment bled over to their child? She couldn't subject an innocent baby to the misery of a divorce, nor would she clip Max's wings, not when he had grand plans for the future.

"What? Why? We love each other, and we now have a baby on the way. Don't you want us to be a family, Belle? Because I do—more than anything in the world."

Belle knew that Max didn't get along well with his family. He told her that they were as good as dead to him. And yes, she felt sad for him. He deserved to be loved and cherished, and she felt both those things for him. She also wanted a family. She always ached to be a part of a large family, but her mother never remarried and never had another child.

"I do want a family, but I don't deserve you, Max. You're too good—"

"Bloody hell! I'm not that good of a person, Belle. Not that I'm—I mean I—that doesn't matter! None of that has any bearing on whether or not we should get married. I love you. I love our little bean; I want to do right by both of you and give you my last name. I want to experience all the highs and lows of parenthood with you by my side, so say yes. Make me the happiest man on this earth and say you will marry me, Isobel Aston."

"Yes," Belle answered, crying and laughing all at the same time.

But she didn't know if the tears were a result of her joy or if the laughter was the product of her fear.

CHAPTER 10

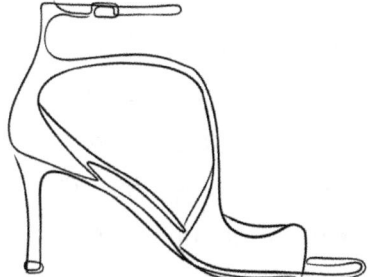

BOTH LITERALLY AND METAPHORICALLY, Belle was starting to have cold feet. Her shoes, a pair of delicate, strappy Jimmy Choos, gave little protection from the chill breeze that kept blowing in under the fabric tent Max's family had rented to serve as her bridal suite.

She couldn't help the resounding voice that was echoing through her head.

What do you think you are doing? It screamed at her over and over again.

She was sitting in the most elaborate wedding tent she had ever seen, the walls made of a thick silk brocade, the ceiling swooping into the high center where a massive crystal chandelier hung. It had been Max's family's idea, much to Max's chagrin. He'd wanted something small and intimate for the wedding. Hell, Belle imagined Max would have been perfectly happy to elope, and while Belle's preferences ran in a similar direction, Max's family had other ideas.

Though she'd heard it from him, Belle could never have imagined how truly greedy Max's family was. Eager for a chance to spend his money, nearly all of his relatives jumped at the opportunity to use their wedding as a spending spree. And while Max had been impressively firm with his aunt and cousins about what he absolutely would *not* be purchasing for the wedding—like a Rolex for all the men and Tiffany diamond earrings for the women—Belle knew that the constant battle was wearing him down. Eventually, one day she watched Max after a particularly hard phone call at the kitchen counter with his head down in hurt and betrayal. He commented that he was feeling done with saying no to all these people, and so Belle had taken it upon herself to handle the phone calls, extending invitations in secret, hoping that he'd be happy to see a group of people so happy for him on their wedding day.

The conflict between his family was something Belle couldn't understand.

Her mom had given everything for her—every day, every penny, every spare scrap of energy went into raising her. And in the end, Belle had given everything back in order to give her mom as long on earth as she could.

Because the ignoble cost of those last few months of her mother's life had been so very, very high, Belle had never considered herself worthy of Max. Not when he'd first started showing interest in her, and not this morning as Chloe had helped her into the simple yet elegant sheath wedding dress that so effortlessly camouflaged her quickly growing stomach, did she feel like she was a good enough woman to walk up that aisle and marry him. But for the first time in their relationship, it occurred to her that, in one way, at least, her life had been blessed with something truly wonderful.

The woman who had been her best friend: her mom.

Belle, who was trying to peek out of a tiny opening in the door of her tent, yelped at the sudden voice she heard behind her.

"I wouldn't do that if I were you," Chloe called from behind her.

Belle placed a hand over her chest and laughed at her own nerves.

"How could I not?" She asked her friend with a shaky laugh, "There are almost three hundred guests out there!"

Chloe came up to her and gave a gentle tug on Belle's elbow, easing her away from the door gently.

"Exactly. Who even *are* all these people?" she said.

Belle groaned, "I only know a fraction of them. After we told Max's family about the engagement, he suddenly started getting phone calls from every long-lost cousin who demanded an invite. Honestly, I think after a while, he was too worn out to keep fighting with everyone. I think his aunt would have invited a few hundred more people if she'd had her way."

"Ugh, but why?" Chloe teased, "I mean, not that I'm complaining, of course. I did get paid to make roughly one million cupcakes for this event after all."

Chloe's face morphed from the cheerful maid of honor to the concerned friend.

"I'm just worried about you. Are you going to be alright out there? You know that you don't need to worry about what any of those people think, right? If anyone dares think anything other than, *wow-she's-so-gorgeous-max-is-so-lucky!* Max would probably destroy them. All that matters today is you two."

She poked Belle's hands which were currently in their new default resting position over her lower stomach.

"Oh! And this little marshmallow, of course!" Chloe laughed.

And at that, a genuine, ecstatic smile blossomed over Belle's cheeks.

The baby. Their baby. While Belle had no idea what she was doing or if she was about to make a horrible mistake and ruin Max's life, she did know that this baby was a blessing.

Chloe was one of the only people who knew about the pregnancy besides Grayson and a couple of Max's other closest friends. There would be tabloids and rumors to ward off after the wedding when the rest of the world found out, but Max and Belle had decided that they wanted their wedding to be special—just the three of them happy and in love, as they celebrated becoming an official family before the rest of the world had their say.

"How could you forget?" Belle teased right back. "You already had to fix my makeup after all the hormonal crying this morning!"

This morning when Chloe had arrived—doing her bossy maid of honor duties and banishing Max's family from the tent for asking the bride if she had put on some weight—Belle had burst into tears of embarrassment, worry, and so much relief.

"Come on," Belle said, "Aren't you curious who's out there? Just one peek!"

"Okay, fine," Chloe sighed, "But just one!"

Together they snuck back over to the door, Chloe being careful not to step on Belle's delicate silk train, and squinted to see what was out there.

White spring flowers filled up the beautiful garden space and created a stunning scent. It would have soothed some of Belle's nerves were it not for the hordes of nameless faces she saw filling every chair. She'd regretted letting Max's family boss them around and force them into having an event this big, many times, by this point. Still, the overwhelming anxiety of the moment seemed to cripple her all over again.

At the entrance, a couple was coming in with the woman's arm clasped around the arm of her husband. She was blonde and petite, a frail and older-looking companion to the man who stood several inches above her. Belle was just thinking about who they might be and how interesting it was to see such a significant height difference in a couple when suddenly every muscle in her body froze.

Paralyzed as she watched them get closer and closer, following the usher to their seats, Belle couldn't believe what she was seeing.

She knew the man. He had been one of her clients.

Dalton hadn't been the worst client she'd ever had, but he wasn't the best either. He'd been all business, telling her exactly what to take off and when, which position she needed to be in, and exactly how long she was expected to blow him before she was allowed to stand up again. By then, she'd learned all the tricks she needed to survive—her gag reflex was gone, lube was applied beforehand, and her emotions remained expertly locked in an unopenable safe in her chest. He hadn't spoken to her at the public charity event he'd hired her to attend with him, and besides the crude commands in bed, Belle hadn't learned anything at all about the man. There was no way she could have possibly known that he would show up a year later at her shotgun wedding.

If she wasn't stiff with fear, she might have screamed at the karmic justice the universe seemed to think she deserved.

Just then, the man turned, clearly taking in the stunning tent, and before she realized what had happened, their eyes met.

She'd always had a great memory, something that had been a gift to her when she was a kid in school. Later though, and especially right this second, that memory felt like a curse. She could recall every cruel sneer his mouth had made that night, every ugly noise he had made as he enjoyed himself on top of her. If she could have burned the memory from her mind, she would have, but instead, the man who had paid her a tip for not complaining when he fucked her mouth continued to stare at her.

The moment passed in an instant. His shock shifted to horror, and then his horror to disgust. In less than a second, she saw the concerned glance he gave to his wife (right, because *he* was the one who should be worried right now) and then the moment he realized that he was embarrassed that he knew her. He didn't look back and hurried forward to catch up with the usher, the expression of revulsion never leaving his face.

Would he say something? Was this, their wedding day, the day Max would find out about her past and leave her at the altar, just as disgusted by her as Dalton was? And what about their baby? What would happen to him after all of this?

An icky blackness oozed through her body, a broken damn of all the fears she had been trying to hold in, finally bursting under the pressure.

"Excuse me, but she's not ready! Please, Ms. Erickson—" Chloe shouted from somewhere behind her.

When did Chloe leave the door beside her? Belle felt like she was in a daze. She turned and saw a flustered Chloe in her blush pink gown swishing her hands back and forth as she tried to figure out what to do. In front of her was an elegant looking woman, dressed in a long white gown, the color only broken up by a sheer pink overlay jacket. Perhaps Belle ought to be concerned, but at the moment, there were much bigger concerns flooding her mind. She knew exactly who this woman was and exactly why she was trying to deflect attention from herself, the bride.

This was Max's aunt, Victoria Erickson.

"Ms. Erickson, I think Belle just needs a minute to—" Chloe tried to say but was interrupted by Victoria.

"Wasn't forcing me out of the bridal suite this morning enough for you, Miss... Cupcake Baker?" Victoria sneered, "I believe one of the staff was calling for your help, dear. Keeping a wedding running smoothly is the maid of honor's duty, isn't it? Forgive me. I'm so out of touch with how the kids are arranging weddings these days. Perhaps I am mistaken?"

To her credit, Chloe didn't quiver under the woman's gaze but merely clenched her jaw and turned to Belle.

"I'll be back in ten?" she said, but Belle could hear her real question. *Are you going to be okay?*

Belle gave a tiny dip of her chin and turned to face Max's aunt as Chloe went out of the tent.

"Hello, Victoria," Belle said, standing up straight with her face a perfect mask of faux calmness.

"Well," Victoria said, gazing down at Belle's wedding ensemble. Belle flinched as her perusal scanned her waist, but thankfully she didn't bat an eye. "You do look beautifully... simple."

Belle's dress was simple, but it wasn't cheap. It was one of the things that Max insisted on—that Belle should have the best of everything and anything at all that she wanted for the big day. She'd chosen a designer dress that looked like something she'd always dreamed of but would never have been able to afford. The cream-colored silk was so fine that it fell in luscious waves down the front of her body, the cowl neckline modestly high and delicate. From the back, two bundles of the finest tulle Belle had ever seen streamed from either shoulder, making her feel like a fairy princess as they fluttered in the breeze that arose from her movement. The low back and generous train added to that feeling, sneaky red heels and matching lipstick completed the look. The best part, however, was her jewelry. It was the gold set that they had seen at the gallery opening months before and that Max had gifted her last week.

He'd been watching her the whole time, noticing what she noticed.

So Belle knew that she looked simple, but she knew that wasn't what Victoria was really trying to say to her.

She thought Belle was simple. Beautifully... simple.

And completely undeserving of Max's love. At least on this one thing, they agreed.

"Thank you," Belle answered Victoria, dipping her chin at the backhanded compliment despite its intent.

"Do you feel ready for today?" the woman asked.

Belle lifted her chin back up, unsure what she meant but knowing that there must be some subtext.

"Yes, of course," Belle said, "I feel very, very lucky to be able to have Max in my life."

"Hmph. You ought to be. He is a very sought-after man, you know," Victoria leaned into Belle until she was only inches away, her voice low, quiet, and unmistakably threatening.

"Don't forget that Max is a very important man," she said, "And society has certain rules that it is not forgiving of. I'm sure you'll find your way eventually. Don't forget in the meantime that families can be easily embarrassed and ostracized. We certainly wouldn't want that for our bright star, Max, now would we?"

"Of course not," Belle said quietly. If this woman only knew what secrets Belle had, how easily Max's life would fall to pieces if anyone found out...

"Well then," Victoria stepped back again, "Enjoy your day, dear!"

And like a dark cloud, she left Belle alone and chilled.

Victoria Erickson was right.

Belle hated to admit it, but she was a hazard to Max in every way. If they got married today, people would gossip about the validity of their relationship, questioning whether or not Belle had trapped Max into marriage by getting pregnant. If someone found out about her past, Max would be ruined by association, and his company's stock would quickly fall as well. If Max found out himself, he'd be painted as a fool who could be easily hoodwinked by a conniving woman.

And if she left, Max would be viewed as a frivolous playboy who knocked up girls from the other side of the tracks for fun.

Their child would pay for it the worst. Max was such a good man that it felt like a crime not to let a child take advantage of that in every way.

For the hundredth time since Max had proposed that day in the hospital, Belle wondered if she was doing the right thing. It didn't feel like there was a correct answer, and as much as she tried to put her feelings aside, she just couldn't.

She loved Max so much. She *wanted* to marry him. She wanted this life for the three of them so badly that she unconsciously curled her arms around her stomach as though she were protecting the little life there from whatever the world would throw at them. Maybe today was all the result of her own selfishness.

Did she even deserve to be Max Erickson's wife?

"Belle?" Chloe said. She had tiptoed back into the tent without Belle noticing. "You okay?"

Belle nodded and hurried to put her mask back on, the one that told everyone that she was just fine.

"I am," Belle said, pasting a smile on, "I just forgot something in the car. I'll be right back, okay?"

"What is it?" Chloe asked, "Your something blue? I saw you weren't wearing that blue ring of your mom's. I can go and get it for you."

Bell shook her head and tried to explain.

"Thank you, but I think I'll go myself. I really just need a minute by myself, if that's okay? To get some air?"

Chloe nodded, seeing through Belle's facade completely. "Don't let her get to you too much. Today is your day. Not hers."

Belle nodded and smiled, but she turned and hurried out quickly before Chloe could see her chin quiver.

The back of the tent let out to a beautiful, private walled garden and a stone home after that. Belle didn't want to see anyone else right now, and so she ducked away to the side of the house, trying to sneak to her car without any of the wedding party seeing her.

Just before she rounded the corner, Belle heard the harsh tones of someone arguing in whispers, the deep dark tones of an angry male voice, and the responding sharp hiss of a woman fighting back.

"I told you not to make a scene today," a familiar voice growled. On instinct, Belle took a few steps back, remembering that Max shouldn't be seeing her before the ceremony started. It was a silly tradition, but something about the romance of it had made Belle giddy and bashful this morning as she got ready. Now listening to Max argue with his aunt, any positive feelings associated with the feeling vanished. Now she *just* felt silly, caught again, unintentionally eavesdropping on one of Max's conversations she wasn't meant to hear.

"Oh please," Victoria scoffed, "This whole, ridiculous wedding is your own version of causing a scene. I bet you're just loving watching your family cringe as you hitch yourself up to your pregnant slut."

Belle whipped a hand up to cover her mouth and muffle the gasp that erupted out of her mouth, her heart lurching in her chest. How did Max's aunt know about the pregnancy? Shame oozed through Belle's abdomen as she wondered who else knew. Did everyone here know? Did everyone think that Max was just marrying her because of their child? Despite all of Max's care, affection, and attention over the last couple of months, even Belle wasn't entirely sure if that's what was happening.

"Don't ever talk about Belle that way again," Max said, his voice having lowered dangerously. "In fact, don't ever talk about her at all. After today, we're done, Victoria. You're never allowed in our home, our lives, or anywhere near our child. I thought I'd heard it all from you, but I never thought you'd sink so low as to say the things about my wife as the words that have come out of your mouth these last few weeks."

Victoria barked out a humorless laugh.

"You really think you can put us aside so easily?" she snarled, "She's not your wife yet. If I didn't know how damn stubborn you are, I would have already made sure she never would be. Please! Just explain to me why you are doing this? Is it to spite me? Or because you think you have to be honorable about the baby? Do you think we haven't had to deal with an illicit love child before? God, you are naive, Max! With all of your money, I would have at least expected you to bring someone home that was befitting the family. Imagine how this looks to everyone? The spoiled little rich boy marrying his pregnant, trash employee and then throwing this lavish party to throw it in everyone's face."

"Lavish party?" Max snapped, "You were the one who made the plans! You were the one who pushed us into this! I should never have let you convince me that this enormous event was something that Belle would actually want. Why would she ever want to be paraded in front of a bunch of miscreants with no moral compass? I can't believe I let this happen to her! Imagine how it looks to *her*? The spoiled, little, rich boy asking her to become part of his spoiled, cruel family of vipers? Either take your seat and keep your mouth shut or get out. I have nothing left to say to you."

"How absolutely typical," Victoria said, "bringing trash into the family just like your father did when he married *your* whore of a mother. Let me guess: you're probably foolish enough to believe that this marriage is going to last too?"

From her spot around the corner, Belle's patience snapped as she listened to the words coming out of this woman's mouth, someone that Max had been forced to depend on after his parents died. What must it have been like for him to be subjected to this kind of scorn and derision on a daily basis? If she was about to become Max's wife, regardless of her feelings about how much she deserved the position, she was going to do everything she could to make sure that he wouldn't be alone in the fight against his family ever again.

Thinking of her mother again, Belle shored up her courage and stepped around the corner of the building with her head held high, a direct contrast to her previous encounter with the woman in her tent only minutes before. She would never let Max's aunt corner her like that again.

"How absolutely typical," she said, intentionally turning the vicious woman's own words around on her and startling both Max and Victoria, "Trying to take all the attention for yourself again, are you, Victoria? I'm disappointed. I really wanted to believe that you had Max's best intentions at heart, but I'm sorry to say that I'm not surprised to discover the truth. It turns out you *are* just the selfish bitch I always suspected you were."

Victoria gasped, her face morphing into a sneer of hatred so intense that her face started to turn bright red underneath her pristine makeup. It was somehow fitting to see that at this exact moment, even the most expensive cosmetics couldn't hide the ugliness that lived inside of this woman.

"How dare you—" Victoria started to say, but Belle wasn't going to give her the chance to hurt Max again.

"Thank you, aunt, for all your help so far," Belle said in a polite voice that reeked of insincerity, "but I think I'll handle any necessary wedding preparations from here. I would take your nephew's advice and take your seat before the ceremony begins. You wouldn't want to walk in late after all, would you? It would be so very... *trashy*. However, there is one point on which Max and I might disagree. Say whatever you want. Make the biggest scene you can imagine. Do whatever you want today. I don't care. This wedding is going to happen whether you want it to or not, and the only person who will end up looking foolish is you."

She walked up to Max, forcing her steps to be straight and sure despite the fact that her heels were sinking ever so slightly into the soft earth. The look on Max's face was nothing like she'd ever seen before, part gratitude, part love, and entirely the look of a man who was swelling with pride.

Even Belle couldn't overthink that look away. Her heart pounded in response, and she gave him a tiny, secret smile to tell him that she was going to always be there for him from now on.

Belle curled her hand around Max's elbow and turned them to leave.

"Don't think that I will stand for this!" Victoria yelled, giving up all pretense of being discreet as her voice echoed throughout the garden.

"Don't you dare try," Belle seethed, this time her voice was the one that sounded dangerous and dark. "Don't you dare think you have a say in Max's life ever again. He doesn't need anything from you. Can't you tell? He never has. From now on, I'll be the one to give him the love you clearly withheld from him. Who knows? Maybe love isn't even an emotion you're capable of. Stay away from our family."

Victoria looked like she wanted to spit on Belle, but instead, she turned and stormed off in the direction of the garden where the ceremony was about to be held.

"Belle," Max whispered, but Belle grabbed onto his arm again and turned them in the opposite direction from his aunt. There was too much adrenaline rushing through her veins from the confrontation to be able to clearly listen to what Max had to say at the moment. She needed to walk it off and just hoped that Max wouldn't mind.

"Come on. It's almost time for things to start. I mean, if you can even still want me after I said those things to your aunt."

As they rounded the corner, though, they were halted by the form of a lazily smirking Grayson, who was leaning against the wall of the stone house, his ankles crossed and his hands in his pockets. He was grinning directly at Belle. If, for even a second, Belle had hoped that Grayson hadn't heard everything, that grin confirmed that he most certainly had, though.

"Here I thought I was supposed to be looking for a runaway bride," Grayson drawled, his smile widening as he did. "Only to find her rescuing our poor little rich boy. Don't you guys know how close you're cutting it to the ceremony time? For shame."

Max sighed. "God, you're smarmy. Grayson, you know that?"

Everyone chuckled a little, relieved that Max's friend was able to alleviate some of the tension from the heightened feelings moments before.

"Belle," Grayson said, suddenly serious and throwing Belle off guard, "I want to tell you something, seeing as how we're about to be prominent figures in each other's lives. I didn't know what to think of you when we first met. All the times I've spoken to you, you've been closed off and hesitant around me. You looked like you were walking around full of deep dark secrets."

Belle flinched, on edge all over again. Was he intentionally trying to make this roller coaster ride of a day even worse?

"I don't know if that's just your personality, or if you had another reason to be so cautious around me, but to be honest, I couldn't have guessed it was because you were hiding this kind of ferociousness," Grayson smiled and dipped his chin at her in recognition. "It suits you. And it suits Max. Thank you for what you just said to that witch. We are always happy to welcome another member to our *Keeping Max's Poor Wittle Heart Safe* team. Hey man! I guess I was wrong after all! I think I might be your wifey's new biggest fan."

Belle scrunched her eyebrows together, confused at what he was talking about, and looked over to Max for clarification.

"No shit, you were wrong, asshole. Don't ever come to me with any more stupid ideas about how you don't trust my judgment," Max said to his friend, laughing despite his words. Belle had gotten more used to the good guy/bad guy bit that they seemed to play in their friendship since her and Max's engagement. In fact, she found the whole thing rather endearing.

Max turned to Belle with a bright, close-mouthed smile on his decadent lips to offer an explanation for what they were talking about. "Grayson told me I needed to get you to sign a prenup," he explained.

Belle wanted to laugh that this was coming up now, seconds before she was supposed to be walking down the aisle. She had wondered herself why she hadn't been asked to do something like that. She gladly would have. She had no intention of ever doing anything to hurt Max's future.

Gray stepped off the wall and raised his hands in front of him as though to plead his defense. "Please don't be upset with me, Belle. I'm his lawyer, and the man is a *billionaire*, after all. If it eases your mind, Max threatened to buy out my side of the business and then fire me as his lawyer if I ever brought up the subject again. He insisted that there was nothing in the world that would ever turn you into another one of his many gold diggers. My words, mind you. I'm sure he said something much lovelier. When I asked him, 'What if you cheated on her and she tried to divorce you for it?', he told me that if he was enough of a fucking idiot to do anything so hurtful to you, that he deserved to lose every penny. I think that one was much closer to verbatim. It was all highly dramatic, whatever it was—lots of romantic declarations. I'm sure doves were flying around him. The sun was setting behind his back while the breeze tousled his hair. *Et cetera*. Whatever. I suppose I should find a seat before your husband finds something else to be pissed off at me about."

And with that, Grayson turned and swaggered off before either of them could respond.

God, that man made flamboyant speeches.

Belle didn't know how long went by as she processed what Grayson had just said. The words just kept echoing through her mind, altered, of course, from the colorful explanation Max's friend had given.

Max loved her. Max trusted her. Max would never do anything to hurt her.

It all swirled there as time stopped having meaning. It could have been seconds or hours that she spent thinking about what it all meant, but her thoughts were making her heart pound so hard that she couldn't be bothered to notice the time.

She thought about it as Max gently wrapped her hand back around his and then silently turned them back in the direction of her tent. She thought about it as she listened to the chatter of the colossal crowd beyond the stone garden wall, something that apparently both she and Max had been maneuvered into when neither of them wanted it. She even thought about it as Max stopped them at the doorway of her tent, placed his hands on Belle's cheeks with all the tenderness that she was feeling in her heart, and turned her to face him.

If what Grayson said was true, then there was no denying it: Max loved her.

Max truly loved her.

Did he really think so highly of her that he wouldn't even flinch at the idea that she had the power in their future to bankrupt him, to take away everything he'd ever worked for? Did he trust her that much?

The reality of that understanding slammed into Belle with the force of a freight train. She might have secrets about her past, things that she never wanted to talk about—never even wanted to think about—again, but that didn't mean that the two of them weren't a perfect match for each other. She thought about all the things they meant to each other. She thought about his passion and her determination to protect it. She thought about their combined loneliness and how in all their lives, no one had ever managed to break through their individual fortress of isolation. She thought about them in bed as they made all of each other's worries, fears, and heartaches disappear.

And then she thought about the child that was growing inside of her, ready to come into this tiny family who was waiting so anxiously for his arrival, and she knew that marrying Max was the right choice.

Max was her family.

Max was her love.

And for the first time, every fear she had about accepting his proposal disappeared for a moment. Because for the first time since that night in the hospital, she realized that she was those things for Max, too.

"Belle," Max whispered as he cradled her face in his hands. "I wish I could kiss your red lipstick off you right now."

Belle laughed quietly, feeling like the two of them were cocooned together in their own personal world.

"I would love that," she whispered back.

Max leaned forward and rested his forehead on hers, both of their choppy breaths now brushing against the other as they took several moments to just be together.

"I love you so much, Belle," he whispered, his voice cracking, "Thank you for what you said. Thank you for giving me a real family."

Belle could see the water that was pooling in his eyes and, in response, tears started to leak from hers too.

"I love you too, Max."

"You know," Max murmured, "In an odd twist of fate, I forgot to give the marriage license to the officiant. It's still in my pocket."

He patted his chest to confirm what he was saying, and a smile spread across Belle's lips as she sniffled and slowly realized what he was trying to say.

"Do we have to go out and tell them all?" Belle whispered, shriveling inside at just the prospect.

Max shook his head adamantly and moved one hand down to run the back of his fingers across Belle's stomach where their little bean was growing, happily unaware of all the drama of the day.

"I'll tell Chloe," Belle said.

"I'm calling Grayson and Anastasia right now."

"The limo is out front?"

Max nodded. "The north entrance. I'll meet you there in ten minutes. No, fifteen. I'm going to grab some of the expensive wine from the bar so those scumbags can't take it."

Belle laughed and then spun toward the entrance of her tent, ready to grab Chloe and run. She suddenly felt lighter than she had all day, all month. Maybe ever. Just before she disappeared behind the door of the tent, Max stopped her with a hand on her arm, halting her steps. Belle glanced at his hand and then up at him, confused at the pause. Was he not as excited about this new plan as she was? But she shouldn't have worried, even for a moment. The look on Max's face was glowing with nothing but pure, undiluted love. He was happiness personified.

"You look beautiful today," he murmured, sounding amazed, "Objectively, you're just this beautiful every day, but today you look like everything good that has ever existed in the world."

He had said it with a teary smile, and then turning with an embarrassed chuckle, he jogged off, pulling his phone out of his pocket as he did.

When they were all in the limo—Max, Belle, and their closest friends—headed toward City Hall, something so warm and comforting took root in Belle's body that she could only compare it to sunshine. Maybe it was the feeling of safety, maybe it was peace, or maybe it was just the blissful joy of being in love and knowing that you are loved in return, but as the small group laughed and ran up the steps of City Hall, Belle knew that she wanted to hold on to this feeling for as long as she could.

Things weren't perfect, but for this moment, there was no Dalton, Victoria, or sneering journalists, or meddling family here to judge Belle for marrying the man she loved. That assurance pounded through her and gave her the confidence to walk up to the front desk, book a slot to marry Max in the most informal wedding ceremony possible, and finally stand in front of a plain wooden podium and listen to the words she had been waiting to hear for months.

"Dearly beloved, we are gathered here today…"

CHAPTER 11

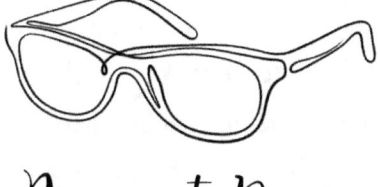

Present Day...

THINKING BACK, the day her life fell apart was rather mundane. There were no clouds in the sky, or lightning strikes, or earthquakes, or any kind of omen foretelling doom that Belle's carefully crafted life was about to come crashing down on her like a ton of bricks.

Although, to say the day was mundane was unfair. Maybe that's how it appeared to anyone outside looking into the Erickson household, but to Belle, her life was everything she could have hoped for and more. People love to say there's no such thing as perfection, but her life was as damn near close to perfect as it could get.

Her lips stretched into a wide smile as Oliver's giggles floated down into the kitchen from somewhere close by. Her son's laughter was so infectious that it was rare for Belle to not find herself laughing along—not at what Ollie was laughing at—but because his laughter was pure, unfiltered joy that rubbed off of anyone within the vicinity.

She heard the low rumble of Max's voice, unable to make out what he said, but whatever it was, set off another round of giggling, this time accompanied by squeals. Belle checked the time on the microwave; they had to leave within the next fifteen minutes if Ollie was to make it to school on time.

"Boys!" she called out. "You better hot-foot it down here, or I'm leaving a certain someone behind when I leave." She chuckled, hearing the rushed footsteps on the stairs, and within a few moments, a familiar head of sandy brown curls appeared in the kitchen doorway.

"I'm here, mommy. Don't leave me!" Oliver puffed out. His red-rimmed glasses were askew and slipping down his nose, shirt buttoned all wrong. Belle pushed off from the counter where she was busy preparing Oliver's lunch box and went to kneel in front of him, fixing up his disheveled appearance.

"You and your dad have been upstairs for ages, and you still haven't gotten ready?" She arched her eyebrows as she smoothed out the wrinkles from his shirt and set his glasses straight.

"Your son takes after you. He couldn't decide what he wanted to wear until that last minute. Then he thought it would be fun to start a tickling war in the middle of dressing," came Max's amused reply as he stepped into the kitchen.

Belle should have been used to this feeling by now, but every time her husband walked into a room, or when she woke up and found his cornflower blue eyes looking down at her, her heart gave a hard kick at her chest. She still couldn't believe that this magnificent creature belonged to her.

"I don't recall ever starting a tickling war while getting ready," Belle replied archly, making way for Oliver to pass through into the kitchen for breakfast. Before she could follow, Max pulled her to him so that their chests were flush against each other. Without any prompting on Max's part, except the heated look he gave her, Belle felt her nipples pebble underneath her bra.

"I seem to recall us running late to the Coopers' party because you needed some tickling," his lips brushed against the shell of her ear as he whispered. Belle's body heated up in response to feeling his cock becoming hard against her stomach. She got on her tiptoes, eyes fluttering closed as Max's arms wrapped around her waist. Their lips had barely brushed against each other when Oliver's whining snapped them back into reality.

"Mom, can I have Cocoa Puffs for breakfast?" he asked, already dragging a stool to the cupboard where they kept the sugary cereal out of reach.

"Go feed the kid before he hurts himself," Max murmured against her mouth. He nipped gently on her lower lip before letting her go. Belle shot him a playful look over her shoulder when he tapped her denim-covered ass.

"You're not staying for breakfast?" she asked.

He shook his head, smoothing down the lapels of his grey pinstripe suit.

"I have an early meeting with the marketing department; I need to be at the office before nine. Let me grab my stuff," he said in a distracted tone and walked out of the kitchen. Belle turned her attention back to her small mountain climber in the making—even though he was struggling to climb on top of the stool without assistance.

"Alright, spider-monkey," Belle said, picking him up and groaning at how heavy he was and how quickly he was growing. Everything pointed toward Oliver taking after his father in height and build, which meant that pretty soon, Belle wouldn't be able to pluck him up into the air like a sack of potatoes. She had conflicting feelings about that; on one hand, she was excited to see what kind of person he would grow up to be, and on the other, she wanted Oliver to remain her baby boy forever, who wasn't embarrassed by kisses from mom and dad in public.

"What did I tell you about climbing up on the furniture?" she scolded, burying her nose into his unruly curls and taking a whiff of his apple-scented shampoo. She had no idea where the curls came from when both she and Max had hair straight as straw.

"That it's dangerous and not to do it?" he answered with a cheeky smile, hazel-green eyes that were identical to hers blinking up at her and comically magnified by his glasses.

"Right," she confirmed, setting him back down. "Next time I catch you breaking the rules, no more swimming lessons." She ruffled his hair, biting her lip to keep from laughing at his adorably chagrined expression. Two red spots blossomed on his apple cheeks, and his pink lower lip jutted out in his childish version of a pout.

"Besides, Cocoa Puffs are for weekends and holidays. Today we're having spinach and cheese omelette... and don't give me that face. I know you secretly love it." She smiled, helping him onto a stool.

"But mommy, spinach is so—blegh!" Oliver exclaimed, face twisted in disgust and tongue sticking out of his mouth. "Tommy's mommy made him drink a yucky spinach drink, and his poop was green for three days," he told her solemnly, holding up all four fingers plus thumb instead of three as he said so. Belle dished out a small serving of the omelette for him and poured a glass of fresh milk into a sippy cup, making sure the lid was screwed on tight.

"I promise your poop won't turn green. Besides, you'll need the energy if you want to keep up at swim practice later," she told him, placing the food in front of him. "Now eat up. We don't want to be late for Ms. McGrady's class."

Max walked back into the kitchen as Oliver took small, measured bites of the omelette. His eyes lit up in wonder when it didn't taste as awful as he thought it would be. Getting him to eat any vegetables besides carrots was becoming a chore, so Belle had to be creative with Oliver's meals.

She made a mental note to look for other recipe ideas to upload onto her lifestyle blog.

"You all set?" she asked her husband.

"Almost," Max replied, placing his briefcase, cell phone, and car keys on the countertop. "Just need to collect my goodbye kiss." He bent down a fraction and pressed his mouth to Belle's already parted lips. She had always found Max to be a walking paradox.

His contradictory nature was his firm lips that only cracked a smile for Oliver and her; his lips were surprisingly soft for a man who spent long hours frowning and grimacing at his employees.

She tried to keep the kiss chaste in front of their son, who let out a loud "Ew!" before returning to eat his breakfast. Max took matters into his own hands—or rather lips. When Belle tried to suck in a much-needed breath of air, he snuck in his tongue, snaking it around hers as one hand grasped at the back of her head and the other curled around her waist, pulling her onto her tiptoes.

She let out a quiet moan, her hands trapped between their bodies, clutching at his chest. Her panties were already embarrassingly damp, and for a brief moment, she longed for the days when all Max had to do was to hoist her up onto the countertop and have his way with her.

She almost lost her footing when he pulled back without warning, eyes blinking rapidly as she tried to clear out the haze of lust blanketing her.

"That should tide us over until later tonight," Max smirked, his blue eyes gleaming with heat and promise.

"You don't play fair, Maxwell," Belle gulped, brushing her fingers across her mouth that was still on fire from that searing kiss.

He gave her a soft peck on the forehead before giving his attention to their son, who was looking up at them wide-eyed and chewing with his mouth open. "Give daddy a kiss and hug goodbye?" he smiled, lowering himself so that he and Oliver were at eye level. Oliver tugged at his dad's ear, indicating that he wanted to tell him something. Belle shrugged when Max gave him a questioning look and proceeded to clear out the dishes and put them in the kitchen sink. She would clean up after coming back from dropping Oliver at school and running a few errands.

"Tommy says kissing girls gives you cooties," Oliver whispered, or tried to since Belle could hear him clearly from her position by the sink.

She rolled her eyes at the comment. This Tommy kid was a character and a half. He had slept over at their house on a few occasions, and the kid was not only an energizer bunny with a loudmouth, but he had no filter and no concept of privacy at all.

"Is that so?" Max chuckled. Belle turned around to see her son nod his head vigorously so that his glasses slipped down his button nose. "Hmm, but you've been kissing mommy loads of times, and you don't seem to have any cooties," he pointed out, making a show of examining Oliver for the so-called girly germs.

"Because she's my mommy and not my girlfriend," Oliver beamed up at Belle as he pushed up his glasses with two of his fingers.

"What do you know about girlfriends?" Max booped Oliver's nose. "C'mon bud, give your old man a kiss," he puffed out his right cheek so that Oliver could give him a loud, smacking kiss.

"I'll try to be back home in time for dinner." He stood back up and gathered his things.

Belle nodded and gave him another short kiss, watching as he left via the kitchen door.

"Alright, bud. It's about time we left. Go get your bag and grab a jacket too!" Belle called out after him as Oliver ran upstairs to his room. She grabbed his lunch box and locked up the kitchen door before meeting Oliver out in the living room.

She helped him into his jacket; it was only October, but the days were starting to grow colder, and Oliver was prone to fevers even with the slightest chill. After packing his lunch box into his Batman-themed bag and making sure he had his asthma inhaler and anything else that he would need, they set off.

"Look, mommy, it's Mr. Cooper and Bambi!" Oliver gushed, waving frantically at their neighbor and his golden retriever, Bambi. He greeted the two, face glued onto the window as he drooled over Bambi. Oliver had been nagging them to get a puppy for months now; she and Max had been discussing adopting one in time for Oliver's birthday.

"We don't have time right now. We'll play with Bambi later. Come now." she encouraged, helping him into the backseat.

Yes, the day had started perfectly. She had taken Oliver to school many times before. Why did her past have to come back to haunt her at this moment? Why did Danton Stanley have to show up at Oliver's school and suddenly ruin her life?

She had a feeling that she would eventually have to explain her past to Max. But to have Danton show up and make demands?

The mere idea of sleeping with Danton again made her sick. She opened the car door, vomiting onto the sidewalk. How did this happen?

In all the years since she's been married to Max, Belle had only run into one of her former clients, and he was wise enough to keep their acquaintanceship a secret, given that he was married too.

Now, when she'd finally laid the demons of her past to rest and accepted that someone as ruined as her could be happy and have a normal life with her perfect husband and even more perfect son, one more demon pops up to burst her bubble.

God, what was she going to do? This couldn't have come at a worse time, just when she and Max were starting to talk about having another baby.

She buried her face in her hands, consciously drawing in her breath. Another set of rapid knocks at her window, this time on the driver's side, made her jump and accidentally press on the horn, startling the traffic monitor who was peering down at her.

Faking a smile reminiscent of the one she would don during her escort days, Belle rolled down her window and apologized for holding up traffic. Belle started her car and made her way back home—all errands forgotten for the day.

Tears gathered in her eyes as she looked up at the huge house she shared with her family. She stared at the tiny bicycle Oliver had left out on the front lawn and realized that she was at risk of losing it all.

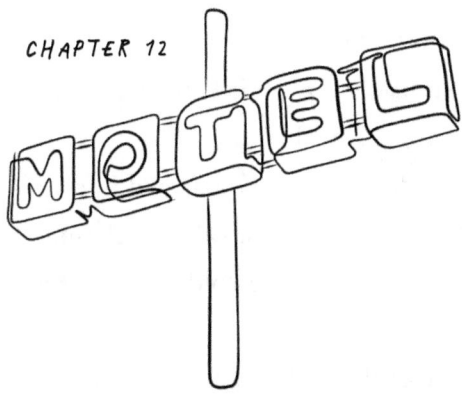

CHAPTER 12

BELLE COLLAPSED ON THE COUCH. Her day hadn't truly started yet, and she was already drained. The silence in the house was deafening, but her mind was a riot of emotions. Danton Stanley, why now after all this time?

She looked at the note in her hand. The Oasis Motel. Why did that name sound familiar?

She pulled out her phone to Google the directions, and what popped up had her rushing into the kitchen and throwing up her breakfast. It was the very same motel Danton always insisted they meet at six years ago, and Belle knew that it would be the very same room.

"Oh, God!" she gasped, smoothing out the wrinkled paper that she still held on to. Not only was there a room number and date, but there was a monetary amount as well for ten thousand dollars.

The fucking bastard was attempting to blackmail her. She went back into the living room and collapsed on the couch once more.

What was she going to do?

She couldn't tell Max that she was being blackmailed. He'd demand to know who and why. Even if Belle lied about her past as an escort, she knew her husband.

Max would hunt Danton down, and the bastard had no reason not to tell Max all the sordid details. Danton claimed he had pictures on top of it all. What if he sold them to the gossip rags out of spite?

Titan recently had a successful IPO launch, rocketing the company into a global powerhouse in the telecommunications business. Max was a reputable and well-respected businessman who guarded his reputation fiercely and their privacy even more so. Having their dirty laundry aired for all to see would destroy him.

Belle would never say that they were famous, but there was more than a passing interest from society about their lives. It was one of the reasons her blog was doing so well, as well as her gig as a freelance graphic designer.

Then the ultimate horror clutched her chest, "Oliver!" she squeaked breathlessly. He knew exactly where her son went to school. What if Danton became so enraged that he kidnapped her son? She could think of nothing worse. And even if Danton never came near her son, the controversy about her would ultimately fall on his small shoulders.

Ugh! This was all so frustrating; her life was a house of cards right now, and it was on the verge of teetering over.

Max would never forgive her if he found out about her secret. He could divorce her and take Oliver away from her. Or... what if Max accused her of continuing with the escort business behind his back and doubted that Oliver was even his? She shook off that idea as soon as she thought it. Ollie was a carbon copy of his father, and a paternity test could easily prove that Oliver was an Erickson through and through. That would not change the fact that people would talk.

Belle went through the rest of the day in a daze, thinking of possible ways to get rid of this Danton problem without him spilling her secret to her husband, and even worse, the media. All roads lead back to paying off Danton and demanding that he give her all copies of the pictures he claimed to have. The problem was, she and Max had a joint account. He would notice if she made a withdrawal for a substantial amount.

"We'll cross that bridge when we get there," she muttered to herself.

Eventually, it was time to fetch Ollie from school and take him to his weekly swimming lessons.

In the car, her son talked her ear off the entire way to the gym. She tried to look interested, but ever since this morning's encounter with Dalton, she'd been off-kilter.

The scent of chlorine hit her nose as soon as they got to the gym. Belle had to hold on to Oliver's hand to prevent him from running off to the locker rooms by himself as she signed them in.

"You know the rules, Ollie, no running in the—"

"No running in the gym, yeah, I know. But Andy's already in the pool. I don't want him to learn the breath stroke before me!" Oliver whined.

"It's breaststroke, sweetie," Belle corrected, letting out her first real smile since this morning.

"Go change. I'll be sitting at the usual spot with aunty Chloe," she told him, taking his bag and coat once Oliver took out his Speedos and swimming goggles.

Andy was Chloe's nephew, and she was the one who brought him to practice so that they could squeeze in some girl time. Motherhood and Chloe's booming cupcake business kept them quite busy. Chloe had recently started seeing someone, though she wouldn't tell Belle who it was just yet.

"Hey, you," Chloe said, removing the coats and her bag on the seat she'd saved.

Belle gave her a side-hug as she sat down and then offered a greeting to all the other parents waiting.

"I see Greg is still padding his Speedo," Belle whispered, watching one of three instructors.

Chloe snorted, tossing back a red curl that fell over her forehead. "I think he made it twice as big as the last time. I don't blame him, though, not with Julio as his competition," she replied with a sly smirk. They both surreptitiously eyed the Spanish instructor, who was the reason why most of the parents present were predominantly female.

Of course, if Julio caught them staring, Belle and Chloe could always use the excuse of keeping an eye on Adam and Oliver since he was the one helping them out today.

Belle managed to relax for the two hours she spent with Chloe at the gym, catching up on the latest gossip, but she nearly had a heart attack as they were leaving when she spotted someone who looked eerily like Danton walking into the weight room.

"You okay? You look pale as a ghost," Chloe commented. "Low blood sugar. I haven't eaten since this morning. I should take this little one home and make dinner before we both die of starvation. You're still coming over for dinner this weekend, aren't you?" she asked.

Chloe confirmed, and they said their goodbyes.

"Babe, are you okay?" Max asked, his brows furrowed in concern.

Belle snapped out of the daze she'd been in all evening. She had basically coasted through getting Oliver cleaned up for dinner. When they sat down to eat, she'd fallen silent and let Ollie take over the conversation as he regaled his father about his day. Somewhere along the way, she had zoned out.

"Sorry, did you say something?" she gave him a neutral smile and hoped he didn't notice the strain behind it.

"I was asking if anything interesting happened today. You look exhausted."

Belle gulped. "Just the usual, cleaning up after you two pigs," she said, tweaking Oliver's nose. "And I worked on a few designs for Chloe's bakery. Now, who wants some dessert?" she asked with forced cheer.

"Me! Me!" Oliver replied, bouncing in his chair.

Belle got up and cleared the dishes from the table and served them each a bowl of Ben and Jerry's ice cream. She made sure to keep up the cheerful facade to keep Max from prying, and it worked, except that she caught him stealing worried glances here and there.

Somehow, she needed to survive through tonight and tomorrow. Once Danton had his money and she had the pictures, everything would go back to normal.

The following morning, Belle went about her usual routine; waking up when Max did. They made love that morning, and if she was needy in her affections, he said nothing about it.

"I've been thinking," he murmured into her hair as Belle threw a leg over his hip and nuzzled into the crook of his neck.

"About?" she asked, placing a soft kiss on his chest before looking up at him. The intent look in Max's eyes stole her breath away and made her feel guilty as well. It was a look full of love, devotion, and absolute trust.

"I was thinking that maybe you should stop taking the pill," he suggested, sitting up and moving Belle so that she straddled his waist. "Oliver is old enough now so we can have another kid without running ourselves into the ground, and we have more than enough money to support another mouth to feed. I miss having a baby in the house—"

"Yes, let's do it!" Belle kissed him, plunging her tongue deep into his mouth. They'd been together long enough that she didn't mind the morning breath.

Max pulled away when things grew too heated.

"Much as I'd like to come inside you right now, I need to work. And you need to get Ollie ready for school. We'll talk more about this later tonight, yeah?" Belle nodded and let him go take his shower as she went downstairs to pack Oliver's lunch before waking him and getting ready for school.

She headed straight for the bank after dropping Oliver off to make a withdrawal. The dopamine boost from this morning's lovemaking had run its course, and Belle was back to being a bundle of nerves. The whole thing was so sordid, like a scene out of a bad movie. The money was in a nondescript envelope, and she wore a cap and sunglasses just in case someone saw her go into the motel.

Nothing about the motel had changed at all in six years since she quit the escort business, from the tacky 80s decor to the same desk manager who was always more concerned about watching horse races than helping out his guests.

Belle walked past him; envelope clutched to her chest as she stopped outside room number six, as instructed, with nine minutes to spare. She froze outside the door. She was once again transported to all those years ago when Dalton had brought her here.

Bile crept up her throat as she remembered all the vile things that he did to her, the humiliating things she was forced to do to please him. There was no way she was going in there, so she knocked and stepped back. A few seconds later, she was face to face with his disgusting smirk and golden-brown eyes once more.

"Right on time," Danton quipped, making a show of looking down at his watch. "Won't you come in? You'll feel right at home," he winked, opening the door wider.

Belle took another step out into the hallway. "We're doing this out here, and I'm not giving you a damn cent until you hand over all those pictures you took."

"No," Danton answered simply, arms crossed.

"Excuse me?" Belle sputtered with a glare.

"You heard me. I'm not handing over a damn thing, and you're giving me my money if you know what's good for you."

"How do I know you won't expose them once I give you the money? Do you expect me to trust you?" she asked, her voice loud and panicked. Danton rattled off a phone number and email address.

"I will be exposing them to your dear husband if you don't hand over that envelope. You think he'll let you see your son once he finds out you were a whore?" he sneered.

"Fine, just don't show them to anyone else. Here, just take the money and disappear!" Belle hissed, shoving the envelope into his chest. Danton started counting while whistling "Beautiful Day" by U2.

She winced; he was off tune.

"All here. Don't look so down, babycakes. It's the least your hubby owes me after all he's cost me," Danton smirked. He went back into the room and shut the door before Belle could ask what he meant.

Instead of demanding answers, she rushed out of the motel. When she got home, she took a long, hot shower, unable to scrub away the lingering scent of cheap cigarettes and cologne off of her. It had been years since she felt this crawling sensation of being unclean. But at least it was done now; she had paid Danton off, and he could crawl back to whatever pit he came from.

Her mood improved with every hour that passed, and by the time Max came back home, she was back to her regular self and couldn't wait to finish their discussion from that morning. She made a mental note to make an appointment with her gynecologist soon; her heart swelled at the thought of having another baby in the house.

"Fuck, your smile drives me wild, babe," Max whispered into her ear, scaring the wits out of Belle as he snuck up behind her and wrapped his arms around her midriff.

"You're insatiable," she giggled, grinding her ass into his erection that was pressed up against her back.

Max nibbled on her ear before placing a hot kiss on the nape of her back. Desire pooled in her core, and Belle swallowed down a moan. "Shouldn't you be grilling steaks in the garden and keeping an eye on that unruly son of ours?" she asked in a breathy tone.

"Steak's done, but I wanted to tell you something first. I invited Grayson over for dinner on Saturday," he announced sheepishly.

"Max!" Belle groaned and whined. "Chloe will be here. Do you want us to play referee all night?" While she didn't exactly like the man, she didn't hate him either.

"I'm sorry, babe, I happened to mention in passing that you're making mac-n-cheese, and you know what a smooth talker Gray is. Next thing I knew, I was inviting him home." He gave her an innocent smile when Belle glared at him. *I'll never be immune to his rugged handsomeness*, she thought when she all but melted at the sight of him in jogging shorts and a hoodie.

"Fine, but you're responsible for cleaning up any blood and destroying the evidence if they kill each other. Now go sit down. I'm about to bring out the salad." She gave Max a light tap on the ass and watched him head back outside.

It was as she was finishing up when the text came. Thinking it was Chloe confirming their next girl's night, Belle picked up the phone. It was an unknown number with the same motel room number, a time, and a demand for twenty-five thousand dollars this time around.

The salad tongs in her hand clattered to the floor.

"What the fuck?" she hissed with wide eyes. The number immediately went to voicemail when she tried calling it. Twenty-five thousand dollars? Dalton was a sick son-of-a-bitch. The time he picked for the meet-up clashed with when she was supposed to be dropping Oliver at school too!

"God-fucking-dammit!" she cursed, biting down on her nail.

"Honey, are you coming or what? Ollie's about to riot if he doesn't eat soon," Max called from the doorway. Belle turned to face him so quickly she felt light-headed, but that didn't stop her from pasting a perky smile on her face.

"Be right there." She picked up the salad bowl and headed out to the picnic table. She did a better job of not betraying her uneasiness that evening and didn't think Max noticed anything was amiss, that is until he cornered her when Oliver was taking a bath.

"Okay, what gives? You've been on edge all evening and last night too. What's going on? You know that you can tell me anything, right?"

Belle looked up at her husband's reflection in the mirror above the sink. She set down the face cream she was applying and turned to him. He sat on the bed and waited. "I promise nothing's wrong, sweetheart. I haven't been feeling well. It's nothing serious."

Max arched his brows, eyeing her skeptically. "Should I take you to the hospital?"

Her heart sank. Her phobia of hospitals wasn't as paralyzing as it used to be. "No! There's no need. Actually, um, could you take Ollie to school tomorrow? I kind of want to sleep in and maybe pass by the pharmacy."

"Sure. No problem." The way he readily agreed had Belle's stomach clenching with guilt.

She quickly changed the subject by telling him that they should go tuck Oliver into bed. The tired boy talked them into reading him a story, and she couldn't put up much of a fight.

"Guh-night, momma," Oliver mumbled, his eyes droopy as he curled into his blankets. Belle kissed him and dragged his blankets up to his chin.

"Night, my little prince," she whispered, blinking back tears. She only allowed them to fall after Max was working in the study downstairs and she was curled up in their bed.

There had to be a way to get rid of Danton. Belle wasn't going to let that lout ruin her life and take her perfect little family from her.

CHAPTER 13

FALL QUICKLY TURNED TO WINTER, and by mid-November, Belle was at the end of her rope. Danton was relentless in his demands, alternating between demanding ten thousand or twenty-five thousand dollars in payment. Soon, she had withdrawn more than seventy-five thousand dollars. It was only a matter of time before Max realized that the money was missing.

In a moment of guilt, she'd almost succumbed and told him the truth. It was late at night after they'd put Oliver to bed, and Belle went into the kitchen to load up the dishwasher. "Babe, you got a sec?" he asked her, sounding unsure of himself.

"Sure," Belle quipped with the fake smile that seemed to be permanently stuck on her face. A few people asked her if she was sick, she had lost noticeable weight since this whole ordeal began, and she bore signs of strain on her face, not to mention she was always jumpy. Belle's sanity was quickly fraying, and she had no idea how much longer this was going on; Danton didn't look like he was going to stop anytime soon.

"I got a call from the bank today—"

Belle dropped the dish she was holding, the ceramic breaking into three pieces and a few tiny shards. She quickly cleaned up the mess, telling Max that the plate was greasy and slipped from her hands.

"Sorry! You were saying?" she asked, smoothing a hand down her abdomen. The helplessness in Max's eyes broke her heart, he knew something was wrong, but she was always quick to brush the subject away every time he asked her about it.

Instead of insisting that she explain to him what was bothering her like Belle knew he wanted to, he asked her if he knew about the repeated cash withdrawals.

This was it. She should come clean and rid herself of the monkey on her back. But when she opened her mouth, what came out was a pithy excuse that left a bitter taste in her mouth.

"Oh, that," she busied herself with wiping down counters. "I started my holiday shopping early this year. I have to admit I may have gone overboard."

Max's eyes wavered between hers, and Belle was convinced he would call her out. The amount of money she'd withdrawn was too much, and there were no new extravagant purchases in the houses.

He laughed, but it rang hollow to her ears.

"Oh, in that case, do you want me to raise the limit on the credit card?" he asked. Belle stepped up to him, cupping his cheek.

"That won't be necessary, but thanks for asking." She rose on her tiptoes and gave him a lingering kiss on the cheek.

Belle collapsed on a kitchen stool after Max left for his study to get some work done. Hunched over with her face buried in her hands, she painted a picture of despair. Her phone chimed, and she flinched. She had come to hate that sound and even resorted to putting her phone on silent at home.

She knew what that message was going to say before she read it, yet her stomach still cramped up, and a searing pain pierced her skull.

Like always, there was a time and a demand for more money. His demands were becoming more and more unreasonable; this time around, he wanted to meet in an hour. He had to know how that would look to Max; his wife going off to meet someone in the middle of the night was suspicious enough.

Belle wanted to scream; she wanted to hurt Danton back so that he could feel the same suffering that she was experiencing. In a fit of rage, she texted him that there was no way she could give him any more money.

A reply came within minutes. Her stomach lurched when she saw a picture of herself from the back dressed in only a lacy bra as she straddled Danton. Both their faces were hidden, but who was to say he didn't have ones where her face could be seen?

Belle blindly ran to the bathroom and threw up in the toilet. She thought she might have blacked out for a few seconds because she woke up on the cold floor a short while later. After washing her face and rinsing her mouth, she went back to the kitchen, where she deleted the picture and sent Danton another text.

This time she made it clear that she could only give him the money next week. Max was becoming suspicious, and she wanted to wait until he eased off.

Danton took his time texting back, leaving Belle unable to relax the entire night. This was just a cruel mind game on his part, she kept checking her phone every few minutes, and a reply finally came as she and Max were getting ready for bed.

Danton was insistent that she bring the money tomorrow morning when she was supposed to be dropping her son off at school.

"Who are you talking to?" Max asked from his side of the bed, noting the anxious look on Belle's face.

"Chloe, she's having some guy trouble." The lie slipped naturally off her tongue. She had no idea what that said about her. She went back and forth with Danton until she negotiated for three extra days. It was a small victory for her, but at least she had room to breathe and to think about what to do. She couldn't live in this state of limbo, being extorted and wondering when Danton would decide that he'd had his fun and enough was enough.

The sword would drop eventually. When it did, she needed to make certain it wasn't going to injure her or her family.

Three days later, Belle stood once again in the hallway in front of room 6B as a disheveled Danton stood across from her. She wondered where all the money was going since none of it went toward his grooming. She buried her nose inside her thick coat, mostly to keep from smelling the stench of alcohol and cigarettes on him.

"Your money," her voice was terse and her expression severe. If she were a braver woman, she would have long taken the gun Max kept hidden in the safe in his study and put a bullet between Danton's bloodshot eyes. Too bad she wasn't a criminal mastermind who could get away with murder undetected.

"You're getting too comfortable, Mrs. Erickson," he sneered. His face twisted in a mask of disdain as if her name on his tongue left a bitter aftertaste. "You're an uppity little bitch, ain't ya? Just like your stuck-up husband," he growled as he advanced on her.

It wasn't the first time he'd mentioned Max so spitefully.

"Unfortunately, after that little stunt you tried to pull, money won't be enough anymore," he crooned in a deceptively calm voice, caging Belle against the wall with his hands on the side of her head.

She gulped, and cold sweat trickled down her spine. "W-what do you mean?"

"I mean," he enunciated, his teeth bared. "That you'll have to pay me back in the best way you know how. On your back with your legs spread," He chuckled, his teeth stained with tobacco.

Belle didn't see his hands move. She just felt his rough palm caressing her thigh.

A scared whimper escaped her as her muscles locked up, giving Danton an opportunity to drag her into the room. She came to herself before they could cross through the door. Snatching away her hand, she kneed him in the crotch when he turned to face her and ran out of there as fast as her legs could carry her. Danton's pained cries and threats chased after her.

Belle was sure she broke a few traffic laws in her haste to get home. Dumping her keys, purse, and coat on the floor, she left a trail up to the bedroom, where she collapsed onto the bed in a heap of tears, the kind that gave you a headache and left your eyes swollen. She curled up into a ball on Max's side of the bed, hugging his pillow to her chest and drawing in his cedarwood and cypress scent.

Instead of offering comfort like it usually would, the familiar scent made her cry even harder.

Belle had no doubt that Danton was going to retaliate soon after what she had done. The sword was bearing down on her neck so close that she could smell blood. If she were the only one in the line of fire, she wouldn't care this much, but once those photos leaked, Max would be a laughingstock amongst his peers. She couldn't bear to think about Oliver and what she was going to put him through. Nothing was ever genuinely forgotten on the internet.

Years from now, when he was old enough to understand, would he hate her? What if he was bullied at school because of her? She had no idea how long she lay there staring forward sightlessly.

She forced her eyes shut when the room was suddenly filled with a blinding light. Max crouched in front of her, his blue eyes narrowed and lips set in a thin line.

"Max? What time is it?" Belle croaked, her voice rough from crying and nose stuffed. Her head felt as if it had been shoved full of cotton.

"You've been crying," Max stated in an accusatory tone. "You need to tell me what's going on, Belle. And don't tell me that you're fine because you're not. Whatever it is, we will get through it together!" he snapped.

Belle's lips trembled, but she swallowed back the tears.

"Period pains and a nasty headache, that's all. I came in here to take a short nap after dropping Ollie off—" she sat up abruptly, remembering that she hadn't picked her son up from school. Her heart fluttered in her chest, "Ollie!" she gasped.

"I picked him up already. The school called to say you didn't show up and you weren't answering your phone. Belle,

I think it's time you see a doctor. Please!" Max begged her, on his knees as he took Belle's hands.

"I'll make an appointment soon," she told him.

He looked like he wanted to argue. "Fine. I'm making dinner tonight. How about you go soak in the bath and come join us downstairs when you're done," he ordered her.

By making dinner, Max meant ordering enough pizza and wings to last them days. They ate in the living room that night, watching one of Oliver's favorite Marvel movies. After dinner, Oliver snuggled between them, reciting every line of the movie word for word.

Despite her stressful day, Belle managed to have fun laughing and cheering with her family when the movie called for it.

Max wrapped his arm around them both as Oliver snuggled into her. Watching her boys watch their favorite movies and simply being themselves made her smile and cry with her happiness. She wiped away her tears before they noticed, allowing herself to enjoy their moment together.

That night, Belle lay awake in bed, listening to Max's soft snores and feeling his heartbeat beneath her palm. Her cheek still tingled from where Oliver had kissed her goodnight. Her thoughts kept circling back around the same point: she could not let Danton win and destroy two innocent lives.

She thought back to her first date with Max when he told her about his vision for Titan. He worked so hard to grow the company to where it was, and he was on the verge of making a groundbreaking deal with a renowned company that would take him and the company even higher. Belle didn't know all the details, only that it had to do with virtual and augmented reality. If Danton leaked those photos, all of Max's hard work would be for naught.

Belle saw how people reacted to scandals. If and when news of her own broke, companies and partners associated with Max and Titan would want to distance themselves, lest they get caught in the fire as well. Belle wanted to protect her family, but she wasn't about to cheat on Max, no matter how Danton threatened her.

An idea began to take shape as she stared up at the bedroom ceiling. Max had given her so much. He'd supported her when she wanted to continue with her studies after giving birth and in her choice to become a stay-at-home mom while picking up freelance gigs on the side.

It was her turn to protect him now and Oliver, too, even if it meant that they would end up hating her in the end. Belle had to do something outrageous to save them, and she had a plan.

CHAPTER 19

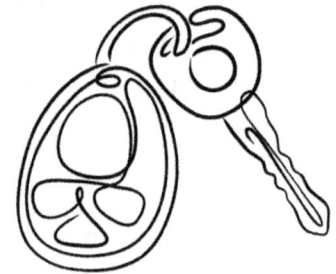

FIVE DAYS PASSED without anything about her past being leaked to the media. Danton attempted to contact her multiple times, but Belle ignored his messages. She knew it was only a matter of time before he exposed her, and quite frankly, she was surprised that he'd waited this long. She wouldn't look a gift horse in the mouth, though. Whatever reason Danton had for holding back, Belle would use this time to put her plan in motion and make sure Max and Oliver were somehow protected from the backlash.

The perfect chance came when Oliver was invited for a sleepover at Tommy's house for the weekend. She hugged him longer than usual when she dropped him off, memorizing his beautiful face. She drew his scent deep into her lungs, savoring the warmth of his little body in her arms for one last time.

She was going to miss him so much.

"Remember to behave, 'kay?" she reminded him, brushing his hair back from his forehead. She should have cut his hair earlier, but she'd fallen in love with the shaggy curls.

When he nodded in response, his sandy brown hair flopped over his eyes, causing her to smile. "Ollie, you know that mommy loves you more than anything in the world, right? No matter what happens, no matter what anyone says, you and daddy are the two most important people to me," she said in a trembling voice, taking Oliver's small mitten-covered hands in hers.

"I love you too, Momma," he replied sweetly.

Belle could tell that he was confused by what she said, but he still gave her a luminous smile and kissed her goodbye as Belle left him in the care of Tommy's parents.

Her heart stuttered in her chest, but she still had one more goodbye left to get through. Max wasn't working in his office for once, but he was playing a video game which he paused when she walked in. Just as she did with Oliver, Belle memorized every single detail on Max's face.

He aged like fine wine, and Belle knew she was tossing her one chance at happiness away. *For good reasons*, she told herself.

"You're back!" Max stood. "So, I was thinking we could order some takeout from that Thai place you love so much. After, maybe we should get to work on giving Ollie a sibling."

Max walked up to her, rubbing his hands together before pushing against Belle's body. He started kissing and nibbling at her neck, sucking at her pulse.

She froze in his arms, her breath hitching as her stomach hollowed and twisted. It was now or never.

"Since we're all alone, we can be as loud as we want. I can fuck you anywhere in the house without worrying about traumatizing our son," Max chuckled wickedly as he began to unbutton Belle's coat. "Maybe we should start against the wall right here."

I can't do this, Belle wavered.

She couldn't bring herself to break his heart and make him hate her, but then she pictured the look of disgust once he found out. Max surely wouldn't want to touch her like he was right now. There would be no more heated touches, no more claiming kisses, no more tender endearments. It would all be gone in the blink of an eye.

So, she donned another mask, wiping off all emotion on her face. She slapped Max's wandering hands away and stepped back from him.

"Babe, what's wrong?" he asked, hurt and confusion flashing in his eyes.

Belle realized she'd fail if she continued looking at them, so she picked a spot over his shoulder and stared at it. Consequently, it was a picture of the two of them on their wedding day; the frame perched on Max's work desk.

"Are you finally ready to tell me what's bothering you?" he asked gently.

Perfect

She drew in a deep breath that did nothing to calm her nerves. It was best just to blurt it out and be done with it. Swallowing down a lump in her throat, Belle coldly declared, "I want a divorce."

Max was visibly confused for a long moment. He let out a nervous chuckle and said, "You have a strange way of instigating intimacy, babe."

Belle frowned and stepped away, crossing her arms over her chest. "It's not a joke, Max."

The silence bore down on them, making it hard for Belle to breathe. When Max remained silent, she turned to leave, but his broken voice stopped her in her tracks.

"What do you mean you want a divorce? Stop joking around, Belle, because it's not fucking funny!" The hurt in Max's voice arrowed straight to her heart. Belle let out a quiet breath, placing a palm against her body. She allowed some of her pain to show on her face, but when she turned to face Max, her expression was one of cool indifference.

"I said I'm not joking! I have done my best to pretend that these last six years were everything I ever wanted, but I can't live like this anymore."

"Live like what?" he scoffed. "You mean with a husband and son who love you? Live in the lap of luxury with all the money and comforts you desire?" he roared, eyes wild, gathering with tears.

"Yes!" she screamed back. "I can't do this anymore, pretending to love you, playing the perfect little housewife for you and your rich, pretentious friends. This is not the life

I wanted for myself! I never wanted to be a mother at twenty-three, but I agreed because you looked so desperate and pathetic, telling me you would do your best to care for the baby and me. Because let's be honest here, if I hadn't gotten pregnant, none of this would be here! We never would've gotten married, and I wouldn't have to put up this front of acting like I belong in this world of money and fame! I thought that—" she broke off to take a deep breath, despite herself, tears were beginning to flow down her cheeks.

"Thought what?" He growled.

She moistened her lips with a swipe on her tongue and continued. "I thought that maybe I could learn to love you. I thought if I gave this a chance, things would turn out different, but I was kidding myself. I'm so tired of pretending. I can't hide it anymore." Her impassioned speech became a matter of truth.

Max stared at her in disbelief, his eyes moist and jaw clenched. At least when Danton finally leaked the photos, Max could claim he divorced her because of her indiscretions. He and Oliver had some partial cover from the scandal coming their way—or so Belle hoped.

"You're lying! You are fucking lying to me, Belle. None of this was pretend. We were happy—we *are* happy together! And what about Ollie, huh? Did you only pretend to love him as well? Are you walking out on your son too?" He spat, reaching forward and grasping her shoulders, shaking her lightly in an effort to make her see reason.

Belle shoved him away. "We'll have our lawyers work out a custody agreement. You don't have to worry about your money; I don't want it."

The thought of abandoning her son nearly had the façade crumbling. Maybe there was something she could salvage out of this. Oliver was her sunshine, he was the song that her heartbeat held its rhythm to, and he was the one thing Belle would never *ever* regret. "I'll be living with a friend in the city for the meantime."

She had her bags in the car, having secretly packed her things and storing them in the trunk of her SUV all week, in anticipation of the right moment.

His voice, broken and soft, forced her to pause by the front door. "Belle, I love you."

She grabbed for the doorknob and told herself to stay strong. "Well, I don't love you," she said simply.

There was only silence behind her. His effort to prevent her from leaving stopped as the door closed. She told herself she was being cowardly; she should turn around and face him one last time. He was due that much, at least.

Licking her lips, she turned her head and caught him staring after her with wide eyes. She expected the cold, ruthless businessman to make a reappearance, but one thing Belle learned over the years was Maxwell didn't exist when it came to her.

He was just Max. He was simply her husband, and she was crushing their six precious years of marital bliss in a matter of five minutes.

She wanted to go to him and pull him into her arms and never let go. Instead, she forced her legs to carry her out of his life.

"Goodbye, Max," she whispered.

It felt strange that he wasn't doing anything to stop her. She thought it would be easier if he were angry with her. She never anticipated the resigned silence that permeated the air.

Belle ran to her car, keeping up her charade of indifference in case Max was watching her leave from the window. She had no idea if she imagined it or not, but she swore her heart slowed down with every mile she put between her and her family. She managed to keep her cool and drive with a clear head, that was until she came upon a rest stop where she parked her and cried for a good two hours.

She kept picturing Max's face when she told him that she didn't love him. She wondered what he was going to tell Ollie if he'd even let her see him again when the truth came out.

Inwardly, she knew he would. He'd never keep Ollie from her, but would her son even want to see her when all was said and done?

"Fuck!" she screamed repeatedly, her forehead resting against the steering wheel. When she was all cried out, Belle cleaned herself up in the bathroom and continued on to the pharmacy. At the pharmacy, she bought eye drops before continuing to Chloe's house.

All that was left to do was wait. Danton would make his move soon enough.

CHAPTER 15

"HEY, YOU OKAY?" Chloe peeked her head through the cracked opening of the guest bedroom door. Belle had been hiding since Friday evening, too ashamed to show her face and too tired to face any questions.

It felt like a lifetime ago when she made the terrible choice of leaving, but really, it had only been three days.

Three long days...

Oliver was supposed to come home that evening. Would Max remember to fetch him from Tommy's house? There were so many times she had to stop herself from picking up the phone and checking up on them both. If this was going to work, her break up with Max had to be easy so he would eventually move on.

She was only kidding herself. How was a divorce easy? God, she was a monster.

Belle felt sick picturing another woman standing by Max's side, sleeping in their bed, living in their house—raising her son. She couldn't stop imagining Max finding happiness with someone who wasn't her; another woman's name falling from his lips as he fucked her, a new baby making an appearance.

The picture-perfect family... a family that didn't include her.

"I'm fine," she told Chloe with a weak smile, putting down her Kindle and burrowing deeper into the blankets. She tried to distract herself by reading, but she'd been re-reading the same line over and over again, getting nowhere.

"No, you're not, Belle," Chloe replied, taking a seat at the foot of the bed. "You've been crying yourself to sleep since you showed up here looking like someone kicked your puppy. If you'd tell me what you guys fought about, maybe I can help. I know a thing or two about fighting and making up," she said with a wry smile.

Belle shrugged. There was no use correcting her; this was more than a lover's quarrel.

"It's... it's more than that. And you'll be the first person I come to for tips on making up if I need it." She laughed, the sound ringing flat to her ears.

Chloe and her boyfriend had the most volatile relationship Belle had ever seen. Sometimes she suspected they were together purely for the drama and the rush that came with their epic fights and even more epic makeup sex. Chloe was an over-sharer, so Belle knew things about their sex life she wished she didn't. She was just thankful that her boyfriend was out of town on business this weekend. Belle didn't have to feel guilty about dampening their romance, but she needed to find somewhere else to live soon.

"You're right. You and Maxwell are a great couple. I've never seen you guys so much as raise your voices. You always get this goopy wide-eyed *I'm-so-in-love* look when you're around each other. It's sickeningly sweet," Chloe huffed, a teasing smile on her face.

"Don't worry. We'll sort this out soon enough. I promise I'll be out of your hair." Belle glanced around the not-so-dilapidated room and smirked, "If I'm lucky, I'll be out of this dump soon enough."

Chloe playfully smacked Belle's leg, completely missing her target. She couldn't make out Belle's legs beneath the blankets. The two of them shared a heartfelt laugh, the first glimpse of happiness she had shown since showing up on her friend's doorstep.

"Trust me, Chloe, the end is within sight," Belle added. Her friend gave her a brilliant smile, assuming that this meant Belle and Max were closer to making up than she thought. If she only knew the truth.

"Whelp, I gotta check in at the bakery and make sure those idiots haven't burned the damned place to the ground. Enjoy your lazy Sunday, but take a shower, will ya? I could smell you from the hallway."

Chloe cackled on the way out as Belle threw a pillow at her head and missed.

She did take that shower and felt a felt a smidge better, more prepared for the call she was about to make. Scrolling through her contacts list, she unblocked Danton's number. "Time to face the music," she murmured as the phone rang.

He wasted no time answering. "You fucking bitch!" Danton growled in greeting. A TV show was playing in the background on his end, something with gunshots and screaming.

"Danton," Belle greeted him calmly, nursing a cup of hot chocolate in Chloe's kitchen. A memory came to her of Max making her hot chocolate at Titan's old offices the night her mother passed. It was that night she and Max made love for the first time. She pushed back the thought and focused on their conversation.

"Don't Danton me," he snapped. "You've been ignoring my calls. I don't know where you get the balls to renege on our agreement, but maybe you need a reminder about who holds the power in this relationship?"

Belle rolled her eyes and sat down at the table, crossing her legs. "Jesus Christ, would you shut up already? The one who holds the power here is me. See, I've grown tired of being jerked around like a puppet, so I decided to change things up. There will be no more threats, no more texts demanding to meet in some shady motel, and most of all, no more money. I don't give a shit if you leak those pictures. You can scream from the rooftops that I was an escort for all I care. I. Am. Done!"

There was a stunned silence on the other end, and then, "What did you say?" Danton stuttered, sounding taken aback by Belle's assertive tone.

"You heard me. I'm done being your personal ATM, Danton. You can go straight to hell." Belle hung up and sat back as she sipped at her hot chocolate. Her phone rang once, but she silenced it and proceeded to block his number.

Strangely enough, she felt free. It took extreme effort to get to this point, but at least she could rest happy knowing that her family would be safe. Her stomach growled, reminding her that she hadn't eaten anything since the breakfast Chloe had forced on her Saturday morning.

It was noon, so she probably should make a light lunch for herself.

Her mind wandered to her husband and Oliver. Did they eat yet? Was Oliver asking for her? And what did Max tell him? Did Oliver think his mother had abandoned him?

She remembered how she resented her dad when she was younger. It wasn't his fault that he died, but sometimes Belle felt like he had abandoned them. If he were still alive, her mother wouldn't have had to work herself to an early grave.

Of course, in Oliver's case, Belle had willingly left him behind, which was far worse than her father dying. She could only hope and pray that one day he would forgive her and understand that she'd only left to protect them.

She attempted to eat the leftover chicken salad she found in the fridge, but the taste was off, and it made her want to throw up. Belle suspected that it was only because she was so depressed that food was unappealing to her, so she made another cup of hot chocolate and trudged back to bed, where she passed the time scrolling through photos on her phone. There were photos of her and Max, but most were of Oliver, going as far back as when he was a baby. She and Max had made it a point to capture as many moments of his childhood as possible.

Belle paused on one photo. The photo was taken shortly after her last birthday. Ollie had surprised her with breakfast in bed. The toast was burnt, and the eggs had no salt, but it was the best birthday she'd ever had. Max woke her with soft kisses, and Ollie cuddled into her side as she ate.

On either side of her were her boys, smiling at the camera and looking like they had it all. Belle was rumbled from sleep, but her eyes were so light and content, and she wanted nothing more than to go back to that moment.

I hope they're okay…

Chloe found her still huddled up in bed, her eyes puffy and red from crying. The smile on her face died as she dropped a paper bag from her bakery on the bedside table.

"Seriously, woman! Did you even leave your bed today?" she scowled down at Belle's curled-up form.

"I took a shower as you requested," Belle mumbled, sitting up when she noticed the bag. She rooted through the paper bag, hoping to find something that could ease her sorrows. "Oh, and I made some hot chocolate," she said, gesturing to the now empty mug.

She picked out a bran muffin from the bag and ate it in three bites. She didn't realize she was hungry until she actually tasted something. It turned out she was starving, so she picked out another muffin.

"What happened? You were in better spirits this morning. Did you talk to Maxwell? Did you guys have another fight?" she asked.

When Belle wordlessly shook her head, Chloe looked to the heavens for help. Convincing Belle to open up about what was happening was like trying to draw blood from a stone.

"I have an idea," Chloe announced, running into the living room. She returned, carrying a pamphlet about a wine tasting event taking place later that evening. "Maybe we should loosen up over a few glasses of Merlot? Maybe you'll be more forthcoming."

"I don't know—"

"Come on. It will be fun." She dragged the blankets off of Belle's body, snorting at the pajamas she wore. They were a bit skimpy for winter, but the sight of them hanging off her already rail-thin form was disturbing. Chloe frowned with concern, realizing how much weight Belle had lost.

"Up, up, up. You and I are going on an impromptu girl's night out," she declared in a tone that brokered no argument.

Belle pleaded her case anyway. "I don't feel like going out. I'm tired, my muscles are aching, and I'm really not the best company right now."

"Nonsense! Once we get a few drinks and food in you, you'll be right as rain. Come on, Bells, it's nothing hectic. It's just a wine tasting and a live jazz band at the country club. You need to let loose for a few hours, and then you can go back to moping."

"It's Sunday, Chloe. Don't you have to open up the bakery tomorrow? How are you going to get anything done when you're nursing a hangover?"

"The beauty of being the boss, Belle, my dear, is that I can order one of my grunts to open up. I'll just sleep in 'til noon if I want. Do you have any more excuses to dish out? Because, mark my words, friend, you're coming with me even if I have to drag you out by your beautiful hair."

CHAPTER 16

CHLOE IS RIGHT, Belle thought, as she watched the band play. Dressing up in an evening dress and heels, as well as getting her makeup and hair done up, did lift her spirits. Her pessimistic self still didn't think that attending a wine tasting was worth the one-and-a-half-hour trip to the country club.

The vineyard was beautiful, but the sights reminded her too much of the events she attended with Max.

There had been awkward moments when Belle and Chloe ran into a business acquaintance of Titan Telecom during the event. The man asked about Max and Oliver, and the little joy Belle felt swiftly died.

Then it dawned on her that this could help her cause; if word got back to Max that she was partying it up days after asking for a divorce—it would crush any hopeful feelings of reconciliation. But then again, Max hadn't attempted to contact her since she left.

Maybe this front she was putting up was for naught.

"Are you having any fun at all?" Chloe asked as she swayed to the music by the buffet table.

Belle shrugged, loading her plate with chocolates, cheese, and fresh fruit. She spotted an empty table near the back from where a small stage was erected in the ballroom. Chloe followed behind so close on her heels she could feel her warm breath fan against the shell of her ear. Stopping abruptly and turning to face her friend, Belle narrowly missed having red wine spilled on her white dress.

"Oops," her friend giggled, tipping the cup back up.

A flare of irritation had Belle's face heating up. The entire point of this outing was for her to drown her sorrows—or so that's what she'd been led to believe. They had been there only an hour, and Chloe was quickly slipping past buzzed and was well on her way to being sloshed, and the night wasn't close to being over.

This meant Belle needed to limit the amount she could drink so that someone was sober enough to drive them home. She didn't mind doing that, but the problem was that in her inebriated state, Chloe was determined to see Belle have fun when all she wanted to do was stay off her feet and enjoy the great music.

"You do know that you don't have to babysit me, right? You can go chill with your other friends; I don't mind hanging by myself," Belle told her in what she hoped was a reasonable and cheerful voice. She didn't want to snap and alienate a friend; she already lost enough people in her life.

Chloe pouted, her blue eyes unfocused and glazed. "I wanna see you having fun, Bells. Is that so wrong?"

"It's not, and I am having fun. Go, chill with your friends. Just don't get too drunk and hook up with strange men in the bathroom," she teased. Chloe rolled her eyes, but she had done that once.

The night of Belle's twenty-fifth birthday, Chloe had insisted that they go clubbing. She had gotten so pissed drunk she thought hooking up with a random dude in the bathroom was a good idea. Belle had had to brave her phobia of hospitals and accompany Chloe to the emergency room a few days later when the girl admitted to having unprotected sex and was freaking out about an STD.

"Alright, alright. But if you wanna leave, come get me, 'kay?"

Belle nodded and went to sit down, hanging her coat over the chair. She checked the time on her phone and saw that it was 8:30, Oliver's bedtime, and she wasn't there to tuck him into her bed and kiss him goodnight.

Loneliness was a feral beast gnawing at her. The last time Belle felt this was after her mother died, perhaps even before that. She nibbled on the snacks, watching the band play. They were really good; Max would have loved them. He would have pulled her out onto the dance floor and convinced her to waltz even though Belle had two left feet and was always stomping on his toes.

She smiled to herself, thinking about how he'd always try to hide his winces when she stepped on him and pretended that he wasn't limping when they walked off the dance floor. "Oh, for the love of—" she mumbled, taking an angry bite out of a piece of Turkish delight when she caught onto her train of thought. Was she going to spend the rest of her life like this? With every little thing reminding her of Max and her son?

She grabbed a glass of white wine and downed it. She didn't bother with any of the etiquettes for wine tasting; she just wanted to be numb for a few hours.

"Guess we're ordering an Uber," she mumbled into her glass, her face snarled in disgust. The wine was dry and stronger than it looked.

Her heart stopped when she saw someone who looked like Max near the stage. She closed her eyes, reopening them to see that it was someone else. Suddenly, the ballroom became too suffocating. Belle slipped on her coat and decided to take a walk in the courtyard. Maybe the cold air would sober her up a bit.

She swayed as she walked, causing her to giggle. A loose stone in her path caused her to stumble, nearly spraining her ankle.

The courtyard was paved with uneven cobblestones. Instead of risking taking another tumble, she took her shoes off and walked barefooted. Several tables were scattered around. A few of the tables were taken by other guests—primarily couples—sat outside for privacy. Light spilled from the open doors of the ballroom and, along with lanterns and fairy lights lining the walkways, lent a romantic feel to the air.

Not wanting to intrude on the couples, she followed the cobbled path to a more secluded area of the vineyard.

The smell of wet earth and fruity and floral scents of the grave wafted her way. The breeze picked up, lifting tendrils of her hair. She walked under an arched trellis away from the courtyard where it emptied to the front of the in-house restaurant of the vineyard. The restaurant was closed, but there was outside seating, so Belle sat on one of the chairs and looked up at the stars making up her constellations. The full moon was out, and it illuminated her lonely form.

She started singing *Twinkle Twinkle Little Star* off tune, her breath coming in choppy gasps and misting when she exhaled.

"Ain't this the most pathetic sight I ever saw?" Came a gritty voice that chilled her blood.

Belle jumped up from her chair and stared slack-jawed at Danton, who, for once, actually put some effort into his looks. He was dressed in a maroon suit, his dirty blonde hair framing his face and golden eyes glittering in the moonlight. Once again, Belle thought it was unfair for someone with a black heart like him to have the looks of an angel.

"What the hell are you doing here? Are you following me?" she hissed, holding one of her shoes in her hands, the heel pointed at Danton to use as a weapon if he tried anything funny.

"What are you gonna do about it if I did? Run to your prick of a husband and have him take care of me again? He couldn't get rid of me the first time. What makes you think he'll succeed now?" Danton sneered.

Belle blinked up at him in confusion. She knew that Danton harbored a grudge against Max, but for the life of her, she couldn't think of a reason why. She was the one who knew Danton; he was her dirty little secret, not Max's. Why did he have a dark and dangerous look in his eyes whenever he brought up Max?

"Why do you keep bringing up Max? You don't even know him. I told you that you won't be getting any more money from me, so leave me the fuck alone, or I'll report you to the police!" she spat.

Danton's emotionless face had goosebumps blooming on her skin. "Know him?" he asked, sounding outraged. "That stuck-up asshole is the reason my life is in ruins! He took everything from me and had the nerve to live happily, making millions and showing off his perfect little family! Except you're not so perfect, are you, my little whore?" Danton accused as he stalked toward Belle.

"Stay back, Danton! I'm warning you!" Belle called out in a tremulous voice, but he ignored her warning and came to stand right in front of her—ignoring the heel pressing into his chest.

"You're just a money-grabbing gold digger, aren't you, little whore?" he hissed, grabbing Belle's chin forcefully in his hand. "Got yourself pregnant so that you could get your filthy little hands on his money. Is that the reason you stopped coming to our appointments? Is it?" he exploded when Belle didn't answer.

"Is the kid even his? You were probably still screwing around behind his back. Now that you have a ring on your finger, you think your pussy's too good for the rest of us lowly commoners. Just like your fucking asshole of a husband who thinks he's above us mere mortals."

Belle raised her hand as the sound of her palm connecting against his cheek echoed in the empty courtyard.

His face was turned away, his expression hidden in the dark, but Belle had an idea of what he was feeling. He spat onto the ground and used his thumb to wipe the blood off his lip where Belle's wedding ring had cut him.

"Not bad. But this is how you slap someone." With that warning, Danton's huge palm smacked against her with such brutal force that it swept her off her feet. She crashed into the side of the metal table with her pelvic bone and collapsed onto the floor. Her ears were ringing, and whatever little courage she had deserted her.

Pulling herself back up, using the table as support, Belle ignored the pain in her hips and her scraped knees and palms. She looked around the courtyard, Danton was blocking her way to the only exit, and they were too far from the ballroom for anyone to hear her call for help.

"If I can't get the money owed to me, how 'bout we make up for all those missed appointments?" Danton asked, his alcohol and cigarette breath fanning against Belle's nose as he pinned her to the table and pressed his aroused length—covered by his pants—against her core.

Belle's stomach sank to her toes as he continued taunting her, "You know... you used to ride me better than my witch of an ex-wife. Your pussy was tighter, too. The only reason I could fuck that ugly bitch was that I already dipped my cock in your soaking cunt and had my fun," he whispered in her ear, pinning her hands on the table behind her as he ground against her core.

Bile burned its way up her throat as she struggled uselessly against his heavy and masculine body.

"You must know that you'll never get away with this, Danton!" she cried.

"Shh—" Danton whispered against her mouth. Belle squeezed her eyes shut when his lips brushed against hers as he spoke. "You forgot your place, little whore. It's beneath me. Your job was to pleasure me, not to play housewife to Maxwell fucking Erickson. Maybe I should film this, what do you think? Even the most hardened men will break down at the sight of the woman they love being violated. It's only fair that I hurt him back, is it not?"

Danton's statement brought a whimper to Belle's lips. "No!" she screamed out. "Let me go!" She tried to kick him in the crotch, but she couldn't even kick her leg up.

She struggled even harder, unable to bear the thought of Maxwell seeing her violated like this just as Danton threatened. It would be too much for him on top of finding out she was an escort.

She sent out a silent plea to a God she didn't believe in, begging him to spare Max and Oliver from any more pain. Somehow, she didn't think she was coming out of this alive. She wished she could tell Max how much she loved him one last time.

Just as the thought entered her mind, a blurred shadow tackled Danton to the ground and began mercilessly punching at his face, letting out angry and wounded screams.

CHAPTER 17

The Friday after Belle left...

MAX STARED BLANKLY at the carnage he wrought in his office. Documents were strewn everywhere, his gaming monitors lying broken on the floor and picture frames he kept on his desk lying in broken pieces. His chest heaved as if he'd been running non-stop, and he felt as if his chest had been cracked open and someone stomped on his heart.

Belle.

Belle had done that, ripped his heart out, and carelessly tossed it aside. And like a fool, he'd stood there and watched her walk away as if the past six years meant nothing at all. His wife. The mother of his child. His heart.

Why did he let her leave? Why did he slam the door and be angry instead of going after her?

Her words kept running in loops through his head, driving him to raid his liquor cabinet. Lying amongst the wreckage in his office, Max tried to pinpoint the moment where it all went wrong. It wasn't like he hadn't noticed that something was up with Belle; he did ask her on multiple occasions what was bothering her. Even when she kept repeating that everything was fine, he figured she needed more time and space and that she'd come clean eventually.

So many theories had come to mind about what could have been bothering her, like an illness perhaps, but not this. Divorce never crossed his mind.

"Fuck!" he screamed to the heavens. What was he going to tell Oliver? Would his son grow up going back and forth between two households? Max drank his Johnny Walker scotch straight from the bottle, relishing the burn on its way down as he drowned the images of Belle with some other prick, acting like one big happy family with his son. His wife.

Max drank until the room spun, even when he was sitting down, and his sight blurred. He somehow managed to climb the stairs to the bedroom without falling and cracking open his skull. Taking off his jeans was a chore beyond him, so he threw his body on the bed and fell fast asleep, thanks to good ol' Mr. Walker.

I am going to kill whoever thought pounding a drum this early was a good idea, Max thought as he flipped onto his stomach and tried to open his eyes. His eyelids felt like they'd been stuck together with superglue, and it took a moment for his sluggish brain to register that the pounding was coming from his head.

He stretched out his hand to Belle's side of the bed to wake her up and ask why he smelt like a bar, except she wasn't there. Her side of the bed was cold. Everything that happened last night crashed down on him, intensifying his pounding headache. His stomach lurched. Before he could rush to the bathroom, Max vomited over himself and across the bed.

"Jesus fucking Christ," he groaned, wiping his mouth with the back of his hand. He wanted to clean up, but there was a disconnect between his brain and body. It took ten minutes lying in his vomit before he gathered the strength to stand and stumble to the bathroom. He was still slightly drunk, but the hot shower left him feeling meagerly refreshed and clear-headed enough to want to get to the bottom of Belle's sudden divorce request.

One greasy breakfast later, he loaded the bedding into the washing machine. He returned to his office, realizing how much damage his triad from the night before had caused.

He was grateful Oliver was away on a sleepover, and he prayed that he'd have Belle back in the house before he came back on Sunday. He still had a hard time believing that she wanted nothing to do with him, but for the life of him, Max couldn't think of a single reason that would drive her to leave. How did they jump from trying for a second kid to divorce?

Maybe there was an answer to her strange behavior somewhere in the house.

After a quick call to his P.A., Ryan, to tell him he would be working from home and that he would be taking a few days off, his assistance panicked.

"But Sir, the deal with Viz Tech," Ryan began, referring to the tech company they were partnering up with for a new virtual reality program.

"There's a chain of command for a reason, Ryan. Emergencies only. Otherwise, I'm firing anyone who calls me about anything mundane. Be sure to pass the message along."

He hung up and went upstairs to a guest bedroom they'd renovated for Belle to use as her office. Searching for any clues was a long shot, but he had to try. Belle rarely used the room, preferring to work where she could keep an eye on Oliver or in Max's office while he was also working.

The room smelled stuffy, so he pulled the drapes and windows open to allow airflow and sunlight to come pouring in. Belle didn't have much in the office except some contracts for her freelance marketing gigs, as well as some itineraries for blogging conventions she had attended in the past. Her laptop was not there; that was the likeliest place to find private information she wanted no one else to see.

Their bedroom and his own office turned up empty as well. Realizing that he'd get nowhere on his own, Max called his lawyer, Grayson Sinclair. The man had a finger in every pie in the city and connections most people could only dream of, legal or otherwise. His shady connections had helped Max a time or two, something Max wasn't proud of, but this time he didn't give a shit where Grayson got the info he needed from.

"I don't work on Saturdays," Grayson answered lazily, his smooth voice roughened from sleep.

"I need your help, Sinclair—"

"Don't you always?" Max could hear the smirk in Grayson's voice. There was a pause, and Max heard sheets rustling and a woman's incoherent voice asking something. Grayson told her to go back to sleep, and then there was the sound of the door closing. "What do you need, boss?"

"I want you to find out everything Belle's been up to in the last three or so months," he instructed in clipped tones. A stunned silence came from the other end.

"You want me to look into Belle? Your wife?"

"Yes," Max bit out.

"Okay... That's unexpected. You think she's screwing around behind your back or something?" Grayson sounded skeptical, even as he asked.

"No," Max answered, confident that whatever else may be going on, Belle was not fucking another man behind his back. He knew it as surely as the sun rose in the east and set in the west. "But she's been acting odd the last couple of months. I think something's got her spooked—" he took a deep breath before telling Grayson the rest, "She wants a divorce."

Grayson released a slow whistle. "That's rough. Is there anything more specific that you can tell me that'll maybe point me in the right direction?"

Max opened his mouth to say no, and then he remembered the call he got from the bank. "Apparently, she's been withdrawing a large sum of money from the bank regularly. She told me it was early shopping, but I know Belle. She normally forewarns me before doing something like that. Find out where all that money went to."

"Got it, boss. I'll give you a ring as soon as I have something."

Max decided to do some digging of his own and logged onto their accounts from his laptop. The transaction records left him stumped by the scope of withdrawals as he stared at the screen. The amount of money Belle had been withdrawing was far above what he'd assumed; starting from ten thousand dollars, the money had slowly increased over time.

"I started my holiday shopping a little early this year and may have gone overboard."

"What the hell kind of holiday shopping costs two hundred and fifty grand?" he mused out loud. Did Belle have debts he didn't know anything about? Max didn't remember seeing any new purchases that cost tens of thousands of dollars. In fact, everything was cash withdrawals. No checks were written, and no charges were made.

If she was really shopping, she would've used one of their credit cards.

He went back to the bedroom and checked her jewelry pieces. At first, he was shocked that she didn't take any with her. However, he didn't see anything new. Belle was a frugal spender. All the jewelry she owned, Max had bought for her, or they were pieces that once belonged to her mother. He looked through her closet, finding nothing new that would justify the missing money. He continued searching through the accounts they had with exclusive boutiques and the like, but he found no receipts of recent purchases that would raise a red flag. So, where the hell had all the money gone?

By the time evening rolled around, Max had lost count of how many times he'd called Grayson only to hear that he was still chasing a lead. During the last call, Grayson snapped at him, telling him that answers didn't come instantaneously and repeating for the umpteenth time that he would call as soon as he had something worth reporting.

Frustrated by the lack of answers, Max threw his phone against the wall. He didn't bother picking it up as he walked out of the bedroom. With nothing more to do, he went into the entertainment room and watched old home videos with the volume muted. As he watched Belle help Oliver blow out candles on his first birthday, his mind wandered to where she was and what she was doing.

Belle said she would be staying with a friend. The only friend she had that was close enough for her to stay with was Chloe Martin. He thought about calling Chloe and checking up on Belle, but he didn't know Chloe's number. He couldn't even know the number to call the Butterson's house to bid Oliver a good night.

His stomach rumbled, but he didn't have the energy to cook anything worthwhile, so he nuked a frozen pizza in the microwave and went back to watching home movies.

When the clock struck 1:00 a.m., he dragged his body up to bed. Throughout the night, he tossed and turned, unable to catch more than a few minutes of sleep at a time. He would doze off only to have his subconscious slap him awake with a reminder that Belle's warm body was not in bed with him.

By Sunday afternoon, Max still hadn't heard from Grayson. Frustrated by not knowing what was going on and not having a clue where else to look, he decided to grab his keys and go to Chloe's house. He was all but ready to drag Belle home, whether she wanted to or not. One way or another, they were settling this before their son returned from his sleepover. Max was almost out the door when the landline phone rang.

It took him a moment to realize what the sound was and where it was coming from. The landline hardly ever rang since everyone always called his cell phone. He quickly backtracked into the living room and picked up the phone, thinking it might be Belle calling. "Hello?"

"Oh, thank heavens!" A woman, who was not his wife, exclaimed in relief. "Maxwell, is that you? This is Amelia, Tommy's mom," the woman said, not giving him a chance to answer. Max knew Tommy, and he had a vague image of his mother in his head. The woman was as hyper as her son, so he tended to zone out whenever they ran into each other.

"Oh, yeah... Did something happen to Oliver?" he asked.

"Um, no. I'm calling because Belle was supposed to pick him up this morning, but it's well past noon now. I was worried when both of you weren't answering your phones." Amelia told him, her words rushing out as though she were in competition for the world's fastest—and chirpiest—talker.

"Shit," Max cursed away from the phone as he quickly thought of a solution. He didn't want Oliver coming back to find that his mother was gone. "Actually," he began, rubbing his fingers over his eyebrow. "My wife and I seem to have caught a bug and we were up all night. We really don't want to pass it onto Ollie. Would you mind keeping him an extra night? I'd be more than happy to compensate you. I'll pick him up from school tomorrow."

"Oh no!" Amelia chuckled. "It's no problem at all. I've been there before, and Belle helped me out. I don't think Tommy and Oliver will mind sharing a bed one more night. Would you like to talk to him?"

"Yes, please." There was some rustling on the other end as Amelia called for Oliver. A few seconds later, his sweet voice came from the other end. Max's mouth naturally curved into a smile at the sound.

"Hi, daddy!" Oliver shouted. No matter how many times he and Belle told him that you didn't need to shout over the phone, Oliver couldn't grasp the concept. He thought because you weren't in the same place as the person you were speaking to, you had to shout to be heard.

"Hey, bud. Your mommy and I aren't feeling well, so do you mind staying at Tommy's a day longer?" he asked.

"Nope. Tommy's mommy said we can make gingerbread men later, and we're putting up Christmas decorations. You and mommy didn't start without me, right?" he asked, alarmed at the possibility of being left out of the annual tradition. Max swallowed down a lump of emotion.

Before Belle and Oliver, Christmas was a regular day for him ever since his parents died and his relatives played hot potato with him. His employees used to especially hate him during the festive season because he used to force them to come to work. That stopped the year Belle and Oliver came into his life.

"No, buddy, we're waiting for you. I have to go now. Remember to thank Mrs. Butterson for looking after you. Love you, bud."

"Okay, I will. Love you too, daddy. Can I speak to mommy?" Oliver asked.

Max squeezed his eyes close, squeezing the phone in a death grip. "Mommy went away on a short trip, but she'll be back soon."

"Oh," Oliver replied in a dejected tone. "I thought you said Mommy was sick?"

Shit, he thought. So lost to his grief, he couldn't keep a lie straight to his son. "Yeah, she is, but Mommy had something she needed to do."

"Oh," he repeated with the same tone.

"Don't be sad, bud. You know mommy loves you, right?" Oliver replied that he knew and said his goodbyes just as someone pounded violently on the front door and repeatedly rang the doorbell.

Max hurried over to the door, opening it to the irate image of his lawyer.

"Why the fuck are you not answering your phone? I called a million times!" An incensed Grayson strolled into the house as if he owned it. Max patted his pockets for his phone to check for missed calls, and then he remembered that he threw it against the wall in a fit of rage.

"It's dead. Why didn't you try the landline?" he asked.

"People still use those?" Grayson asked, a stupefied look on his face.

"Apparently," Max shrugged. "You have anything for me?" he asked, stomach twisting in knots.

"At least offer me a drink first, sheesh! You have no sense of hospitality," Grayson groused. Max glared at his friend and led him to his office, where he kept the good stuff. Grayson arched a brow at the pile of wreckage but wisely kept his smart mouth shut.

"So?" Max prompted after Grayson took a satisfying sip of his scotch.

"We managed to find out that Belle has been visiting a certain motel three days a week for the past six weeks. Same room but at different times, mostly when you're at work. And... she's been meeting the same guy every time." Grayson delivered the news in a matter-of-fact tone as if he hadn't just blown Max's world to smithereens.

Max was so certain that Belle would never cheat on him, but this changed everything. He sank into his gaming chair, feeling sick to his stomach thinking of Belle. How could she be intimate with another man then coming back home to share a bed with him? She wasn't lying when she said she didn't love him. Where did she meet this guy? What if she wasn't staying at Chloe's like he initially thought, but her lover's place?

"Whoa there, buddy! It's not what you think," Grayson rushed to say when he saw the green tinge of Max's complexion. "We managed to find a camera snapshot of a man. He always shows up on the same day Belle goes to the motel, minutes before she arrives. Take a look at this," Grayson said, handing Max his phone to show him the video. "Does he look familiar to you?"

Max took the phone with trembling hands, still feeling dizzy from the doubts he'd had about Belle's fidelity. His mental state was suffering from whiplash over everything that had happened the past three days.

He looked at the black and white picture that showed a relatively smarmy man in profile. Something about him niggled at him, but Max couldn't place him. He frowned and looked up at Grayson who remained standing. "Am I supposed to know him?"

Grayson took the phone and scrolled to another photo, this one looked like an ID of some sort, and it was in color. The man had chiseled features, dirty blonde hair, and eyes the color of aged whiskey. Max racked his brains trying to remember where he'd seen him before and came up empty.

"You seriously don't remember this fucker?" Grayson sighed.

"Stop beating around the bush and tell me who he is already!" Max growled. He stood and went to his bar to pour himself a glass of scotch. All the while, he ignored the way his stomach clenched in protest, remembering his bender after Belle left.

"Danton Stanley, ring any bells? He was the former CFO of Greenlight Tech, which Titan took over three years ago. You fired him after an audit revealed that he was embezzling company funds. You had him blacklisted. Word is the fucker never recovered from that. He lost everything from his flashy cars to his wife and kids," Grayson informed him, sounding disturbingly gleeful about the entire thing.

Something clicked in Max's brain. This useless waste of a human being was using Belle to get revenge on him. He must have been coercing Belle for money. But how did Belle become involved in all of this? Something wasn't adding up.

"Belle stopped working at Titan long before I took over Greenlight. Why is Stanley targeting her and not me directly? As far as I know, the two of them have never met, There's no reason for him to go after her. And how the fuck did he convince her to leave me?" Max asked.

"Ah, but that's where you're wrong, Maxy-boy!"

Max gave Grayson a warning look for the childish nickname and got an impish smirk in return.

"Before he was broke as fuck, Stanley had a taste for high-class escorts. Coincidentally, his wife left him because of his serial cheating and not because you fired his ass. Anyhow, Danton was a regular client of one Romero Marino. I'm sure you remember him?" Grayson asked, brows arched.

"Son of a bitch!" Max hissed as a jolt of recognition zapped through his body at the mention of the name. "He was Belle's—" he choked. He couldn't bring himself to say the word pimp.

"Employer?" Grayson chipped in sarcastically. His face had never looked like it needed to be punched as it did at that moment. He was the one to tell Max of Belle's second job besides being a data clerk in Titan's formative years.

Max never told Belle that he knew she used to be an escort. When they first started dating, he thought it was a wise idea to look into her past. He felt bad for invading her privacy, but he needed to protect himself, not to mention his company. He meant to mention it to her, but he knew she was ashamed of her past. She sometimes had this dark look of self-loathing in her eyes when she thought Max wasn't watching. He thought she would eventually tell him on her own, but when she didn't, he let it go.

Her being a former escort didn't change how he felt about her. No, he didn't like the idea that Belle was once an escort. However, Max knew she only did it to pay for her mother's treatments and hospital bills. He saw the pile of hospital bills in the living room the morning after they slept together the first time.

"So, this Danton guy, he was—" he trailed off again and finished his scotch. Just because he didn't mind Belle's former occupation, it didn't mean he could stomach thinking about all those men touching her. Max had known men who sought the company of escorts, and more than one of them were absolute pigs without a shred of respect for women.

"Client?" Grayson chipped in again, seemingly enjoying Max's discomfort. "Yes, he was. I reached out to Romero. He told me that Danton stopped seeking his services around the time you fired him and all but disappeared off the face of the earth until a few weeks ago. The guy has been spending money on whores and booze like it's going out of fashion. My guess is that he's been blackmailing your wife, using her past against her to take your money."

"Motherfucker!" Max cursed, kicking the foot of his office desk. If he had just told Belle that he knew about her past, this bastard never would have had any leverage to use against her. Just because it didn't matter to him, he assumed Belle was over it as well. Though, she must have still have been ashamed and scared of him finding out after all these years.

Max remembered the first time he'd seen her at a gala event. He was bored out of his mind that night; the only reason he didn't leave was because of the networking opportunities. There were many influential guests there who helped him build his business to where it was today.

Max was brooding on the outskirts of the dance floor when he first saw Belle in the arms of another man. The man was old enough to be her father. She was a vision in white, an angel among rats, except her white dress did not invoke any pure, virginal images. Her dress complimented her curves perfectly, stopping below her butt and showcasing her toned thighs and calves. The way she looked that night could have tempted an angel to sin. But it wasn't her body that reeled him in, but her perfect, innocent smile.

After getting to know her for some time, Max realized that the smile he saw on her that night was nothing compared to the genuine, carefree smiles she'd given him since they were together.

He obsessed over her that night, wanking off to the image he had of her in his head. Two nights later, he saw her hard at work in his company and nearly creamed his pants. After finding out her name from one of his other employees, he had Grayson conduct a background check on her.

Max was floored to find out that she was an escort, especially since he'd been finding excuses to visit the floor she worked on to observe her secretly.

At the time, Belle was one of the most reserved staff members, always diligently doing her work and going home when her shift was over. Because her job as an escort offered her opportunities to connect with other influential businessmen, he wondered why she kept working at Titan. A desk clerk was surely paid a lot less than being an escort.

The possibility that she was a spy for a competitor entered his mind. Max requested that Grayson dig deeper. If she was betraying him, Max was going to deal with her the same way he dealt with other traitors, his little crush be damned.

The pieces of the puzzle all clicked into place when he found out that her mother, Annaliese, was terminally ill. He figured Belle was moonlighting to take care of her mother and somehow, that made him fall for her even more. Since losing his parents, Max had forgotten what it was like to be loved by someone who would walk over hot coals to keep him safe and make him feel loved. He wanted to experience that again, wanted someone like that for himself. Later, after finding her crying alone in that cramped space between the vending machine and the potted plant, Max realized that he needed Belle for himself.

Soon after, he began courting her as he was working on his trust issues. He could tell that Belle was reluctant to be with him and had doubts about their relationship despite his best efforts to show her that he wanted no one else but her. The day he found out that Belle was pregnant, he was beyond ecstatic. He felt like he'd been offered the perfect solution to his problem.

He knew Belle was terrified out of her wits, thinking that he would accuse her of entrapping him when it was really the other way around—Max was the one who trapped her. He was never a subscriber to the whole 'love conquers all' adage, but after meeting and falling in love with Belle...

They would overcome anything in their way, and Danton Stanley would learn never to cross him again. There would be no one else but Belle for him. She touched places in him that he didn't even know existed. She saw through the bravado and all the trimmings to the man within and loved him still, even though he could be inflexible and pig-headed sometimes. They should have been more forthcoming with each other, but they were going to work on that, hash this out, and come out the other side with their marriage not only intact but stronger.

"Find Stanley and bring him to me. But first, I'm getting my wife back."

By the time he arrived at Chloe's apartment complex, it was after six in the evening, and there was no one in the house. His phone was broken, so he couldn't call Belle or Chloe. Max debated going home and returning in the morning. Better yet, maybe trolling the bars and restaurants in the area in case they went out. He was walking to his car when Grayson's silver sports car skidded to a stop mere inches away from running Max over.

"You need to fix your damn phone and save me the inconvenience of hunting you down," Grayson complained.

"We tracked Danton to a vineyard on the outskirts of town. It just so happens that your wife and the damn red-headed friend of hers is there as well."

Max knew the vineyard he was talking about. It also served as a country club. They hosted a lot of events, from weddings to parties, there. He and Belle were members, though they rarely visited.

Wanting to put this whole ordeal behind them, Max slid into his car and sped off with Grayson behind him. It couldn't have been a coincidence that Danton was there the same night as Belle. Max deduced that the reason Belle insisted on divorce was so that Danton didn't have any leverage over her anymore. The fucker must not have liked that.

"Come on. Come on." Max tapped his fingers impatiently on the steering wheel, urging the traffic light to turn green. He couldn't shake the feeling that Belle was in danger, and he couldn't even call to warn her.

Stepping on the gas, he made an hour and a half's worth of a drive in fifty minutes. It was a wonder he didn't total the car in an accident. The car had barely rolled to a stop when Max tossed the keys to a valet. He ran to the large ballroom where the event was being hosted.

Spotting Chloe Martin was fairly easy; she was the only redhead in the room, her flaming hair like a beacon. She was plastered to some guy who was most definitely the man she'd introduced as her boyfriend a month or two ago, but then again, Chloe's love life was a revolving door of men.

Her glazed gaze landed on Max as he weaved his way toward her through the crowd. She quickly detached herself from her dance partner, a wide, albeit drunk smile plastered on her face.

"'Bout damn time you came for your girl. I knew you two wouldn't be on the outs much longer. I don't know how you two do it, but fuck, if y'all broke up for good, I woulda stopped b'livin' in love," Chloe rambled on drunkenly.

"Where is she?" Max asked, not seeing any sign of Belle or Danton in the ballroom room.

"Who?" Chloe blinked owlishly at him.

"Belle," Max gritted out impatiently.

"Right, the white knight's here for the princess. She's here somewhere... No, no. I saw her go out into the courtyard."

Max cursed under his breath. Danton must have followed her out. Saying nothing further, he ran out into the main courtyard in search of Belle. He saw no sign of them among the small number of people out there.

He followed the cobblestone path under the arched trellis. If he remembered correctly, this path led to the restaurant, which also had another, smaller courtyard. He heard the voices before seeing them. The courtyard was hidden from view by the hawthorn hedge on either side of the trellis.

"No! Let me go!" Belle's terrified voice came from the other side of the hedge.

Max picked up his pace as he finally came to the entrance of the courtyard. His blood ran hot when he saw Danton pinning his wife against a table, groping, and pawing at her. Without another thought, he ran toward them, tackling Danton Stanley to the ground and unleashed his anger on him.

CHAPTER 18

THE SOUND OF FLESH HITTING FLESH echoed in Belle's ears like bombs exploding one after another. Her hands covered her mouth to keep the screams bubbling up her throat. She gawked at her savior, who was pummeling Danton into the ground. His back turned to Belle, but she could recognize him even in her sleep.

"M-Max?" her voice was barely audible as she stumbled over to the man who was straddling Danton. She stared in frozen shock as Max beat Danton to within an inch of his life. Then she horrifyingly realized that Max wasn't going to stop until he killed Danton. His life would be ruined despite her best efforts.

Belle knelt beside them and grabbed Max's hands. He shook off her grasp easily and continued with his vicious attack.

"Max! Max, stop! You'll kill him!" Belle pleaded, trying to pull Max off Danton, whose face was barely recognizable under all the blood and swelling.

"I don't give a fuck! After everything he put you through—" Max roared, the air in front of him fogging as he panted.

"Max, stop. He's not worth it," Belle pleaded.

The dark and cold look in his eyes morphed to one of pain and despair as he turned to Belle. Her hands dropped limply at her sides, and her mouth moved, but no words came out. A stabbing pain pierced through her heart and the frigid air felt ten times colder. A choked sound escaped her as she sat down on the cold pavement and stared at Max, shame and hopelessness falling over her in waves.

"You... you knew?" Belle shaped the words rather than saying them out loud. She scuttled back on her hands when Max reached out to touch her. His hands may have been bruised and bloodied, but Belle felt like the one who was hurt.

"Belle!" Her name on Max's lips sounded like both a blessing and a curse. "After everything he's done, why do you care if he lives or dies?" Max questioned; the words tumbled off his tongue as he stood from Danton—who was now half unconscious. He knelt before Belle, lacing their chilled fingers together on the cold ground. He held onto her when Belle tried to shirk off his touch.

"I don't give a shit about whether he lives or dies, as long as it's not by your hands. I don't want to cause you more problems," Belle told him, shoulders slumped and head bowed in submission.

Max let out an exhausted sigh as he cupped her cheek. He forced Belle to look up at him, but her gaze focused on a point beyond his shoulders. "Look at me, Belle," he commanded gently. Her hazel eyes held a hint of wariness and a hard-edge Max didn't recognize, but they softened when she finally looked him straight in the eye. Whatever Belle saw on his face had her breaking down into sobs that tore at his heart as she buried her face in his chest, her hands fisting his hoodie.

She kept repeating her apology over and over.

Max wrapped his arms tightly around her and lay his head on her shoulder as tears silently trekked down his face. Every time he closed his eyes, he kept seeing Danton groping her. He kept seeing the copies of text messages and pictures Grayson found and became pissed off all over again. He almost lost her, and the only reason he wasn't finishing off the job was because he was afraid Belle would disappear again if he let her go.

She was trembling in his arms, her tears soaking his shirt. Still, she continued to apologize for something that wasn't her fault. He thought of all the times she went off to meet Danton by herself, willingly putting herself in harm's way.

"You stupid fool. Don't ever do something so dangerous ever again," he mumbled into her hair. He kissed her on her forehead to ease the sting of his words.

"I'm sorry for lying to you," Belle said, looking at him with huge teary eyes that shone brightly in the moonlight.

Max wasn't sure which lie she was apologizing for, but he'd like to think she meant when he tried to convince him that everything she felt for him was a lie. Looking into her eyes now, no one would ever doubt the depth of Belle's feelings for him. As if she read his mind, Belle spoke up. "I love you so much, Max. You and Oliver both... more than my own life." She declared, reverently snuggling deeper into his warmth. Before Max could say anything, Grayson chose that moment to step in.

"Well, isn't this quite a touching moment?"

Belle looked up, frowning when she saw Grayson—Max's lawyer—and three other men she knew to be his fixers. Belle saw them from time to time in Max's office when he was working on a particularly huge deal. What were they doing here? And how the hell did Max know where she was in the first place?

"Took you long enough!" Max growled, glaring at his friend, who was never without that shit-eating smirk on his face. He stood, pulling Belle up with him.

"Not all of us are inclined to drive like a maniac in the middle of the night. You took off like a bat out of hell, and you're damn lucky there were no traffic cops on the way here," Grayson commented. He forced his hands in his pockets as he nodded to Belle, a knowing glint in his eyes. She flushed, realizing he knew. She tried to tug her hand free from Max and keep some distance between them, but his hold was a vice grip.

Danton chose that moment to let out a loud groan as he attempted to sit up. Grayson's gaze skated past her to the injured man on the ground. He let out a low whistle of appreciation.

"Is this your handy-work, Erickson?" he asked, sounding impressed. "You never cease to amaze me. Hey, maybe you can help me out, for once? I know another psychotic bastard that—," he said, looking up at Max as if it was the first time seeing him.

"I think I'll pass," Max chuckled. "What about this sack of shit?"

"Max won't get in trouble, will he?" Belle asked Grayson, then turned to her husband. "This is my fault! I never meant to drag you into any of this. I left to protect you. I never wanted to crush your dreams and destroy your or Oliver's future. I am so sorry, Max!"

"Save your apologies, sweetheart. This dirtbag was after Maxwell the entire time. You were the easy target because of your past as an escort," Grayson explained to Belle.

She flinched at the mention of her past job, lowering her gaze. At that moment, she wished she was invisible. Max clicked his tongue at Grayson for his callous remark. His severe expression melted as he looked at his wife. A bruise was blooming on one side of her face, and her color looked washed out from all the shock. Max sighed. It was time for both of them to come clean and clear away the dark cloud hanging over them.

"Belle, there's no need to be ashamed. I knew that you were an escort before we started dating," he confessed, stroking her hair. His lips curved in the barest hint of a smile. Belle gaped at him, mouth parted and eyebrows raised. "That's not possible. Ha... how?"

Grayson, once again, stuck his nose where he was not wanted and completely ignored Max's murderous stare. "This sucker saw you at a gala and fell headfirst into love. It was funny to watch the usually unflappable Maxwell Erickson lose his shit over a woman. Then he had us track you down after that night. I always thought the whole love-at-first-sight thing was a load of bull, but..." he shrugged. "You should have seen him when he found out you worked at Titan... it was like the stars aligned for him. Anyway, it wasn't hard to dig up info on you. Plus... Romero is an old, uh... let's say he's a friend of mine," he winked at Belle.

"Romero?" Belle repeated. She hadn't seen or heard from her former boss in years. She had cut off all contact with that part of her life when she quit.

"Don't you have a job to do?" Max snapped, lightly shoving Grayson away. "I'm sorry I never told you that I knew what you did for a living. I realize now that it was a mistake. All these years, it must have been eating you up inside."

Belle walked over to one of the chairs, giving Danton and the men who were crouched over him a wide berth. She picked up her discarded shoes and placed them on the ground next to her as she sat down. Max pulled up a chair beside her.

Belle chewed on her lips as she watched Max watching her. There were so many questions and thoughts running through her mind, she could barely keep up. "I don't understand," she told Max, squeezing her hands under her thighs. "If you knew all along, why did you marry me? I slept with men for money, Max, and lied to you about it. I wasn't—I still am—not fit to be your wife. A man like you should have married a woman who didn't have a murky past, someone pure."

"Bullshit!" Max hissed. "I married you because I love you. I don't care what you did before we were together because I know you love me, and you've been faithful to me. I know you did what you did for your mother, and I don't think less of you for it. When we started dating, you never broached the subject. I decided to let it go. In hindsight, I see now that we should have been forthcoming with each other. If we had, Danton Stanley would not have used you to get to me."

More tears fell down her cheeks. Belle thought she would have been all cried out by now. Unfortunately, she cried at the drop of a hat lately. Max squeezed her knees and continued, "None of us are perfect, Belle. Even I've done things I'm not proud of," he said with a glance at Grayson before looking back at her. "However, I won't let any of those things hold me back from achieving my goals, and you shouldn't fret over it either. Besides, the company and all the riches in the world are worthless to me if I don't have you and Ollie by my side. I would gladly give them up if I had to—but I'd really rather keep both," he joked, drawing a small laugh from Belle.

Feeling elated, Belle leaned in to kiss him. It was meant to be a short peck, but the moment their lips touched, Max cradled her face and deepened the kiss. Belle sighed as he snuck his tongue into her mouth. He tasted like whiskey and home, the uneasiness she'd been feeling in her gut finally settled, and her blood heated up in her veins, warming her from the inside out.

"I love you, Max. Forever and always."

"Ditto, Tinkerbell. Let's get you home," Max said. "Sinclair, I trust you'll take care of everything. I'm taking my wife home."

"I came with Chloe; we need to take her too," Belle told Max.

"Don't worry about that, love. I'll take care of the redhead and see that she is safely delivered to her home." Grayson smirked at Belle, making her grimace at the thought of a drunk Chloe and Grayson together. Every time those two were around each other, something bad always happened.

"Let's go. Ollie misses you." Max said as he helped her put her shoes on.

Belle clasped her hands together. "I abandoned him. He must hate me."

"You've only been gone for two days. I told him that you went on a short trip. He doesn't think you left him."

Her heart was in danger of bursting from happiness and love as they left Grayson talking to a barely conscious Danton. "How did you even know where I was?" she asked

Max as they waited for the valet to bring his car around. She had left her car keys with Grayson.

"I had some help from Grayson," he explained.

"I just love happy endings, don't you? But damn, I have the most troublesome clients." Grayson mused out loud as he watched Maxwell leave with his wife. It never ceased to amaze him what extremes people would go to in the name of love—and money, for that matter. The easygoing smile on his face melted away as he turned to face Danton Stanley, who could barely stand and was being held up by Underling One and Two, as he referred to his assistants.

"Yo, Stanley. Remember me? You've gotten yourself in quite the pickle, haven't you? After the last time, Maxwell asked me to deal with you, you'd think you would know better, but nooo! You had to go and create more work for me when my cock should have been buried balls deep in some bitch's pussy by now," he said conversationally, taking leather gloves from his coat pocket and putting them on.

"Here's what's going to happen," he said, coming to stand in front of Danton. The latter struggled weakly against the men holding him up, his one good eye brimming with fear. "You have made an enemy out of a very powerful and very angry man, not to mention one of the few people on this earth I consider to be a friend. And you tried to hurt his wife, too. You're going to skip town. Better yet, leave the damn continent, and don't ever think of approaching the Ericksons again. You won't get off so easy the third time around. And those pictures you were using to blackmail Mrs. Erickson? Gone." Grayson said, snapping his fingers.

"I had someone hack into your computer and delete all evidence. You will also find that there's no trace of this meeting ever happening, so if you even think of incriminating Maxwell or myself, know that all the security cameras in the area are down."

"Clean him up and get him on the first flight out of here," He told his assistants as he pocketed his gloves and went in search of a certain redhead.

CHAPTER 19

THE DRIVE HOME was filled with silence and simmering with tension; unspoken thoughts and feelings still lingered between Belle and Max. However, Max found himself unable to let go of Belle's hand, choosing to steer with one hand, which made signaling difficult.

"I'm never going to leave again, Max," Belle teased him, but her hazel eyes were deadly serious and carried a hint of guilt.

"I know, my love. I just love the way your hand fits in mine," Max replied with a smile and brought Belle's knuckles up to his mouth, where he placed a soft kiss.

"Home sweet home," he murmured, ushering his wife inside their home. He watched silently as she went from the foyer to the living room and then the kitchen as if she was checking that nothing had changed in her time away.

"Everything up to snuff?" he asked, leaning against the doorframe of the kitchen, his hands in the pocket of his hoodie. Belle walked up to him and placed her hands in his pockets too.

"There are dirty dishes in the sink, so I might have to dock some points." She gave him a short smile and her gaze strayed to the ceiling or rather upstairs. "When can I see Ollie?" she asked.

"He stayed an extra night at the Buttersons' place. We'll both pick him up from school tomorrow. I took a few days off from work. I was thinking that we should pull him out of school before Christmas break and go somewhere, the three of us, alone?" he suggested.

"That sounds nice. I can't think of anything better than getting away for a few days," Belle answered, her head burrowed into his chest. "But can you afford to take time off right now? What if—what if Danton leaks the pictures anyway? You'll be ruined," she said, lacing her fingers through his cramped pockets.

"He won't. Grayson will make sure of it. And if my subordinates can't operate my business without me ordering them around, then I need new staff, don't you think?"

Belle didn't answer, and Max frowned when he realized that she was crying. "I'm so sorry, Max," she began, her voice muffled by his chest. "None of this would have happened if I'd told you the truth from the start. Danton would have never targeted me, and I wouldn't have lost all that money."

"Hey, hey," Max soothed, cradling her face in his hands. "You need to stop apologizing. There's nothing to forgive. Besides, you're not the only one at fault. I should have let you know that I knew instead of allowing you to agonize over this for so long. The real villain here is Danton, but we don't have to worry about him anymore."

Belle turned her face to kiss his palm. "From now on, I promise one hundred percent transparency—" she paused, her nose cutely scrunching over. "Make that ninety-five percent... a girl has to have some secrets. However, if there's anything that seriously affects all three of us, I'll let you know."

Max opened his mouth to say something, but his stomach growled embarrassingly loud.

"I'll order takeout. Why don't you go up and take a shower?" He suggested, caressing the scraped skin of her palms with the pads of his thumbs.

Almost an hour later, their bed was laden with Chinese takeout, their eyes trained on the TV as a movie played. Max was amused by Belle's clinginess; she couldn't stop snuggling up to him or finding any excuse to touch him—not that he minded. She was too cute, but the thoughts her innocent touches inspired were the furthest thing from cute.

"You know," he smirked as he cleared the cartons from the bed and put them on the floor. "We still have the house to ourselves." He paused and frowned. "The last time I said that to you, you not only left me brokenhearted but horny as well. I had big plans for our short moment of privacy before the little terror returns."

"That's not funny," Belle slapped him on the back. No matter how many times Max told her she didn't need to ask for forgiveness, the guilt would not loosen its grip on her. She opened her mouth to apologize again and was stopped by a finger pressed to her lips, and a wicked smile tossed her way.

"If you're going to apologize again, then I can think of a better way to do it," he rasped.

Belle's throat went dry, and she could feel her pulse all the way in her core. She walked over to the vanity and grabbed a hair tie, pulling her hair back into a loose ponytail. "Very well, the best way to ask for forgiveness is on my knees, right?" she asked, returning Max's wicked smirk as she knelt at the foot of the bed and waited for Max to come stand in front of her.

"So, they say. Come, show me how sorry you are, wife." Max growled, freeing his erection and guiding it into her mouth.

Belle placed her hands on either side of his thighs, sliding her hands up and helping him out of his jeans and his boxers. Once he was completely naked, she looked up at him through her lashes. "Sometimes, I still can't believe how big you are."

He grinned at her, rakish and handsome. Max grabbed her by the hair, pushing her face toward him. "Why don't you show me how hard it is for you to fit your mouth around my thick cock?"

Belle did as she was told, curling her tongue around the thickness of his cock. She lapped at him, making a mess on purpose, spit dripping from the sides of her mouth as she all but worshipped his length.

"Look at you," Max said, his voice low and rough. He stroked his hands through her hair, rubbing fingers gently into the back of her neck. He spread his legs wider, so she could settle more fully into place between them. "Sucking my cock like a good little wife. You know your place, don't you? Right here between my legs."

She hummed, her face hot and covered in a blush. Even after all this time, the things that Max said could still get her all kinds of worked up. It was amazing how far they had come over the years and yet how little anything had changed.

By now, Belle knew all of the right ways to really work Max into a frenzy. She knew where to lick and suck, where to put her hands and when to hollow out her cheeks. She knew how to tell when he was close, from the way his cock swelled in her mouth to the way his sounds turned deeper, more guttural in his chest.

He took her by the hair again, all but ripping Belle off of his dick and pulling her onto her feet. Max kissed her fiercely, his tongue claiming every part of Belle's mouth in a truly passionate kiss. In a matter of moments, she found herself turned around and shoved onto the bed, face first. She bounced against the mattress with a yelp. "What?"

"I think there are more than a few ways you could make things up to me," he growled. He grabbed her by the hips, pulling her up onto her knees. Roughly, Max tore off her clothing until she was completely nude. "Say you want my cock."

Belle's voice trembled. "I want your cock."

"Make me believe it."

"Please, Max! Let me make things up to you. Fuck me!"

"That's better," he said. He shoved two fingers roughly into her cunt, thrilled to find that Belle was already wet for him. "You're practically dripping. Just thinking about getting railed by me is enough to do it, huh? I bet you could get off on the thought alone. Should we try that?"

Belle shifted so she was half-propped up onto her elbows. She shook her head. "No! Please, don't do that. I... I just want to feel you, Max. I want to feel you close to me."

Oh, that did things to Max. His stomach twisted up pleasantly at the sound of her voice—at the thought of her needing him, of her wanting him.

"Alright," he purred. Max ran a hand along the length of her back, soothing her. "I won't do that today. But one of these days, we're going to try it. It can just be us today. Just me and you."

He kept up the motion with his hand, fucking her steadily with his fingers. He wanted to do this right today. He wanted her not just wet, but dripping by the time he slid his dick into her. Max added a third finger alongside the first two. He stroked the inside of her walls, fucking her nice and slow.

Max pressed kisses to the small of her back, shifting his other hand around so he could rub at her clit while still finger-fucking her. She was as loud as always when she came, her pussy tightening around his fingers. He pushed them into her a few more times, lengthening the pleasure of her orgasm.

She had barely been able to collect her breath before Max was lining himself up with her. It was the first time that they had fucked without a condom. He knew that she was on the pill, and nothing would come of it, but there was still a certain amount of thrill in the thought of splitting Belle open on his cock and spilling his seed into her.

"Alright, princess," he told her, voice a low drawl. "Say it one more time."

"I want you," she said, still trying to catch her breath from her last orgasm. "I want you, Max. I want you inside of me!"

He took her roughly, both hands on Belle's hips, yanking her back onto him. He didn't give her any time to adjust, delighting in the fact that he could finally, truly feel her. The softness of her walls. The wetness of her cunt. There was nothing between him and her. No more misunderstandings. No more arguments or fights.

No barriers—metaphorical or physical.

Keeping one hand on Belle's hip as he plowed her, he used the other to reach out and grab hold of her ponytail. He yanked her head back by it, and she yelped, but the sound turned into a moan partway through. She had to struggle up onto her palms to prevent herself from being bent in two, and even then, she had to keep her head tilted back at a sharp angle.

"Look at you. Letting me take whatever I want," growled Max. "Letting me use you like a good little wife. You know what else wives are good for?"

Belle moaned in response. She rocked backward, meeting his every motion, and grinding herself on his dick. The flush spread down the back of her neck and over her shoulders. Max wanted to bite her, to leave purple hickies blossoming along the side of her neck so all the world could see exactly what they did.

It was a tempting thought, but he didn't want to let up his punishing pace for that. Instead, he released her hair and abruptly pushed down on her shoulders instead, forcing her upper half onto the mattress once more, then curling over her, plastering his chest against her back. The change in angle let him reach even deeper inside of her.

Max plastered her shoulders in kisses, the sweet touch a sharp contrast compared to the fast way that he claimed her. Belle was brought to orgasm a second time, but he didn't stop. He kept fucking her, looking to reach his own peak.

She gave an over-pleasured sob. The sensations were so much that she couldn't help herself, tears brimming in her eyes. It was everything that she wanted, and still, it was almost too much.

"You know what else good wives are for?" Max finally said. He bent to her ear, whispering, "making babies." The thought sat inside of him like an overheated weight. It made his heart beat faster thinking about it. "How about that, Belle? How's that for an apology? I'll knock you up right here, fill you up with my cum so many times, there's no way you won't walk away from here pregnant. Fuck, you won't be walking away at all."

She made a low noise in the back of her throat, pressing against him. Belle was clearly as turned on by the thought as Max.

He kept going, kissing one shoulder and then biting down hard. He told her, "I'll breed you up nice and heavy, make you so swollen with my cum you'll look like you're already pregnant. That's what you're good for. Giving me a kid. Fuck, I could just..." He groaned, pulling out almost completely and then slamming into her pussy with a wet squelch, "... keep you knocked up. Fuck you like this every night; make you take my seed."

Oh, that made her twist and moan. And then a thought hit Max.

He pulled out of her completely. Belle jolted at the sensation of suddenly being empty. On shaking limbs, she pushed herself up and turned toward him, "Max?"

"Roll over," he ordered, leaning back and watching her.

Belle hesitated a moment, confused, and then rolled onto her back. She had barely settled down before he was on her. First, claiming Belle's mouth in a heated kiss, he licked at the backs of her teeth and sucked at her lower lip. Then Max dropped his head, leaving the dark bruises he'd been thinking about peppered over her skin.

Belle tangled a hand in his hair, holding his mouth against the side of her neck. She tilted her head, letting him have more access to her throat. Then, he dropped lower, so he could press open-mouthed kisses first to her left breast, then to her right breast.

"Look at you, all spread out for me," he murmured, words muffled against her sweat-damp skin.

"Always," she told him.

The word sent a thrill through Max. *Always*. That's what he wanted, too. To have Belle this close to him, always.

He nipped at her tits, palming the one that wasn't occupied by his mouth, and then straightened up. Max took hold of her hips, lifting her partially off the bed. Belle hooked a leg over his shoulder, letting the other one splay out to the side. It made her look positively indecent.

Her cum dripped from her stretched, fluttering pussy. Belle's whole body ached for him, and Max was more than happy to fill that ache. Once more, he lined himself up with her—this time pushing in slowly, savoring the way it felt to cleave her innermost folds open with his cock. When he was fully hilted inside of her, Max looked down, marveling at the sight of his wife.

From this angle, he could see the slight outline of his cock through the thin skin of her lower stomach, the way it made her bulge around him. He could see the bruises that he'd left on her throat and the way her whole face burned with blush. He knew that it was a sight he would never be able to forget.

Finally, Max began to move again, fucking into her slow but deep. With every roll of his hips, he changed the angle until he was able to find that sensitive bundle of nerves inside of her that had Belle screaming out his name.

"Max! Max! Right there, right there," she said, her words reduced to babbling nonsense and desperate-sounding moans.

Max held true, banging into her with each push. It was slow but no less fierce for it. Max held her gaze the entire time that he fucked her. When she came again, her eyes rolled, tears of pleasure streaming down her cheeks. Her mouth parted, and her body shook.

The walls of her cunt went tight around him. Max grit his teeth, fucking into her a few more times. He made sure that he was as deep inside of Belle as he could when he finally came, letting the heat of his cum fill her. She moaned at the sensation of his cum inside of her, and he held himself there, keeping it in her, for as long as he could.

When he pulled out, Max held onto her, keeping her angled so that he could watch his cum slip from her—then with two fingers, he pushed it back in, pressing his fingers as far in as they could reach. The sound it made was obscene but not nearly as lewd as the one that left Belle's mouth. It was as if the sound had been punched out of her.

"Too much," she said.

Max told her, "I think you can cum one more time, don't you?"

She shuddered. "Max!"

"One more time," he insisted and then started to slowly fucking her with his hands, taking great joy in the sheer amount of slick that dripped out around his fingers. She sobbed, worn out and overcome with pleasure. She was whining and mewling, shifting so hard and so often it was amazing she didn't manage to wiggle right out of his hand.

Max kept the pace steady and rhythmic, slipping a third finger in beside the first. He wondered, briefly, how many he could fit into her, whether he could stretch her open. Whether she would take all of him. But then he focused back on the task at hand, so to speak. With his free hand, Max petted Belle's hip, at her side, then reached down and rubbed his thumb firmly against the soaked nub of her clit.

It barely took more than a touch before she was spilling again, her whole body wracked in orgasm. Before she had even stopped shuddering, Belle was squirming away from him in earnest, unable to handle any more pleasure for the moment.

Max let her, holding his hand up, making sure that Belle was watching him, and then licking his fingers clean. He took each one deep into his mouth, laving them with his tongue, and pulling them out with a wet pop. He was very tempted to lean down and clean Belle's pussy with his mouth but was wary of pushing her too far tonight. Instead, he leaned over Belle and kissed her instead. No tongue or tooth. Nothing messy or hard. Just his lips against hers, as he tried to impart on her exactly how much he loved her and how much they had needed a night like this.

A night where it was just the two of them, and nothing mattered outside of that. Where he could take her apart, piece by piece, and Belle would trust him to put her back together again afterward.

"Beautiful," he breathed, between kisses.

She laughed and threw her arms around his neck, curling as close against him as she could. "Love you."

"Love you too," said Max. And then, just for the fun of it, "my pretty little wife."

In the aftermath, they laid together. Belle pressed up against her husband's chest, with his arm draped over her side. He ran his fingers along the curve of her back, letting his hands splay out over her skin, and pressed gentle kisses to her cheeks, the side of her face, and the corners of her mouth.

It was quiet, and the late hour stretched out around them. Belle let her eyes drift shut. Typically, it was Max who fell asleep first, but she found that she was truly exhausted. More than that, she also wasn't sure what to think about the turn that their evening had taken: was that something she really wanted, to have a kid? Or was it just a nice thought at the moment?

A little bit of both, she decided, and something that could be thought about at another time. Maxwell wasn't thinking about anything past the fact that he thoroughly enjoyed his wife. Loved her. Was glad that they had been able to work out their problems and share a good evening together.

She closed her eyes and fell asleep, and he laid there a few minutes longer, watching her until sleep claimed him as well.

Epilogue

TWO MONTHS LATER...

Max's cheeks ached from smiling so hard as he stared at Belle in front of him. She looked beautiful and radiant with the Hawaiian sunset at her back, giving her a halo over her chocolate brown hair. She was dressed in a flowy, peach wedding dress that brushed her ankles, her bare feet digging into the beach sand. Max was barefooted as well, the hems of his suit pants rolled up over his ankles and jacket discarded somewhere, leaving him in his shirt and waistcoat that matched the color of Belle's dress.

Standing beside him, Oliver was like a miniature version of Max and looked very proud of himself, with his chest puffed out and holding the new wedding bands that Max bought for renewing their vows. They didn't have many people attending the ceremony, only Grayson and Chloe, as well as the Justice of The Peace who was officiating the ceremony.

When the Justice of The Peace gave them the chance to recite their vows, Max dug out a note from his pocket and breathed in deep, letting the salt and brine scent of the sea calm his nerves.

He frowned at the vows. He'd been struggling to put his feelings into words ever since he convinced Belle that they should do this and what he'd written down was a load of crap, so he crumpled up the paper and pocketed them.

Belle's eyes shone with amusement at his flustered state. He gave her a soft smile and let the words pour out of his mouth.

"Belle... My Tinkerbell." Someone snorted, Max suspected Grayson, but he didn't have it in him to look away from Belle long enough to confirm. "I honestly cannot put into words what you mean to me. Before I met you, I was just wading through life, going through the motions, and finding minimal joy in everything I did. There was a quote in your bedroom before we moved in together. *'All you need is faith, trust, and a little pixie dust,'* and I believe I've found all three of those things in you, in the love we have for each other, and in our son. You are my heart, Isobel Erickson, you are the north point my compass is always searching out, and I wake up each day thankful that I was the one to find you crying and the one to offer you comfort on the darkest day of your life. May we continue to pull each other through such days, but most of all, may we continue to bask in the light and create even happier memories together."

She swallowed down the lump in her throat at Max's words. She wanted to pull him down for a kiss and lock him away in the hotel room for the next few hours to show him how much she loved him.

Taking a deep breath, she began, "I used to think that to stand by your side as an equal, I had to be perfect. The perfect wife, perfect mother, and a perfect hostess. For so long, I perceived any flaw of mine as yet another piece of proof that I didn't deserve your love. I know now that there is no such thing as perfection and that love is indeed blind because I love you without reserve, Maxwell Erickson. Even though you're up at the crack of dawn during weekends and whistle off-tune in the shower, or that you're a workaholic and gaming addict, and I always have to drag you away from your computer screens. I love you despite the fact that you always fart in the bed and pretend you didn't—" Oliver giggled at that, almost dropping the rings. "And I know now that you don't need me to be flawless or a superwoman, and I love the fact that you love me, imperfections and all," she said in a trembling voice, her eyes misting up.

The two of them exchanged rings and kissed to seal the deal, Max forgetting to keep it PG-rated.

They dined by the beach in the company of their friends and other vacationers, who came out to watch the fire dancers. Oliver was so mesmerized by them that he hadn't touched a single bit of his food yet.

Belle felt like she was in paradise and felt lighter and content. She rubbed softly at her still flat stomach as she watched Grayson tell her son some fantastical tale about a fire goddess while Chloe rolled her eyes at him.

"You haven't touched your champagne, babe. Do you prefer red wine instead?" Max asked.

She bit her lower lip.

"Actually," she began, her mouth stretching into a smile. "I can't drink any alcohol or caffeine for the next eight-ish months."

Confusion marred Max's blue eyes. When understanding crept in, he jumped out of his chair and swept Belle into his arms, drawing curious stares from other diners.

"Sinclair, keep an eye on my son. My wife and I need a moment to celebrate in private."

Belle's laughter was carried away by the sea breeze as Max carried her away to their hotel room.

www.ingramcontent.com/pod-product-compliance
Lightning Source LLC
Chambersburg PA
CBHW051335020726
47501CB00007B/2092